What I'd mista   ly a black coat. Drago was sprawled on the pavement, one hand clutching at his chest, his face pale and contorted with pain.

"Drago?" I knelt on the pavement, afraid to get too close. With one finger, I gave him a little nudge. He groaned, and I figured it was a good sign.

"Drago, my name is Annie. My friend Eve went for her phone. We're going to get somebody to help you."

His eyes flickered open. His gaze wandered aimlessly, to the Très Bonne Cuisine building, then to the tree Eve and I had hidden behind to watch him and Beyla argue. Just thinking back to everything we heard and saw made a chill race up my spine. It turned to ice when Drago's gaze fastened on me. He reached for my hand, and when he found it, he hung on like there was no tomorrow. For all I knew, for Drago, there wouldn't be.

"Al . . . bas . . . tru." His voice was no more than a breath, and it was even more heavily accented than Beyla's.

"Alabaster?" I wondered if that was his dog's name.

"Alba . . . stru." Drago gasped from pain. His breaths came quicker, each one a little more shallow than the last. He groped for the breast pocket of his coat, and when he brought his hand out again, he had a piece of paper clutched in his fingers.

"This . . . is important. You will see." He pressed the receipt into my hand, and I glanced at it. It was from a restaurant called Bucharest. Important? It didn't seem likely, not unless Drago had been counting calories . . .

Cooking Up
Murder

MIRANDA BLISS

BERKLEY PRIME CRIME, NEW YORK

THE BERKLEY PUBLISHING GROUP
Published by the Penguin Group
Penguin Group (USA) Inc.
375 Hudson Street, New York, New York 10014, USA
Penguin Group (Canada), 90 Eglinton Avenue East, Suite 700, Toronto, Ontario M4P 2Y3, Canada
(a division of Pearson Penguin Canada Inc.)
Penguin Books Ltd., 80 Strand, London WC2R 0RL, England
Penguin Group Ireland, 25 St. Stephen's Green, Dublin 2, Ireland (a division of Penguin Books Ltd.)
Penguin Group (Australia), 250 Camberwell Road, Camberwell, Victoria 3124, Australia
(a division of Pearson Australia Group Pty. Ltd.)
Penguin Books India Pvt. Ltd., 11 Community Centre, Panchsheel Park, New Delhi—110 017, India
Penguin Group (NZ), Cnr. Airborne and Rosedale Roads, Albany, Auckland 1310, New Zealand
(a division of Pearson New Zealand Ltd.)
Penguin Books (South Africa) (Pty.) Ltd., 24 Sturdee Avenue, Rosebank, Johannesburg 2196, South Africa

Penguin Books Ltd., Registered Offices: 80 Strand, London WC2R 0RL, England

This is a work of fiction. Names, characters, places, and incidents either are the product of the author's
imagination or are used fictitiously, and any resemblance to actual persons, living or dead, business establishments, events, or locales is entirely coincidental. The publisher does not have any control over
and does not assume any responsibility for author or third-party websites or their content.

PUBLISHER'S NOTE: The recipes contained in this book are to be followed exactly as written. The
publisher is not responsible for your specific health or allergy needs that may require medical supervi-
sion. The publisher is not responsible for any adverse reactions to the recipes contained in this book.

COOKING UP MURDER

A Berkley Prime Crime Book / published by arrangement with the author

PRINTING HISTORY
Berkley Prime Crime mass-market edition / November 2006

Copyright © 2006 by The Berkley Publishing Group.
Cover art by Stephanie Power.
Cover design by Rita Frangie.
Interior text design by Kristin del Rosario

ISBN: 0-425-21291-2

BERKLEY® PRIME CRIME
Berkley Prime Crime Books are published by The Berkley Publishing Group,
a division of Penguin Group (USA) Inc.,
375 Hudson Street, New York, New York 10014.
The name BERKLEY PRIME CRIME and the BERKLEY PRIME CRIME design are trademarks be-
longing to Penguin Group (USA) Inc.

PRINTED IN THE UNITED STATES OF AMERICA

10 9 8 7 6 5 4 3 2 1

For Peggy
Thanks for a place to brainstorm,
the Goat White,
and the salt and vinegar chips!

One

✕

 I WAS IN THE KITCHEN BURNING A POT OF WATER when Eve leaned on the buzzer down in the lobby of my apartment building.

How did I know?

About Eve? Or about the water?

I knew it was Eve because she's the only one with a sense of humor warped enough to try to play "Love Hurts" on the buzzer. And the water . . . well, I'd been so lost in my own miserable thoughts, I'd forgotten that I put it on the stove. It didn't cross my mind again until I dragged myself into the living room and buzzed Eve in. A minute later, she swept into my apartment, a vision in a tight black skirt and a purple tank top that hugged every inch of her surgically enhanced to perfection chest.

The door closed behind her, and I braced myself for a hug. Eve hugs everybody. Friend or stranger, male or female, it doesn't matter to Eve. A hug is as natural to her as the chirpy "How are you?" that's sure to follow, a greeting she somehow manages to turn into one word with two syllables.

But this time, when what I needed more than anything was both a hug and an inquiry into my well-being, so that I could answer that I was lousy, Eve didn't do either.

She stopped dead in her tracks and wrinkled her nose. "What is that smell?"

You can take the girl out of North Carolina but you can never take the Southern belle out of the girl. At least not a girl like Eve. Even here in Arlington, Virginia (which is, after all, technically the South, even if it has been overrun by Yankees), her accent is as thick as honey and as noticeable as Eve is herself.

Eve is tall. A good four inches taller than me even when she's not wearing some outrageous pair of heels that puts her up in skyscraper country.

Eve is blonde and blue-eyed. Her hair is poker-straight, and she makes a trip to her hairdresser at least once every couple weeks to make sure her do is as chichi as the latest issue of *Vogue*.

I've got shoulder-length brown hair that I usually end up piling on top of my head because it's curly and unmanageable. My eyes are plain ol' brown, too. Not a combination that makes me stand out in a crowd.

Eve is gorgeous.

And me?

Well, guys always tell me that I'm "cute." I guess it's my heart-shaped face. Or my turned-up nose. Maybe it's because instead of being pencil-thin like Eve is and like the media says all women should be, I'm unfashionably curvy.

Cute?

I knew the truth. *Cute* is a code word guys use because it's kinder than coming right out and saying that though I'm the girl they want to be best friends with, Eve is the type they all fall head over heels for.

Every guy except for Peter.

I couldn't help it—I sighed. Maybe it was the sound that got Eve moving again. She pivoted, looking all around at the same time she sniffed again.

"Something smells weird. Annie, is something burning?"

That's when I remembered the water. And suddenly, the metallic aroma that had been building too slowly for me to notice hit my nose and the back of my throat.

Eve and I took off for the kitchen at the same time. I might not be as graceful or as sylphlike as she, but I was faster. Probably because my bunny slippers provided better traction than her Pradas.

I got to the stove just as the last drop of water boiled away and my not-so-good cookware went from an ugly shade of gray to an uglier and very burned black. I turned off the stove and stepped back, thinking about the best— and safest—way to keep things from getting any worse.

Eve stepped right between me and the stove. Like a surgeon awaiting a scalpel, she held out one hand. "Pot holder," she said.

Call it habit—when Eve tells me to do something, I listen. But not because I'm a pushover. Eve and I have been best friends since we were in preschool together, and more than thirty years of thick and thin have taught me to face the truth: I'm the cautious one who evaluates every situation to death. Look before I leap? I look, all right, from every angle. Eve is the mover and shaker.

I was self-aware enough to know I'd never be the take-no-prisoners type like she is, but I also knew that while I was still thinking, considering, weighing, and justifying, she was already doing. And whatever she was doing, she was usually right.

If she wanted a pot holder, damn it, I'd give her a pot holder.

It was only when I'd turned to grab one that I remembered

that Peter had taken all the pot holders with him when he left.

Talk about adding insult to injury. The realization hit me like a kick in the stomach. I dropped into the chair by the kitchen table and propped my head in my hands, watching as Eve grabbed a dish towel, folded it in two, and without a moment's hesitation, moved my ruined-beyond-being-cleaned pot from the hot burner.

When she was done, she brushed her hands together and sat in the chair next to mine. She cocked her head, and when she spoke, her look and her voice were compassionate. "You were making a cup of tea. I hope it was that aromatherapy brand I gave you. You know, the one that's supposed to boost your mood and enliven your spirit."

"I was making chicken soup." I pointed to the box on the counter. Eve looked that way and took in the empty container of Cherry Garcia, the crumpled bag of Chips Ahoy, and the half-eaten bowl of pretzels that weren't there when she dropped me off the night before.

Well, like I said, we'd been friends a long time. Never having gone through what I'd been through, she might not understand. But I knew she wouldn't pass judgment, either.

"Oh. Comfort food." Eve patted my hand. Maybe she did understand after all. "You know, you should have used the teakettle to boil the water. It's far safer."

"Except that Peter took the teakettle."

She winced. "Sorry. I keep forgetting—"

"Yeah, me, too," I lied. If I was busy forgetting, I wouldn't have nearly burned down the apartment building because I was so busy obsessing about the fact that as of yesterday, I was a divorce statistic.

I was a terrible liar, and nobody knew it better than Eve. She leaned forward. "It's OK to get it all out," she said. "Why, it's only natural that you'd feel—"

"Like I'd like to wring his neck?"

She slumped back in her chair. "I thought we were past the anger stage and working on acceptance."

So did I.

Until I realized I didn't own a pot holder.

I scrubbed my hands over my face. It was two o'clock on a Saturday afternoon, and even though it was June and outside the Virginia air was hotter than my just-about-combusted saucepan, I was wearing jammies and a flannel robe. Comfort food, comfort clothes. I cinched the belt a little tighter around my waist.

"I've been working on acceptance for just about a year now," I reminded Eve and myself. "Ever since the day Peter told me he never really knew what love was until he met that girl at the dry cleaner's. News flash! If the knot in my stomach means anything, acceptance is not working."

"Well, of course not!" Eve popped out of her chair and rummaged around in the cupboards. She came back to the table with a jar of peanut butter, two spoons, and all that was left (it wasn't much) of the giant Hershey's bar she'd bought me the day before, on the way back from the courthouse where Peter and I had signed the papers that said our marriage was officially over.

Eve broke off a piece of chocolate, slopped peanut butter onto it, and handed it to me. "He's a slimeball," she said.

I popped the whole piece of chocolate into my mouth. "Sure he is." I would have sounded more convincing if my words weren't stuck together with peanut butter. "And honestly, she's welcome to him."

"Annie, it's not what you say . . ."

"It's what I feel," I finished for her. I'm not sure it exactly proved my point, but I emphasized my sincerity by grabbing a spoon and a piece of chocolate. I ladled peanut butter on it and this time chomped the piece of candy in half. I licked peanut butter off my fingers. "If he cheated on me, he's going to cheat on her," I told Eve. "Maybe not any time soon, but someday. I'm better off without him."

"You are."

"I'm happier without him."

"You've got to be."

"I've got a bright future in front of me."

"You do."

"I'm . . . I'm . . ." I paused, desperately hoping the endorphins from the chocolate would kick in at that moment.

My shoulders drooped. My spine folded like an accordion. I dropped my head on the table. "I'm alone and miserable!" I wailed.

"There, there." Eve patted my back. "You have so much to look forward to."

"No." I sat up, pushing my hair out of my eyes. "*You* would have something to look forward to if you were divorced. If you were divorced—"

She cocked her head. "But I've never been married."

"But if you were. If you were married, and then you were divorced. You'd have something to look forward to. Guys would be lined up around the block to date you."

"And they're not for you?" Eve rolled her eyes. "Why, that nice Ed Downing at the bank—"

I cut her off with a groan. "That nice Ed Downing is fifty-four and still lives with his mother."

"He's saving to buy a house."

"He's a loser."

"He likes you."

"He likes me because every time he screws up his drawer, I'm able to make sense of it before the head teller shows up and he gets his ass fired." I got rid of the thought with a shake of my shoulders. "I don't know why I even mentioned it. It's not like I care. Mr. Right could walk in here right now—"

"No." Eve's eyes twinkled with mischief. "Let's have him drive in. In a red Jag."

"OK, Mr. Right. In a Jag. He could drive in here right now stark naked—"

Eve giggled. "And with a nice, tight ass."

"And he could ask me to rip off my clothes and—"

"Ask?" Eve pooh-poohed the very idea with the wave of one manicured hand. "We don't want him to ask, honey. We want him to beg. Mr. Right. Jag. Naked. Begging. If you're going to fantasize, you might as well go whole hog."

"I still wouldn't want him." I folded my arms over my chest and *harrumphed*, just so Eve would know I meant business. "I'm never going to look at another guy. I'm never going to date another guy. I'm never going to get married. Not again."

"Of course you are." Eve took a bite of chocolate, and because she forgot to spread it with peanut butter first, she dipped her spoon in the jar, scooped up some extra crunchy, and swallowed it down. "Annie, really . . ." She pointed at me with the spoon. "You're talking crazy. You make it sound like your life is over. You're only thirty-three."

"I'm thirty-five," I reminded her. She was just trying to be kind, and I wanted none of it. Kind would make me feel better, and right now, I was too busy wallowing in my misery. "I'm a thirty-five-year-old bank teller and my hips are too big and my hair is too curly and I have the most boring life in the world and—" My voice wobbled, and I screeched, "I don't even own a pot holder!"

Eve didn't mind the screeching, probably because she'd been overemotional herself a time or two. Sometimes it was because her job—whichever one she happened to have at the moment—wasn't going right. Sometimes it was because she'd missed a sale at Macy's or put a run in her last pair of hose.

Mostly it was because of men.

Fact is, Eve's affairs, like everything else in her life, are the stuff of grand opera. There's always plenty of uncontrollable passion at the beginning and usually, just as much angst at the end. Hence, the screeching.

Me, on the other hand . . . well, the truth of the matter is that I wasn't used to these sorts of gut-wrenching emotions. My life before, during, and after I'd met Peter had been pleasant and largely uneventful. We'd been introduced by friends, and I liked him instantly. Maybe because unlike all those other guys, he'd never once said I was cute. Maybe because unlike all those other guys, Peter really liked me.

Was it any wonder that I really liked him back?

Peter was a high school chemistry teacher. He had a good job, a low-key sense of humor, and an appreciation for all the things I valued. Things like stability and a balance in our savings account that promised that someday, we'd own a home of our own. We dated for two years before we got engaged, and then we had a wedding that was as pretty as a fairy tale. We were married for eight years and were finally at the point of looking for that home we'd spent so many nights talking and dreaming about.

Then he made that fateful trip to the dry cleaner's.

Call me a wimp, but I sighed again.

"Speaking of pot holders . . ." Eve's eyes lit the way they did when she's excited about something. "I think I've got just the thing to make you feel better."

"A lifetime supply of pot holders?"

She was as good as anyone at ignoring sarcasm. Rather than respond, she disappeared into the living room and came back a minute later, Kate Spade bag in hand.

"No pot holders. I'll let you buy your own." She dug through the purse, and when she didn't find what she wanted, she began the unloading process. Wallet, checkbook, comb, compact, blush, lipstick, eyeliner, lip liner, nail polish. After less than a minute, my kitchen table looked like the cosmetics counter at Saks.

"Ah! Here's what I'm looking for." Grinning, Eve pulled a piece of paper out of her purse.

"That better not be a confirmation for a trip to anywhere," I warned her, backing away to put some distance between myself and whatever she might have planned. "You can't afford a vacation, and I can't take the time off from work. I've already missed enough days going back and forth to court."

"No trip." Eve waved the paper. "And you won't need to take any time off from work. This is in the evening. Every evening for ten evenings, starting this Monday."

"A book discussion group."

Eve rolled her eyes. "You know better than that! A girl with my busy social schedule doesn't have time to read."

"A visit to a spa."

"For ten days in a row? Don't I wish!"

"Then what?" I drummed my fingers on the table, annoyed and, I admit, intrigued in spite of myself. "Oh, I know. It's Peter's new address. That place he bought with Mindy or Mandy or whatever her name is. We're going to stake out the house, wait until he leaves one night, jump out of the bushes, and—"

"Now, now. Remember: acceptance." Eve tapped my arm with the paper. "This," she said, "is my receipt. Enrollment for two. You and me, honey, we're taking a cooking class."

I would have laughed if there was anything funny about it. Instead, I aimed a laser look in Eve's direction. Sometimes that could get through to her.

This time, it didn't.

"Earth to Eve!" I waved my hands in the air. "Do I need to remind you? You live on carry-out Chinese. And me?" I looked over my shoulder at my ruined saucepan. "I can't even boil water!"

"All the more reason to take the class." She set down the paper and swept her things off the table and back into her purse.

I took the opportunity to scoop up the receipt and look it over. "Ten Nights to the Perfect Ten-Course Meal," it said, right above the part that said the class would be held at Très Bonne Cuisine.

I knew the place, all right. Fancy-schmantzy kitchen shop on the ground floor, upscale cooking school above. It was in the Clarendon neighborhood of Arlington, one of those rare spots in town where old storefronts stood in unexpected but peaceful coexistence with million-dollar condos, trendy boutiques, and restaurants with sidewalk cafés out their front doors.

I knew the place well, but not because I was a social climber. Très Bonne Cuisine was the home of Vavoom! seasoning, a cult icon in Maryland, D.C., and beyond. Like thousands of others, I was addicted. I used Vavoom! on everything from popcorn to chicken wings. I knew exactly how much a two-ounce jar of it cost and, if I wasn't heavy-handed, how long it would last me. And going on how expensive those two ounces were, there was no doubt in my mind that ten days of classes would be exponentially pricey.

I dropped the receipt like it was on fire. "No way, Eve. No way am I going to let you—"

Her mouth puckered. "Like it or not, you're going to do it."

"Like it or not, you're going to get a refund. You can't afford to pay for a cooking class for me. You can't even afford to pay for a class for you!"

"Afford has nothing to do with this. Haven't I always told you, Annie, it's not the necessities in life we need to worry about. They'll be provided somehow. It's life's little luxuries that are important. Right now, we need to get your mind off Peter. This is one way to do it."

"No." I could be just as stubborn as she was. "Get your money back."

"Can't." She pointed to the line on the bottom of the printout that said all enrollments were final. "It's paid for, Annie. I know the way your logical little mind works. You know it's better to take the class than waste the money. Besides, it will be good for you to get out."

"So I can embarrass myself in front of a class full of chefs? You know I'm a terrible cook!"

"Don't be silly." Eve got up, slung her purse over her shoulder, and headed for the door. "You'll get an e-mail," she said. "We all will. Tomorrow and every night before class. They'll let us know what ingredients to bring. That way, they'll be nice and fresh. And don't worry about driving. I'll pick you up. Monday, six fifteen."

She knew I was going to keep on arguing—that's why she didn't give me a chance. Eve swept out the door and left me alone. In my jammies and my bunny slippers, the caustic tang of burnt metal still sharp in the air.

"Cooking class?" I'd already heard my own voice echo back at me before I realized I was talking to myself.

When Peter was around, I at least made an effort to cook. Spaghetti sauce, omelettes, the occasional blueberry muffin (always from a box). Since he'd been gone, I hadn't done even that much. I lived on soup and cereal, and when I tried to cook . . . well, all I had to do was catch a whiff of the metallic odor in the air to know how things usually turned out.

But I couldn't be mad at Eve. She was my best friend, bless her, and she was just trying to make me feel better. For that, if for nothing else, the least I could do was cooperate.

I told myself to get a grip and did a mental check through my schedule for the next ten days. It didn't take long: Class was in the evening, and I didn't have a social life. All I had to worry about was embarrassing myself or burning down the cooking school.

But after all, there would be professionals at class, guiding us through each step. There would be cooks—real cooks—telling us what to do and what not to do and how to make sure we never burned pots of water.

How dangerous could a cooking class be?

Two

✖

 WE WERE LATE FOR THE FIRST CLASS. JUST FOR THE record, it wasn't my fault.

Like I did every day (except for Fridays when the bank was open until six), I arrived home at exactly five twenty-five. By five thirty, I'd sorted through the day's mail. I filed the bills in their proper slots in the accordion folder I kept nearby, threw away the junk, and made a separate pile for the letters that were still arriving addressed to Peter. As usual, my plan was to rip them into tiny little pieces and toss them out but—as usual—I relented. I wrote "forward" on his mail along with the address of the school where he taught, and stuck the letters by my purse so I could drop them on the table in the front lobby as I was leaving.

I wasn't sure what cooking students wore, but after a sweltering weekend that culminated in a Sunday afternoon thunderstorm, the temperature had cooled considerably. I changed out of my black pantsuit and into jeans, a green long-sleeved T-shirt, and sneakers. After a minute, my nervous energy got the better of me and I swapped the green T-shirt for a white one. Chefs wore white, didn't they?

About a minute later, I switched back to the green.

Just before I walked out the door, I grabbed the groceries I'd picked up on my lunch break.

"Chicken stock. Broccoli. Cheddar cheese. Cream. Butter. Spanish onion." Even though I'd checked and rechecked earlier, I peeked in my grocery bag and did an inventory, making sure that I had everything mentioned in the e-mail that arrived the night before from someone named Jim at Très Bonne Cuisine.

Thirty minutes later—twenty minutes after she promised—Eve careened into the parking lot on two wheels and slammed on the brakes right next to where I was pacing in front of the cement pad outside the lobby door.

"Forgot to shop," she said breathlessly as I climbed into the car and fastened my seat belt. "Had to stop on the way. Had a heck of a time finding cauliflower. Did you get cauliflower?"

I had printed out the e-mail shopping list. I pulled it out of my bag and I pointed to a line on the ingredients list. "It was supposed to be broccoli."

"Oh. You're right. I always get those two mixed up." Eve's plucked-into-submission eyebrows dipped. "I thought—"

"That's OK. I've got enough for both of us."

Like all of the D.C. Metro area, Arlington traffic has a bad reputation, and for good reason. By the time Eve negotiated her way through the crush of commuters between my not-so-stylish neighborhood and Clarendon and found a parking place around the corner from Très Bonne Cuisine, we had exactly three and a half minutes to make it into the store. That meant getting to the shop, climbing the steps, getting ourselves and our supplies organized . . .

I pulled in a breath, forcing my heart rate to slow. Late

was not the end of the world, I reminded myself. But even that bit of good advice wasn't enough to stop me from snapping out of my seat belt the moment Eve put the car into park.

I jumped out and then grabbed my bag and my jacket. Eve calmly leaned over, checked her makeup in the rearview mirror, put on a little more lipstick, ran a brush through her hair. To make matters worse, when she finally did get out of the car, her cauliflower tumbled out of her bag, and we had to chase behind it as it rolled toward the street. Needless to say, I wasn't exactly cool, calm, and collected when we arrived at the shop.

Maybe that's why I didn't hear the man on the other side of the front door.

Just as I reached for the knob, the door flew open so hard and so fast, I had to jump back or risk getting my nose smashed.

The dark-haired man who stomped out of the shop was as broad as an I-beam and tall enough to fill the doorway. He was dressed in black pants, a black turtleneck, and a full-length black leather coat that was open and flapped around him like the wings of a bird of prey.

His eyes reminded me of a hawk's, too. They were small and dark and so intense, they were narrowed to slits. His cheeks were an ugly color between red and purple, and he was breathing hard, as if he'd just gone a couple rounds in a prizefight.

The fact that he didn't pay any attention to me wasn't surprising. After all, I was pretty quick on my feet, and even after my initial surprise melted, I made sure I stayed as far out of his way as possible. But Eve was standing not six feet away, watching the whole thing, and he didn't give her a second glance, either. And let's face it, in her short, short khaki skirt, flamingo pink top, and hot pink stilettoes, Eve was hard to miss.

That more than anything told me the guy wasn't thinking straight. Every step was fueled by the anger that shivered around him like the heat off a wildfire. He marched over to a black BMW double-parked at the curb, got in, and slammed his keys into the ignition. I swear he didn't even look over his shoulder to check traffic before he rocketed away.

"Have a nice day!" Eve waved. After my close call with the front door, I was grateful for her irreverence. Something about the man in the black leather coat sent a chill up my spine and across my shoulders. Eve, on the other hand, wasn't about to be intimidated. Not by anyone. It was one of the reasons I liked her so much, and I couldn't help but smile.

Still grinning, I peeked into Très Bonne Cuisine. The coast was clear.

I'd been there before (remember the Vavoom!) so I was familiar with the store. Glossy hardwood floors. Sleek cabinetry. Gleaming chrome. The place was a kitchen-aholic's dream come true, stocked floor to ceiling with the latest and greatest gadgets, the priciest of high-priced cookware, jars of mysterious spices, and books that taught special cooking techniques for every food I'd ever heard of and some that I hadn't.

Of course, I am not a kitchen-aholic, or even a wannabee. I live on Lean Cuisine and wash it down with ice cream and the occasional peanut butter and banana sandwich. Grilled, of course. Here in the land of Proper Cooking Technique, I was nothing more than a once-in-a-while customer who spent as little as possible every time she did show up. Which I never did unless I needed a Vavoom! fix.

That's probably why the shop owner didn't recognize me when I walked in.

In fact, he didn't even acknowledge me.

Jacques Lavoie was the genius behind Très Bonne Cuisine and the inventor (is that the right word for a chef?) of Vavoom! He was also a one-man publicity machine, at least if the billboards that advertised the man, the store, and his product on every city bus and at every Metro station meant anything. In fact, his face was on the Vavoom! package in the form of a black-and-white caricature that emphasized his round-as-apple cheeks and his sparkling eyes. His smile, as long as a baguette, pretty much jumped out and said, "*Écoutez!* You must buy this stuff, *s'il vous plait. C'est magnifique!*"

The success of Vavoom! had made him a legend in both cooking circles and among local entrepreneurs, a French immigrant who cashed in on the American dream. And folks in D.C. like nothing better than a Cinderella story.

Monsieur Lavoie was charming and talkative. At least he always had been every time I'd paid a visit to the shop. Even when I was only spending a measly twelve ninety-five for a two-ounce jar of Vavoom! (Like I said, I was addicted.) This time, though . . .

"Monsieur Lavoie?"

He stood behind the cash register, his hands clutching the counter in front of him so tight, his knuckles were white. His breaths came in short, shallow spurts. His face was as pale as the apron he wore over pressed-to-perfection Dockers and a crisp long-sleeved shirt. Whiter than the shock of salt-and-pepper hair that stood out around his head like a fuzzy halo.

Eve was right behind me when I took a step toward the front counter. She raised her voice to try to get through to him. "Monsieur Lavoie, are you—"

"Oh my! How you did startle me!" He jumped as if he'd touched a finger to an electrical line. He pressed one still-shaking hand to his heart and forced a smile. "I did not hear you come in," he said, right before he bent and tucked something under the counter. He popped right back up. "I did not know anyone was here."

"What about that rude man who just left?" Nobody ever

said Eve was good at playing politics. She raised an eyebrow in an elegant little gesture that pretty much came right out and told the old guy that we weren't buying his story. "You know, the one who nearly knocked my friend down when he rushed out of here?"

Monsieur waved one hand in a very Gallic gesture of dismissal. "Customers!" He rolled his eyes and laughed in one of those deep-throated *ho-ho-ho*s that sounds risqué even when nobody's talking about sex. I'd always thought it was a stereotype—but I guess stereotypes have to come from somewhere.

"Some customers, they want to be treated so special. And that one . . ." Again, he laughed, and again, we didn't believe him. For one thing, the man in the leather coat hadn't been carrying one of Tres Bonne Cuisine's trademark mint green shopping bags. For another, he was more than just a little annoyed.

"But you are not here to listen to my complaints. No! No!" Monsieur Lavoie looked at a list on the counter in front of him, made two broad check marks on it, and hurried over to where we stood. He gathered up Eve and me, one of us under each arm, and I couldn't help but notice that he held Eve a little closer than he did me. That's all right. I didn't hold it against him. He was French, after all, and he did smell like Vavoom! I breathed in deep, comforted by the familiar aroma.

"You are Mademoiselles Annie Capshaw and Eve De-Cateur, no? You are here for class, yes? You must hurry, or you will be late." He ushered us toward the back of the store and a closed door tucked between a shelf of pastel-colored martini glasses and a display of color-coordinated, seasonal-themed kitchen linens. The towels were a pretty, summery green. The dishcloths were the color of cantaloupe. The pot holders . . .

The pot holders came in shades of pink, from magenta

to blush. They were arranged on the wall like a rainbow. They were perfect, quilted squares, and the colors were breathtaking. Suddenly, I was glad I didn't own any.

Until I saw the pricetag.

I gulped down my horror and promised myself a trip to WalMart.

Monsieur Lavoie brushed aside the pot holder at the bottom of the rainbow to reveal a security pad. "You are the last two. Everyone else is here. You do not wish to miss a thing, yes?"

"No. Yes. I mean . . ." While he punched in a security code for the door that led to the upstairs school, he explained that the school door was always kept locked so that customers who weren't signed up for classes couldn't wander up there. The lock clicked open and I tried to get my thoughts in order. "We just wanted to make sure that you were OK. That nothing was wrong. After the way that man—"

"Wrong?" He chuckled. "What could be wrong, *cherie*? The night is young, and you are about to have such a wonderful experience. Cooking, *nes't pas*?" He kissed the tips of his fingers and winked. "Except for love, this is the greatest adventure of all!"

Monsieur Lavoie waved us up the stairway, and just before the door closed behind us, I saw him bow. After a quick climb, Eve and I stepped into an airy room every bit as stylish as the shop downstairs.

I know it sounds crazy, but suddenly, I knew exactly how Dorothy felt when she took that first Technicolor step into Oz.

Along one side of the room, a floor-to-ceiling window overlooked the street. Mellow evening light poured into the room like clarified butter. The whole scene reminded me of a photograph in a slick gourmet magazine, the golden light glancing against each two-person workstation with its state-of-the-art stainless steel stove, its charcoal-colored granite cutting surfaces, and cookware that gleamed the way my cookware at home had never gleamed, not even on the day it came out of the box.

Eager students sat side by side, their broccoli out and waiting, green and dewy. Their sticks of butter and globe-shaped Spanish onions added just the right warm touch of yellow to the picture.

In fact, the only false note in the room was the woman who stood looking out the front window. Against the back-drop of gilded light, she looked like she was cut from black paper. When Eve and I walked farther in, the woman spun around. She was pretty in an exotic sort of way, with pale skin and hair as black as a crow's wing. Her eyes were dark, too, and right then, they were wide with horror.

For one mad moment, I thought word of my cooking prowess had preceded me, and she was about to announce that if Annie Capshaw was going anywhere near fire, she was outta there.

She didn't, thank goodness. Instead, she took one look at us, and the worry in her eyes cleared. After just one more glance at the front window, she took her place at her cook station.

Eve and I found our place, too—at the last remaining stove in the far right corner. Back of the room. Out of the line of the instructor's eye. Just fine with me.

"I told you this was going to be wonderful." Eve's voice snapped me out of my thoughts. She dragged in a deep breath and let it out slowly, savoring the moment and the rarified atmosphere. She pulled her assortment of ingredients—minus the cauliflower—out of her bag, and I took the opportunity to glance around the room. Out of a class of twelve, there were four men. Eve must have noticed them, too, because she elbowed me in the ribs. "What do you think, huh? Told you this would be a great place to meet somebody."

"Except that I don't want to meet somebody." I made sure I kept my voice down.

"Which doesn't mean somebody doesn't want to meet you." Eve's eyebrows shot up, and I looked where she was looking—which was at each one of our male classmates.

Two of them were together, and since they were holding hands, it wasn't much of a leap to figure they were gay. They didn't spare me a look, but they did check out Eve's outfit. No doubt they were critiquing her color choices. The other two I wasn't so sure about. One of them was a nondescript guy with pleasantly bland features. When I looked his way, he pretended he didn't notice. The last man was a middle-aged cross between a sumo wrestler and the Incredible Hulk. If he was cooking, whatever he was cooking, no way anyone was going to refuse to eat.

The wall over on the right side of the room was painted with a mural of a Parisian café. In the center of it, right under a sign that said it was the Café Jacques, there was a door. At that moment, it popped open, and the man who I assumed was the Jim who had sent our shopping list walked into the room.

This time when Eve elbowed me, I sat up and took notice.

I should explain that we have wildly different taste in men, Eve and I. She likes her guys big and hairy. Usually light-haired. Always with money to burn.

I, on the other hand, am a little more discriminating. The one and only time I filled out one of those online dating surveys (at Eve's urging, and only because I knew she'd give me no peace until I did, and because I deleted the whole thing as soon as she left), I'd checked off all the things about a man that were important to me. Things like a good sense of humor, a steady job, a sense of self-worth that wasn't tied to what kind of car he drove or how he made his living as much as it was to who he was way down deep inside.

I wasn't shallow, and I was proud of it.

But, hey, I wasn't dead, either.

I looked over Jim and nodded my approval. I smiled at Eve. Eve smiled back. For once, we were in total agreement.

Our cooking instructor was, to put it in the vernacular, one hot hunka hunka burning love.

Apparently, we weren't the only ones who recognized a cooking Adonis when we saw one. A sort of hush fell over our little crowd as Jim made his way to the front of the room where he had a stove and work surface bigger than ours, and a mirror hanging over the whole thing so that we could watch his hands while he worked.

"Good evening! I'm Jim. Jim MacDonald. I'll be your instructor."

"Ohmygosh! A Scottish accent! My knees are weak." The words hissed out of Eve, and she grabbed onto the edge of the granite countertop.

Though I was (as always) a little more circumspect, I knew exactly how she felt. Jim MacDonald was tall and rangy. Long legs. Long arms. Long, lean body. He had a crop of hair the color of mahogany, and though I couldn't tell for certain from this distance, I thought his eyes were hazel. There was no mistaking the impact of his voice, though. Deep and edged with a bit of a burr, it was one of those voices that wraps itself around its listeners. It was soothing and exciting, all at the same time. It was sexy. Oh, yeah. It was sexy, all right. And there wasn't a woman in the room (as well as those two gay guys) who wasn't completely enthralled.

Jim took it all in stride, giving us a one-sided smile that revealed a dimple in his left cheek.

"Now you know me, so let's meet all of you. Let's go around the room," he said, "and get to know each other. Tell me your name and why you're here. What kind of cooking do you like to do? Then tell us something interesting about yourself."

Interesting?

My mind glommed onto that one word and froze. I swear, as my fellow classmates introduced themselves one by one, I didn't hear half of what they said. I knew the gay couple were Jared and Ben, that they loved to grill seafood, and that they spent their weekends when they weren't rock climbing tending to the garden behind their eighteenth-century row house in Old Town Alexandria.

The young girl and older woman directly in front of us were mother and daughter. Their specialty was pastries, petit fours, and tortes. The bland man with the pleasant face was John. He was an accountant—no big surprise there—and a meat-and-potatoes kind of guy.

The dark-haired woman was next.

"Beyla," she said by way of introduction. Her voice was low and accented. Eastern European, I guessed. At the bank where I worked, we had a lot of customers from that part of the world. "I am here because cooking is . . . how do you say it . . . important to me. Important to my family. I am wanting to cook better."

"And can you tell us something interesting about yourself?" Jim asked.

Beyla blushed from the tip of her chin to the tops of cheekbones I would have given my last pink pot holder to own. Her fingers were long and slim, and the gesture she made with them was as delicate as butterfly wings.

"I am good cook already," she said. "In Romania, where I am from, my people say I am very good. But American food . . ." She shrugged the way women do when they're walking that fine line between being modest and blowing their own horns. "I need practice," she said. "I am wanting to learn to cook like an American."

"That's something I've been wanting, too," Jim admitted, and the class laughed.

Just a few minutes later, it was Eve's turn.

"Miss Arlington, Virginia," she said with a little curtsy. "I won't tell y'all how long ago that was. As for why I'm here . . ."

She looked my way, and I held my breath. She wasn't going to tell, was she? About Peter? About me? About how I'd been feeling like a hamster on a wheel, going nowhere fast and not getting any younger and how she saw this class as my first step back into the world?

"Why, I'm here to meet all of you," she said, looking around at the crowd with a smile. "Learnin' to cook, why, that's just a big ol' bonus."

Everyone laughed and smiled. Of course. Eve had a way of putting people at ease.

I don't want to sound as if I hold that against her. I don't. Honest. I'd spent the last thirty years wishing I could be more like Eve. More bubbly. Prettier. More outgoing. And every time I thought about it, I promised myself I was going to make it happen. Right then and there.

It was my turn.

This was my chance. I pulled in a breath for courage and reminded myself that this was the time and place of new beginnings. I was just the girl to do it. I was ready to leap off that wheel that was going nowhere and explore the new horizons spread out before me, awash in golden light and the heady smell of Vavoom!

Everyone in class was staring at me, including Jim, the hunkiest thing out of Scotland since Mel Gibson donned a kilt.

My throat went dry. A bead of sweat broke out on my forehead.

"Interesting?" I croaked out the word. "The most interesting thing about me is that I'm the world's worst cook."

Three

✖

 FORTY-FIVE MINUTES INTO CLASS AND COUNTING, and I hadn't burned anything yet.

I congratulated myself as I checked the onion happily sputtering away in the saucepan in front of me. It was just starting to go limp and translucent, and following Jim's instructions, I dumped in the carrots and celery I had chopped so carefully only moments before. Every little piece of every single veggie was exactly the right size, and there was enough space around them so that they didn't sit on top of each other and steam but instead seared nicely. Just like Jim had explained they should.

I breathed a little easier. So far, so good.

Speaking of Jim, he'd spent the last few minutes going around from stove to stove, peering in saucepans, offering advice. It was our turn now, and he stood at my shoulder, right between me and Eve. "Do you remember what this is called?" he asked.

"What it's called?" Eve assumed the question was for her, and that was just fine with me. I was keeping an eye on my carrots and celery. I didn't have time for a pop quiz.

Eve's veggies were anything but perfect. They weren't chopped and diced, they were minced and mangled. She'd used too much butter, and her carrots (hunks, not neat little matchsticks) were drowning.

Still, when she looked from her pan to Jim, she smiled. She batted her eyelashes at him and fanned her face with one hand, eyeing him with what I called "the look," which has been known to drop guys at twenty paces. "Why, it's hard to know what to think. Especially when it's so very warm in here."

I was in awe of Eve's flirting skills. Always had been, always would be. But even I knew when she was going too far. I could see that her tactics weren't working on Jim. Instead of melting into a puddle of mush the way most guys did, Jim rocked back on his heels, his hands in the pockets of his just-tight-enough jeans and a knowing smile on his face.

I'd seen this game before. Eve and the flavor of the month. No way did I want to get in the middle of it.

Hoping to short-circuit the electricity that crackled in the air, I jumped right in and hoped my French pronunciation was right. "It's called mirepoix," I said. I admit it, maybe I wanted to show off a little, too, and prove I was paying attention when Jim told us what to do to get started on our broccoli and cheese soup. "It's a mixture of sautéed vegetables and what you called aromatics, like bay leaves."

Jim smiled and nodded his approval.

I stood a little taller and dared to smile back. Now that he was standing this close, I could see that I'd been right about his eyes. They were hazel, as clear as amber. As rich and as warm as the rolled *r*'s in his voice. As attractive as his slightly squared chin, his thick hair, his—

"And how long do you cook it?"

His question snapped me out of my thoughts. Good

thing. I was getting way too poetic. It must have had something to do with the evening light. Outside the big front window, the sky had gone from golden to a deep periwinkle, and the muted color crept into the room like a whisper. Or maybe it was the heady aromas that filled the air, the ones that made me imagine what it would be like to be sitting at a sidewalk café in Paris. A glass of wine in one hand, Jim's hand in the other. I would smile across the table at him and—

I twitched away the notion and got back on track. "About five more minutes," I told him, repeating back the advice he'd given when he first demonstrated the technique. I hoped he didn't detect the dreamy note in my voice that betrayed the fact that I'd been thinking of anything but cooking.

"We cook the vegetables until the onion is just a little brown around the edges," I continued. "When it is, we remove the vegetables from the skillet and then deglaze." Since Jim didn't say anything, I figured he was waiting for more. "That's when we add a cup of stock . . ." I pointed to the can of chicken stock that sat ready next to my saucepan. "We swirl it around to get the bits of flavor out of the pan, and the whole thing becomes the base of our soup."

He smiled again and walked over to the next station. "Very good," he said over his shoulder.

And it was, in a warm and fuzzy way that nothing had been since Peter walked out on me.

Smiling like a lunatic, I watched Jim chat with John, the bland man. I saw him peer into the Romanian woman's pan and nod his approval. I heard the low rumble of his voice as he spoke to the mother and daughter in front of us. My smile got wider when that rumble wormed its way deep down inside me and made me feel warm all over.

Not as warm, however, as my veggies.

When I finally realized something smelled funny, they were burnt to a crisp.

* * *

 "DON'T LOOK SO DOWN AND OUT. IT'S NOT THE END of the world."

It was good advice. Too bad I wasn't in the mood.

In the passenger seat of Eve's car, I hunkered down, my hands in my jacket pockets, and looked out the car window. "Not the end of the world for you," I told Eve. "You didn't look like a total loser in front of Jim. Plus your soup was great. You know what? I just don't get it!" I slapped a hand against my thigh and turned to her. "Your veggies were lumpy. You bought the cheapest chicken stock you could find. You used stolen broccoli."

"Not exactly stolen," she reminded me. She smiled as she kept an eye on the traffic in front of us. "You did offer it."

She was right. And because I needed to get rid of the first batch of burned mirepoix and start all over . . .

Because by that time I was so nervous and so embarrassed that I took way too long . . .

Because I'd screwed up royally, I never did get to the add-the-main-ingredient stage of tonight's recipe. Eve ended up using all my broccoli.

"Jim said not to worry."

"Jim." I grumbled the name. "None of that would have happened if it wasn't for Jim."

Eve laughed. "Are you blaming him for being scrumptious?"

"I'm blaming myself for being stupid." I crossed my arms over my chest. "I should know better. If I wasn't so easily distracted—"

"Oh, honey, guys like Jim are what easily distracted is all about! Don't feel bad. You acted like any other woman would have acted."

"I'm not every other woman."

"Then maybe you should try to be. Lighten up. You're

too hard on yourself. Relax and just have fun. You were never like this until Peter the Jerk stomped all over your self-confidence. Stop thinking about him. Stop worrying about what other people think of you."

"People like Jim? You were worried about what he thought of you, weren't you?"

"Was I?" By the way she said it, I could tell that Eve hadn't seriously considered this part of the equation at all. "I wasn't making a play for him, if that's what you think."

"Which is why you practically hung out a Come-and-Get-It sign."

She laughed so hard, she had to catch her breath before she could reply. "He's not my type. You know that, Annie. A cooking instructor?" She wiped a tear from her eye. "So he's cute. So he's more than cute! I don't have him in my sights, if that's what you're worried about."

"I'm not."

"Uh-huh."

"Really!" I defended myself so vehemently that even I wondered if I was telling the truth. "Guys like Jim don't look at women like me."

"Because you're cute."

"Because I'm not . . ." I screeched my frustration. "Because he's sexy and gorgeous and has that accent that makes my toes curl. That's why. I'm not his type."

"If you tell yourself it's true, you will never be his type."

I chewed over the thought, and I have to admit, I didn't like the way it tasted. Mostly because I knew everything that Eve said was right on the money.

"Oh, rats!" She slammed on the brakes, effectively jarring me out of my thoughts.

"My watch is gone." Eve fingered her bare left wrist. "It's back at Très Bonne Cuisine. I took it off when we were washing up, and I know just where it is. On the counter next to the sink."

I thought about Monsieur Lavoie and the way he kept the door between the shop and the cooking school locked. I shrugged. "It'll be there tomorrow."

"Well, yes, I know that." Eve chewed on her lower lip. "If it was only that . . ."

The driver behind us laid on his horn, and Eve started up again. "I'm having lunch with Clint tomorrow," she said by way of explanation.

Clint.

I did a quick shuffle through my mental Rolodex.

It wasn't easy keeping Eve's love life straight. Or the legion of guys who always seemed to be hovering, like bees around an especially beautiful flower.

There was Joe, the professional football player. Michael, the attorney. Scott, the architect. And Clint . . .

I squeezed my eyes shut, thinking, and the pieces finally clunked into place.

"Oh, Clint. The jeweler," I said. "He's the one who gave you—"

"The watch. Exactly. If I don't wear it, he's going to notice. And if he notices, he's going to ask why."

"And you're going to tell him that you left it at your cooking class."

"Practical as always, Annie." As if *practical* were a dirty word, she tsk-tsked away the very idea. "If I don't wear it, Clint is going to think that I don't care."

I thought back to the conversation we'd had only a few days before, the one in which Eve complained about everything from Clint's choice of aftershave to Clint's decision to trade in his BMW roadster for a sedate and sensible Volvo.

"You don't care," I reminded her.

Eve squealed a laugh. "Of course I don't! But there are better ways to deliver the news. No, no. I could never be that cruel. Not to Clint. After all, the shine may be off our relationship, but the boy does have exquisite taste in jewelry."

Eve wheeled left at the next street, ducked into the nearest driveway, and turned around. Before I could protest further, we were headed back toward Clarendon.

Fortunately, it was a Monday night, and the streets
weren't as crowded as they can be later in the week. Between that and the fact that it was after nine and most of the
stores in the area were closed, traffic was pretty light. We
cruised past the Cheesecake Factory, where there was still
a line outside waiting to get in, and the Whole Foods Market that sold the yogurt that I loved so much. We turned left
at the cross street closest to the shop. It must have been our
lucky day (or night), because we found a place to park
within sight of Très Bonne Cuisine's back door.

When we got out of the car, the first thing we heard was
a woman's voice raised in anger.

"No! I will not listen. I will not change my mind. You
know what I want."

"That's Beyla." I recognized the voice and the accent
that belonged to the beautiful, dark-haired woman in our
class. And in the glow of the security light near the shop's
back door, I saw her, too. She was facing off against a man.
He was farther from the light, and all I could see was a
hulking silhouette. Though he kept his voice down and I
couldn't make out what he said, there was no mistaking the
anger in his voice when he replied.

"You say this? To me!" Beyla shot back. She raised her
chin, and when she snarled, I could see her teeth glint in
the light. "I'll kill you, Drago. I swear it on the souls of my
ancestors."

Apparently, Drago wasn't buying any of this, and just to
prove it, he closed in on Beyla. He stepped into the circle
of light, and for the first time, I saw his face.

Eve had come around to my side of the car, and I
grabbed her arm, automatically drawing her into the protection of the shadow of a nearby tree. "It's the big guy," I

hissed. "The one who almost knocked me out cold when we got to class!"

"Yeah, and he's even more pissed than Beyla." Eve leaned forward, trying to hear and see more. "What do you suppose they're fighting about?"

"Something tells me it's none of our business." I tugged her toward the front of the shop. "I think we should get out of here."

"And miss all the fun?" Eve shrugged out of my grasp. "I'll bet they were lovers in the Old Country. You know, one of those family feud things. Forbidden pleasure and all that."

I heard Drago's voice again and saw him pull back his shoulders. He was a big guy. Call me a wimp but if I had been in Beyla's position, I would have been intimidated. She looked more defiant than ever. I could practically feel the bad blood between them all the way over where we were.

"That doesn't look like love to me," I told Eve. "Think we should call the police?"

"Don't be silly! And tell them what? That a man we never met and a woman we barely know are having an argument about something we don't know anything about? The police have better things to do."

No doubt, they did. But I couldn't help but worry. "She said she was going to kill him."

"And you know she didn't mean it. Not like that."

"Then maybe we should go into the shop and tell Monsieur Lavoie what's going on by his back door." I latched onto Eve's arm, and when she didn't budge, I played my trump card. "If we don't hurry, the store will be locked up, and you won't be able to get your watch."

She recognized the ploy for what it was and made a face. "Party pooper."

"No, that would be you if you show up tomorrow at lunch with Clint without your watch," I reminded her.

She knew I was right, even if she didn't like it. Eve took one more look toward the verbal knock-down-drag-out going on by the back door and followed me to the shop.

There was a light on inside, and we could see Monsieur over near the front counter. But we had to knock twice before he looked our way, and another time to get him to open the door a crack.

"Yes, yes?" he asked. He peeked around the edge of the door. "What is wrong? What is it you want?"

I was all set to tell him about Drago and Beyla, but Eve didn't give me a chance.

"Well, maybe I just wanted another look at your smiling face, sugar!" Eve slipped inside the store. I had no choice but to follow or end up standing out on the sidewalk by myself. "What we really want is just to pop upstairs." She displayed her empty wrist. "My watch," she said with a little pout. "And I was just devastated when I realized it was gone. You wouldn't make a poor girl spend the whole night without her very favorite piece of jewelry, now would you?"

Something told me that Monsieur Lavoie was tempted to say he would do just that.

Except that he seemed to have something else on his mind. He glanced toward the front counter where he had a tall spice jar opened, along with a measuring cup, a funnel, and a few smaller jars.

"Yes, yes, you must get your watch." One hand on each of our backs, he hurried us over to the door that led to the cooking school. "Jim is gone. Everything is cleaned up for the night. I must leave soon. But if you hurry . . ."

We did. A couple seconds later, we were at the top of the stairs.

With no light except for the glow of the streetlights

outside, the room looked like a negative of itself. The stainless steel stoves still glinted, but all the golden warmth was lost in heavy shadows.

Automatically, I felt along the wall. "I don't know where the light switch is." Don't ask me why, but I was whispering. Must have had something to do with the after-hours atmosphere and the dark. "How are we going to—"

"Don't you worry. I told you I know exactly where I left the watch." Eve stepped into the classroom. "I'll just—ow!" I saw her stoop to rub her knee. "Forgot that bench was in the front of the room."

"And I forgot this." I felt around inside my purse for the pint-size flashlight I always carried with me. I flicked it on and arced the beam around the room. "Better?"

We had our bearings now, and flashlight in hand, I led the way toward the door in the mural of the Café Jacques. On the other side of it was a kitchen that included the sinks where we'd cleaned up our saucepans and soup bowls.

"You're amazing, Annie. Honestly." Eve's voice came out of the dark behind me. "What else do you have in that purse of yours?"

"Antacids. Gum. Pain relievers—aspirin and ibuprofen." I went through the list. I don't know why. Even though we had Monsieur Lavoie's permission, something about being in the school alone after closing made me nervous, and reciting the familiar litany calmed my nerves. "Paper and a pen. My address book. A roll of quarters, just in case." I stopped at the door and Eve caught up.

Shaking her head, she pushed open the door. "Like I said, amazing. Have I ever mentioned that? Next time I need to pack for a long trip, you're the first person I'm going to call."

It was a threat, not a promise. Every time Eve went out of town—anywhere—she called me to help her pack. It was not a pretty thing, stuffing seven days' worth of outfits into a bag she was taking for a two-day trip. Still, I always managed to make it work.

Eve headed into the kitchen. I aimed the light in the right direction, and soon after, I heard her satisfied purr. "Ah, here it is! Right where I thought I left it." In the glow of the flashlight, I saw Eve slip the watch on her arm. She checked the time. "Nine twenty-five already. Can you believe it? The evening went so fast."

One person's *fast* is another's *interminable*. I tried not to think about it or the fact that I had to show up here tomorrow and risk embarrassing myself again. Jim had promised to send us an e-mail tonight for tomorrow's class: appetizers. I wondered if chips and dip counted.

"Ready?" Eve was already back at the door, and we made our way across the classroom. "We can stop for coffee if you're in the mood."

I remembered what she'd said about the time and shook my head. "This late? I'll never sleep. And I have to get to work early tomorrow."

There was just enough light coming through the front window for me to see Eve grin. "How did I know you were going to say that?"

We weren't upstairs that long, but when we got back downstairs to the shop, all but the front window lights were off, and there was no sign of Monsieur Lavoie. For one panicked moment, I thought we'd been locked in. I was already formulating what I'd say to my head teller the next morning to explain why I was late when we heard a noise near the back door.

I peeked outside. Beyla and the man she called Drago were gone. The only one around was Monsieur Lavoie. I was just in time to see him toss something in the Dumpster near the door.

He saw me and just about jumped out of his skin. "Oh! You are done. Already!" He tried for a smile that wasn't exactly convincing, then waved us outside. "We will lock the door behind you, yes? You have what you were looking for?"

Eve held up her arm, displaying the watch.

"Very good. Then we are ready to say good night, no?" He backed away from the Dumpster, distancing himself from whatever he'd been doing. "I will see you both tomorrow, yes?"

Even before we had a chance to answer, he locked the door and scampered into the shadows.

"Well, that was odd." I peered into the dark, but the chef had disappeared around the side of the building. In fact, the only sound I heard was that of a car door slamming and an engine starting up. I had no doubt it was Monsieur Lavoie hightailing it out of there.

"Maybe he's got a hot date." Eve laughed. "Wish I did. We could head over to that bar on Wilson and see who's there tonight."

"Or not." We stepped out of the circle of light thrown by the security lamp near the back door and into the shadows, heading in the opposite direction from Monsieur Lavoie. "Early morning tomorrow, remember? We're getting ready for the yearly audit and—"

The rest of my words dissolved in a little squeal of surprise when I tripped over something.

Something big.

I regained my footing and looked over to where Eve had stopped to see what was wrong. She'd been walking on my right, and whatever I stumbled over, she skirted without incident.

I spun around, squinting through the darkness to make out what I had run into. But all that I could see was something that look like a black garbage bag lying right in what had been my path.

"Except it's too big to be a garbage bag," I mumbled.

"Huh?" Eve came a couple steps closer. "What are you talking about, Annie? Of course it's a garbage bag. What else could it—"

My flashlight was still at the top of my bag. I dragged it out and flicked it on.

I slid the beam along the hulking shape and saw that what I'd mistaken for a black trash bag was really a black coat. Leather.

Drago was still inside it. He was sprawled on the pavement, one hand clutching at his chest. His face was pale, covered with sweat, and contorted with pain.

Four

✖

"ANNIE?" EVE LATCHED ONTO MY ARM SO TIGHT, I knew I'd have bruises by morning. Her breathing was fast and shallow, her eyes wide. "Is that what I think it is? Is it who I think it is? Is he—"

I swallowed hard and reminded myself not to go bonkers. That wouldn't help anybody. Besides, it looked like Eve was on the edge of bonkers herself. And that was plenty for both of us.

I skimmed the light over the body on the pavement. "It's what you think it is," I told Eve. "It's who you think it is. I don't know if he's—"

Once upon a very long time ago, I had thought about being a nurse, and I'd done some volunteer work at a hospital. It was the summer between my junior and senior years of high school. Like I said, a long time ago. But some things you learn you never forget.

I bent and felt for a pulse the way I'd seen the nurses on the floor do it. "It's weak, but it's there," I told Eve. I looked over my shoulder at her, my own panic forgotten in light of the fact that now I knew that we had to act, and fast. "Call 911."

"Call?" In the gloom, I saw the whites of Eve's eyes. She blinked, stunned and afraid. "Maybe we should just get out of here, huh? Beyla said she was going to kill him, Annie. And it sure looks like she tried." She darted a look around the dark back lot. "What if she comes after us?"

It would have been easy to buy into the argument and the panic. Except that we didn't have time for theories, especially ones as goofy as that one.

I made sure to keep my voice level and my words neutral. What Eve needed right now was reassurance. Like it or not, the only place she was going to get it was from me.

"Nobody's coming after anybody," I told her. "No matter what she said, Beyla didn't do this." I glanced over to where Drago lay. "I'm no expert, but I'd say that it looks like he's having a heart attack. And she couldn't have caused a heart attack, could she? We can't run off and leave him, Eve. We need to help him. Give me your phone."

My words didn't penetrate, and I cursed Eve for being hypersensitive and myself for leaving my own cell phone at home. Except for my mom and dad down in Florida and my brother, Larry, out in Colorado, no one ever called. The way I'd figured it, there was no way I'd need my phone at cooking class.

I'd figured wrong.

"Phone," I said again, slower this time so she'd get the message. "He's still alive, Eve. But he's not going to be if we don't do something and do it fast. We've got to call an ambulance. He needs help. Now."

"Help. Right. Gotcha!" Eve shook herself out of her daze. Her hands trembling, she patted down the side pockets of her khaki skirt. "Not here," she said. "Left my phone in the car."

"Then maybe you should go get it?"

"Get it? Yeah."

But Eve was rooted to the spot.

"Eve!" I didn't want to do it, but I didn't have a lot of choice. I raised my voice. "Eve, go to your car. Get your phone. Call 911."

"Call. Yeah." She nodded. But she didn't move.

"All right. Give me the keys." I held out my hand. "I'll get the phone and make the call. You stay with the dying guy."

"Dying?" When she turned them on me, Eve's eyes were filled with tears, and her face was as ashen as Drago's. "You mean, you think he's gonna . . ." She swallowed hard. "I couldn't stay here. I mean . . . I would but . . . but what if you're not back and . . . what if he . . . I mean . . . I couldn't. I—"

"Right." I grabbed her shoulders and turned her to face the street where we'd parked. "Then go get your phone."

"Phone. Yeah. Right." She took off toward the car.

With that taken care of, I concentrated on Drago. And Drago . . . well, he wasn't doing well.

"Drago?" I knelt on the pavement, afraid to get too close to a stranger, but reluctant not to offer what comfort I could to a fellow human being in need. With one finger, I gave him a little nudge. He groaned, and I figured it was a good sign.

"Drago, my name is Annie. My friend Eve went for her phone. We're going to get somebody here to help you."

His eyes flickered open. His gaze wandered aimlessly, to the building where Très Bonne Cuisine was housed, to the stars that twinkled in the navy blue sky above our heads, and finally to a tree just over my left shoulder, near where Eve and I had taken cover so that Beyla and Drago wouldn't see us as we watched them argue.

Just thinking back to everything we heard and saw made a chill race up my spine.

It turned to ice when Drago's gaze fastened on me.

He groped for my hand, and when he found it, he hung

on like there was no tomorrow. For all I knew, for Drago, there wouldn't be.

"Al . . . bas . . . tru." His voice was no more than a breath, and it was even more heavily accented than Beyla's.

"Alabaster?" I wondered if it was the name of his favorite dog. Or his wife. Or if he had some weird lapidary thing going on. "Is that what you said? Alabaster?"

"Alba . . . stru." He didn't so much speak the words as they leaked out of him on the end of a sigh. He reached up and touched my cheek.

His hands were icy. I jerked back, startled.

Just as quickly, I felt as guilty as hell.

Human being in need, remember?

I told myself to get a grip and pressed Drago's clammy hand between both of mine. "Alba Stru? Is it someone's name? I don't know any Alba Stru, but I'll tell you one thing, Drago, I'll find her if that's what you want. When you're better. Right now, though, you don't need to worry about that. We're getting help. You just hang on—you're going to be all right."

Drago gasped from the pain. His breaths came quicker, each one a little more shallow than the last.

Where he found the strength, I don't know, but he pulled his hand from mine. He groped for the breast pocket of his coat, and when he brought his hand out again, he had a piece of paper clutched in his fingers.

"This . . . important. You will see." He pressed the paper into my hand, and I glanced at it. It was a receipt from a restaurant called *Bucharest*. Important? It didn't seem likely, not unless Drago was counting calories and wanted to prove he had a sensible diet.

I turned the receipt over. Scrawled on the back side was what looked to be an address. But what did it mean?

I was just about to ask when Drago moaned. His body convulsed. I shoved the paper into my jacket pocket so that

I could hold his hand again. I squeezed his fingers, and he took a sharp breath, holding it in a long time. Then, with a sound that reminded me of the murmur of wind through the trees, he slowly let it out.

It disappeared into the night air, and on the end of it, Drago went still.

"Drago?" I rubbed his hand between mine.

No response.

"Drago, can you hear me?"

I was talking pretty loud, but he didn't respond.

"Drago, you've got to hang on for just a couple more minutes."

I looked into the eyes that were open and staring right through me, but there was nothing happening behind them.

"Drago?"

I don't know how long I knelt there beside his body. I don't even know if I cried. I do know that I felt helpless.

It wasn't until I heard Eve come huffing and puffing into the lot that I leaned back on my heels.

"Too late," I said, glancing up at her.

Eve's expression fell. "What do you mean, too late? I called 911. They're on their way."

As if on cue, we heard the distant sounds of sirens. They got closer, and before we knew it, the area behind Très Bonne Cuisine was awash in pulsing red light.

The paramedics were gems. They moved in and moved us back so they could get to work administering CPR. When that didn't work, they shocked Drago with one of those portable defibrillators. But the whole thing went on too long. Five minutes. Ten. Fifteen. I knew it wasn't a good sign, even before I heard one of them say something about "no use."

At some point, I realized Eve was crying. I put an arm around her shoulders and together, we watched the flurry of activity and the expressions of the paramedics that started

out with so much intensity melt into despair and then resig-
nation. Through it all, I felt drained and strangely ghoulish.

Was it right for us to stand there and watch?

Should we have minded our own business and gotten on
with our lives and left these men to their work?

Was there anything we could have done? Anything that
would have changed the outcome? Anything that could
have kept poor Drago from . . .

"I'm calling it." Wiping one hand across his forehead,
the paramedic in charge backed away from the body.

I gave Eve's shoulders a squeeze. "You're shivering."

She sniffed and scrubbed a finger under her nose. "I've
never seen anybody die before."

"No. Me, neither." Technically, of course, Eve hadn't
seen Drago die, but I wasn't about to argue. In this case,
close definitely counted. "It's so sad. Dying in a parking lot
with nobody around but strangers."

"Beyla probably planned it that way," Eve murmured.

I rolled my eyes, but I couldn't be too hard on Eve.
Though she tried for a tough-girl exterior, I knew that right
below the surface, Eve was as soft as a marshmallow. Wild
theories or no wild theories, just being this close to
death—even the death of a man we knew only in passing—
was bound to throw her for a loop.

"Beyla had nothing to do with this," I reminded her. As
they laid a white sheet over Drago's face, I remembered his
last, labored words.

A couple of the paramedics went back to the ambulance
to get a stretcher and I hurried over to the head paramedic,
whose nametag identified him as Sean. He was a muscular
guy with a serious face and buzz cut. He had a clipboard in
his hand, and was filling out a report.

I stepped around the white sheet and the shape beneath
it. "He was asking for someone," I said. "A woman, I think.
Are you going to be able to find out—"

He put a hand on my arm. "You were here, right? You're the one who called us?"

"That was me." Eve moved up behind me. "I did do the right thing, didn't I?"

Sean stepped back and looked Eve up and down. "Oh, yeah. You did great. It takes one amazing woman to keep her head when something like this is happening."

"It was nothing." Eve sighed. "I just couldn't stand by and watch another human being suffer and not take action. You understand. I'm sure you do. I know that's exactly why you chose your noble profession."

I figured I had to put an end to things before the flirtation got out of hand.

"Let's not forget Alba," I exclaimed. They both looked at me like I was nuts. "Alba. The woman Drago mentioned right before he died."

Sean checked his clipboard. "Drago. Yeah, Drago Kravic. That's the name on the driver's license in the guy's wallet. I'm a little mixed up. You knew the deceased?"

"We don't." Eve piped up before I could explain about the cooking school or how we'd heard Beyla and Drago argue. "He told us his name. Right before he breathed his last," she murmured, heaving another sigh. I turned to her in disbelief, ready to protest, but she gave me her best *keep your mouth shut—or else!* look, and plowed ahead. Luckily, Sean was still looking at his clipboard. "We didn't know him at all. We were just walking through the parking lot and there he was. It was . . ." She blinked rapidly. "Well, I don't know if I'll be able to sleep tonight."

"Maybe Alba won't either, when she learns the news," I suggested. I turned to Sean. "Alba Stru. I think that's the name he mentioned. Will you be able to find her?"

He consulted the clipboard again. "We found his wallet. That means we've got all his vitals. Name. Address. Phone. If this Alba is next of kin, you can be sure we'll find her. In the meantime . . ." He signaled to his crew, and they lifted Drago's body onto the stretcher and slid it into the ambulance. Sean gave a wave as if to say that he'd be right there.

"There's going to be a police officer here in a couple minutes," he said. "Just routine. They always send out a patrol car when something like this happens. Actually, they should have been here by now—there must have been some delay. If you could just stick around and give the officer your names and addresses . . ." He looked at Eve when he said it, and I thought he was going to ask for her phone number, too, except one of his buddies called to him, and he turned toward the ambulance.

"There's the officer now," Sean said, as he hopped in. He pointed toward the green-and-white patrol car just pulling into the lot. "Thanks for your help, ladies."

"Oh, no. Thank *you*!" Eve put a hand up to wave.

I slapped it down. "This isn't a speed dating event," I told her from between clenched teeth. I figured we didn't need one of Arlington's finest to find us fighting. "And why did you make up that story about how Drago told us his name as he breathed his last? Why didn't you just tell him the truth about Beyla and the argument—"

"Now, hold on." Eve straightened her shoulder, posing, no doubt, in preparation for meeting the police officer who had stopped the patrol car. "You're the one who insists that Beyla didn't have anything to do with Drago's death. So why mention it? Besides, it made for a better story, don't you think? The dying guy breathing his last words to the women who came to his aid."

"Woman," I reminded her, preparing to launch into a speech about the consequences of lying to a paramedic. But then I realized Eve wasn't listening. Which wouldn't have worried me so much if I hadn't caught a glimpse of the expression on her face.

Eve's gaze was fastened to the patrol car that had just

pulled into the lot. The door swung open. Eve's jaw dropped. For a moment, I couldn't tell if she was surprised or angry or—

She grabbed my arm. Tighter than she had when we first found Drago.

More bruises. Just what I didn't need.

I glanced from my friend to the officer just getting out of the car. It was a woman, and though she was wearing a standard uniform hat, I could tell she was a redhead. She also just happened to be gorgeous. The officer was a few years younger than Eve and me. She had a thin nose, high cheekbones, porcelain skin, and a body that didn't have an extra ounce of fat anywhere on it.

"Eve? What's wrong?"

Eve's muscles clenched. She raised her chin and pasted a smile on her face that reminded me of the one I'd seen her use in every beauty pageant she'd ever been in over the years.

The officer closed in on us. Eve spoke, adding a dollop of Southern accent to her voice until her words were as thick as hominy.

"Why, if it isn't Kaitlin," she said. "Officer Kaitlin Sands."

And the pieces fell into place.

 I SHOULD EXPLAIN RIGHT HERE THAT EVE HAS HAD what might be called a checkered love life.

Or maybe *interesting* is a better word.

Remember Clint? And Joe? Michael? And Scott? Well, that's nothing new.

The thing is that guys love Eve, and Eve loves them back.

She also loves being engaged. She currently was what I charitably called *between engagements*, but I had no doubt there would be another big announcement sometime soon.

As always, it would be followed by a flurry of wedding plans that included me getting fitted for a matron of honor dress that was cut too skintight/was too clingy/showed way too much décolletage for my round figure. But I never worried.

I knew I'd never have to march down the aisle in any one of those dresses.

Why?

Because I knew the engagement would be called off. Or more specifically, that Eve would call off the engagement.

Just like she'd done five times before.

But here's the kicker . . . If my memory serves me correctly (and it always does), Eve's been engaged six times.

It doesn't take a rocket scientist to do the math. Or to figure out that it was the One Who Got Away who had gotten under her skin and was still causing her to itch.

His name was Tyler Cooper, and at the time of their engagement, he was an Arlington patrol officer. Tyler was smart and cocky. He was dedicated to his career, a real up-and-comer within the department. In fact, I'd heard through the grapevine that since their break up, Tyler had been promoted to detective and was working homicide.

I'd also heard that he was newly engaged to another cop.

A woman by the name of Kaitlin Sands.

Five

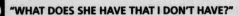

"WHAT DOES SHE HAVE THAT I DON'T HAVE?"

It was the next evening. We were back at Très Bonne Cuisine. And Eve was still obsessing about Kaitlin Sands.

It's not that I'm not sympathetic to Eve's romantic troubles, but let's face it, there's only so much a girl can take. I made a face.

Not to worry, Eve didn't see it. I had my head inside a grocery sack. I was searching for the small (and expensive) packet of fresh chives I'd bought for tonight's three appetizer recipes: grilled goat cheese bundles, vegetables on skewers, and something Jim called "pinwheels under wraps" in the e-mail we'd all received the night before.

I grabbed the chives and looked over at Eve. "A gun?" I suggested.

"That's not funny, Annie, and you know it's not what I mean." Eve reached into her own grocery bag and pulled out a jar of dried chives, a loaf of white bread, and a pound of bacon. The wrapped-in-plastic kind, not the pricey bacon from the butcher counter like I'd bought. "There has to be a reason Tyler chose Kaitlin over me."

This time I couldn't help myself. I sighed, not caring if Eve sensed my frustration. There's a limit to everyone's patience, even a best friend's. I had been listening to her stew for the past twenty-four hours—not to mention the fact that I was still a little uncomfortable with the way Eve had conducted our question-and-answer session with Officer Sands. Eve gave her the same reduced, two-minute version of events she had given Sean the paramedic before dragging me off to the car. I realized Eve would rather eat nails than talk to Kaitlin longer than she had to, but lying to a police officer was serious trouble, even without an ex-boyfriend thrown into the mix.

"We've been through it all before," I reminded Eve. "Tyler didn't choose Kaitlin over you. He'd already broken up with you before he ever met Kaitlin."

Far be it from me to bring up the fact that Tyler had spelled out his reasons at the time of the big breakup: Eve was shallow, he said. Eve wasn't career-oriented. She wasn't the woman of his dreams because the woman of his dreams was smart, and clever enough to reason her way past more than just what color lipstick to wear with which outfit.

"Tyler has mush for brains," I said instead, and my heart went out to my best friend in spite of myself. Eve had a heart as big as Texas, and even though she sometimes exhibited an ego that was just as large, she truly cared about people. OK, so she wasn't a deep thinker. And she wasn't a career woman. So she'd had four different jobs at four different department stores in the last two years. Was it her fault that the economy was sputtering and retail establishments were cutting staff? Besides, the fact that when one employer let her go, another always picked her up proved that her personality outshone her résumé.

"He doesn't know what he's missing," I said a little

more forcefully, and this time, it was the absolute truth. "He'll live to regret it."

Fortunately, I didn't have to go any further—at that moment, Beyla walked in the room. Eve's eyes narrowed. She leaned in close to me and whispered, "You think she knows?"

"You mean about Drago?" I was whispering, too. I guess there's something about death that demands reverence. "What do you think?"

Eve stood back and cocked her head, studying Beyla. Tonight, just like the night before, she was dressed in black. She wore a black skirt that skimmed her ankles, a long-sleeved black top, and black open-toed shoes. Most women would have looked frumpy in the outfit. Not Beyla. Even with her hair pulled away from her face and not a speck of jewelry or any makeup that I could see, Beyla looked elegant.

But she sure didn't look upset.

Eve wrinkled her nose. "It's the ones who look like they don't know and don't care who you should always suspect."

"Suspect?" I was shocked by her use of the word, and my exclamation came out a little too loud. I slapped my hand over my mouth and looked around, afraid that someone might have heard. None of my fellow students paid me any mind, except for Beyla. When I looked her way, she was staring right back at me, those dark eyes of hers focused on mine as if she could read my mind.

I turned my back on her and lowered my voice.

"Get over it, Eve. Beyla didn't have anything to do with Drago's death. Not unless she knows some mumbo jumbo magic that can cause a guy to have a heart attack even when she's nowhere around."

"But they were fighting. Remember? And he was plenty upset. And sometimes when people get upset, their blood pressure rises and their heart races and—"

Have I mentioned that I've known Eve a long time?

Long enough so that when she's thinking, plotting, and planning, I can just about see the wheels turning inside her head. I saw them turning now, and I didn't like where those wheels were headed. Not one bit.

As usual, before I could choke out a protest, Eve had already made up her mind.

"Let's go ask Beyla about Drago." She grabbed my hand and dragged me across the room.

Beyla didn't look surprised to see us. In fact, she basically ignored us. She kept unloading her groceries, carefully grouping them: the goat cheese with the collards, the wooden skewers with the veggies, the bacon with the cream cheese. How she knew what went with what, I hadn't a clue, but then again, she had mentioned that she was a good cook. Maybe that sort of thing is instinctive to someone who knows her way around a kitchen.

"Oh, Beyla . . ." Eve put a sympathetic hand on Beyla's sleeve. That got her attention. She stopped her unloading and turned to us, her expression wooden but her eyes sparking with curiosity. "We . . ." Eve looked my way. "We just had to tell you how sorry we were to hear the news."

Beyla set down the eggplant she was holding and brushed her hands together. "You are talking about what?" she asked. She looked at her little pile of groceries and frowned. This has something to do with the food I have bought?"

Eve's smile was just sympathetic enough. Not too personal, not too flip. "Not about the groceries. About Drago. We heard the news. It's very sad."

A vee appeared between Beyla's perfectly arched eyebrows. "Drago? I know no one by this name."

Eve moved a step closer and lowered her voice. Every one of her words dripped Southern charm. "I know it's hard. When someone dies, I mean. I know you're probably trying to pretend—"

Eve's hand was still on Beyla's arm; Beyla shrugged it

away and stepped back. "I do not know what you are talking about."

I could see that Beyla was uncomfortable. "Eve." I tugged my friend's arm. "Beyla doesn't feel like talking about Drago right now. Maybe we'd better—"

"Who is this Drago person you ask about?" Beyla's voice was edged with irritation. "Why you insist on bothering me? I told you, I do not know this man."

Eve raised her chin. I knew we were in for trouble. "Then why were you fighting with him in the parking lot last night?" she asked.

Beyla's top lip curled. On her, it looked good, but it sure wasn't a friendly expression. Though her dark eyes sparked, her voice never wavered. "I do not hang around—that is the expression, yes?—in parking lots. I do not talk to men I do not know. And I do not know this Drago."

"Then you didn't have anything to do with him dying?"

Beyla's eye's snapped. This was too much, even for Eve. I had to stop her before she made the situation even worse.

"We're sorry for your loss," I interjected, jerking Eve's arm. For a moment, I thought she wasn't going to budge. But then, after one last cold stare, she turned and stalked back to our station.

I closed my eyes, took a few deep breaths, and wished the floor would swallow me.

Eve was back at it the moment I rejoined her. "Well that proves it, doesn't it," she hissed. "If Beyla's not guilty, why is she acting so innocent?"

Did I mention that Eve isn't the most logical person in the world?

I shook my head, certain that there was a morsel of reasoning somewhere in her theory. Maybe I just didn't get it. Or maybe Tyler had been right all along.

"Of course she looks innocent," I shot back. "She is innocent. She said she didn't know Drago."

"But we saw them arguing."

"Maybe we made a mistake. Maybe it wasn't her."

"Maybe she's lying to us."

"Maybe she is. Maybe because it's none of our business."

"Maybe because she killed him."

"Maybe she's just innocent."

"Or she's guilty, and she doesn't want us to know."

"Or she didn't have anything to do with it. She *couldn't* have had anything to do with it, because it was a heart attack, remember?"

"Or she knew he had a heart condition, and that's why she picked a fight in the first place."

"Don't forget, we saw Monsieur Lavoie having words with Drago, too."

"Yeah, but that was long before ol' Drago kicked the bucket. Beyla was right there minutes before. I'll bet she said something she knew would get him all upset and then he'd have a heart attack and it would kill him and she wouldn't be anywhere near when it happened so nobody would ever suspect her."

"Or—"

"Uh, ladies?"

The moment I heard Jim's voice, I realized that both Eve and I had gotten so carried away we weren't paying attention to what was going on around us. Class had started.

My cheeks caught fire. I groaned and made an oh-my-gosh-I-can't-believe-how-stupid-we-look face at Eve before I turned toward the front of the room.

"Now that I've got everyone's attention . . ." Jim smiled our way, and that dimple showed up in his left cheek.

Not that I was looking or anything. Even before my blood started a warm thrum through my veins, I'd come to terms with the reality of the situation, which was as plain as the expression on Jim's face when he looked toward our cooking station.

His smile was meant for Eve.

Of course.

I could stop worrying about looking like a dope. Chances were, Jim didn't even notice I was in the room. Or on the planet, for that matter.

I told myself not to forget it and prepared to get down to business.

"Appetizers." Jim swept a look around the classroom. "How many of you depend on chips and dips and maybe the occasional bag of pretzels?"

Honest to a fault, I raised my hand. Everyone laughed.

"Dump the grease and the fat grams," Jim said. I suddenly wished I could hide all the evidence of the fat grams I'd been consuming lately inside jeans and a baggy sweatshirt instead of the green capris and orange summer top I'd chosen in honor of the on-again, off-again warm weather.

"It's easy to make excellent appetizers that don't involve saturated fats and don't come straight out of the bag," Jim said. "Tonight, we're going to learn how."

That didn't sound so hard. I breathed a little easier and reached for the bacon that was still tucked in my grocery bag.

"Except . . ."

The single word from Jim froze each and every one of us in place.

"We're going to mix things up a little," he said.

I was all for that. Maybe I'd be so busy mixing, I'd forget Eve's crazy accusations as well as how mortified I'd been to be part of her confrontation with Beyla.

"I want you out of your comfort zone," Jim continued, and I snickered under my breath. If he thought comfort had anything to do with me in the kitchen, he had a lot to learn.

"Tonight," he said, "we're going to change cooking partners."

A murmur went through the classroom.

"Oh, come on!" Jim laughed. "It's not the end of the world. If you can cook with your friends, you can cook with anyone. So let's get to it." He moved closer to our cooking stations. "You . . ." He pointed to the Incredible Hulk. "With you." He took the mother from the station in front of ours by the hand and moved her into place. "You . . ." He pointed to another student. "With you. You—" He turned toward Eve, but he was already too late. Before he could assign her a partner, John, the accountant, had already staked his claim. As if by magic, John's groceries had already displaced mine. He and Eve were chatting like old buddies.

Which pretty much left me out in the cold.

"You . . ." When Jim pointed my way, he grinned. I felt a little warmer. "Let's put you . . ." He glanced around the room. "Let's put you over there with Beyla."

"Maybe that's not such a good idea." It slipped out before I could stop myself. Beyla kept staring straight ahead, and I could only imagine the thoughts going through her head.

It was bad enough that Jim had paired her with the woman who'd set off the smoke alarms in the classroom the night before. But also the woman who had been party to practically accusing her of murder?

Maybe I could make it up to her.

I took comfort in that thought as I stepped around John to repack my chives and my bacon and my goat cheese. I sidestepped my fellow students who were busy playing musical cooking stations. I'm not very tall, and it was hard to see across the room, and the next time I caught sight of Beyla, she was reaching into her purse, apparently putting something away. As I approached, she tossed the purse aside and stepped away from the cook station.

She greeted me with, "We will use your stove."

It was better than I deserved, which, as far as I could

tell, was more along the lines of *Get out of here; I don't want to work with a woman who has crazy ideas about me murdering a man I didn't know.*

"Can't." I shrugged and set down my bag. "Eve and John have already started to work over there."

"We will tell them to move."

Why is it that beautiful women think they own the world?

I bit my tongue and got out the pan we'd be using to boil water and cook the collards. There was a small sink between each of the two-stove stations, and I filled the pan with water and set it on the stove.

"Let's just get to work," I suggested.

Beyla took another step back. She ran her tongue over her lips. "We will find another place."

"There is no other place. In case you haven't noticed, all the other places are taken."

"Then we will say we cannot—"

I wasn't listening. I didn't blame Beyla for not wanting to cook with me, but we didn't have any choice. Better to get this over with than to stand here and argue.

I turned my back on her, vaguely aware that when I reached to turn on the stove, she moved away.

I flicked on the burner.

And the stove blew up in my face.

WHEN I CAME TO MY SENSES, I WAS ON MY BUTT with my back against the wall. I had a vague recollection of a noise that sounded like the base line of a Metallica song, and of a wall of fire bursting out of the stove. Fortunately, it came at me with enough force to knock me off my feet. I was stunned but not burned.

My ears were blocked, though, and my head pounded. I think the funny aroma that tickled my nose had something to do with my singed eyebrows. It all must have happened pretty fast, because for a nanosecond, I was alone, and everything around me was perfectly quiet.

Then all hell broke lose.

My fellow students ran to surround me, their words a jumble of noises I couldn't decipher. I saw Eve fight her way through the crowd. She knelt at my side.

"Annie? Are you OK?"

At least that's what I thought she said. It was hard to tell, considering that her words sounded like they came from underneath a thick feather pillow.

I shook my head, hoping to clear it. All the motion did was make it pound harder.

"Annie?" This time it wasn't Eve's voice—it was lower and richer. I turned to find Jim kneeling on my other side. "What the hell—" He glanced up toward the stove, where Beyla was standing just outside the ring of soot around the cooking station where I was supposed to be working. She shrugged, and the simple gesture made it clear that she had no idea what had happened or what I'd done to cause the conflagration.

"I turned on the stove." OK, so that much was obvious. I wasn't exactly thinking straight. My voice sounded like it came from far, far away, and I spoke a little louder. "All I did was turn on the stove."

"I know. I saw it." Jim offered me a hand and helped me to my feet. The room wobbled a little, and I guess I did, too. He put an arm around my shoulders.

"I swear," he grumbled, the burr in his voice more pronounced than ever, "if that no good son of a bitch Lavoie isn't taking care of the equipment the way he should be—" He remembered where he was and swallowed the rest of his words. "Are you all right?"

I was when he was holding me like this.

"I'm fine," I told him and reminded myself not to get

carried away. "My ears are just a little . . ." I shook my head again and the rushing noise inside them settled down a bit. "The stove . . ." I looked that way and cringed at the mess. "I blew it up."

"It wasn't your fault."

Jim was being kind. He patted my shoulder. "I don't want you to get discouraged."

Now he was being delusional.

"I almost destroyed the entire school."

"There's no real damage." He shooed everyone back to their places. When I tried to take a couple steps, he stood at my side just to be sure I made it. "As long as you're all right . . ."

"I am." I tried another couple steps. "Nothing broken," I assured him. "Nothing burned. Nothing—" I glanced down at my capris, which were covered with black soot. "Almost nothing ruined."

"Don't you worry about that. What's important is that you're not hurt. All right," he raised his voice so he could be heard above the hubbub. "Annie's fine, and we'll get the stove fixed. She and Beyla can work up front here with me tonight. Before any of the rest of you get started, I'm going to come around from station to station and test the stoves to make sure we don't have any more surprises."

I smiled at Eve to assure her that I was all right. Knees still shaking, I headed to the front of the room. It wasn't until the last second that I realized I'd left my ingredients back at Beyla's stove.

My grocery bag was crisp around the edges, but nothing inside sustained any damage. Rather than leave a trail of ash, I took out the ingredients one by one and piled them in my arms. I was all set to return to the front of the room when I dropped my collards. I stooped to retrieve the bundle of greens, and stopped cold.

There was a fragment of a piece of paper on the floor

just in front of the stove. It was partially burned, which told me that it had been somewhere in the vicinity of the stove when it blew. The top line had gone up in flames but I could read the block letters of the second line well enough. And what I read didn't exacly make me feel warm and fuzzy.

"You are next."

Six

 WAS THE NOTE MEANT FOR ME? DID IT REFER TO Drago's death?

And if so, was it a warning?

It was the next night, but questions still swirled around my brain.

Fortunately, between that and the headache that felt like it was going to rip apart my skull, I didn't have a chance to think about how the rest of the class had progressed after the explosion.

Perhaps I should say regressed.

My goat cheese bundles turned out soggy. My skewered veggies were limp. And the bacon pinwheels? Well, let's just say they gave the term *crispy* a whole new meaning.

Which I suppose in the great scheme of things was better than how crispy I would have been if the explosion hadn't thrown me back and out of the blast range.

Just thinking about it all brought me back around to the note.

And that made my head hurt all over again.

I massaged my temples with the tips of my fingers while I listened to Jim get us started on night number three: Superb Salads and Dazzling Dressings.

"Freshness, that's the key." Jim stood at the front of the room, a bunch of romaine in one hand and an expression on his face that was almost transcendent. This guy loved to cook. I mean, he really loved it. Go figure.

"You always want your vegetables to be as fresh as possible," Jim said. He rolled the *r* in *fresh*, and the sound tickled its way up my spine. "They need to be nice and crispy."

There was that word again.

I groaned.

"Are you all right?" At least Eve remembered to keep her voice down. Neither of us wanted to be caught talking in class again. "You look worried."

"I'm fine," I whispered back.

Eve didn't look convinced. She shot a look across the room toward the stove where I'd nearly been fried the night before. It had been fixed, Jim assured us, and it was as clean as a whistle. Still, Beyla had refused to work there again, and I for one couldn't blame her. The Incredible Hulk had taken her place, and Beyla and her cooking partner, John, were working one station closer to us. I made sure I kept my voice down so she couldn't hear me.

"I'm just thinking," I told Eve. "That's all."

She nodded. "I know just what you mean. I've been doing a lot of thinking, too."

I'd told Eve about the note, and I knew it had only cemented her theory about our mysterious classmate's guilt.

Eve was 100 percent positive that it all came down to Beyla.

"I'm telling you, Annie, she looks as guilty as hell," Eve said.

"She doesn't." I knew this for a fact, because I was looking right at Beyla, and Beyla was calmly going about her business as usual, unpacking her ingredients and setting up her cooking station.

But Eve wasn't about to take logic into consideration.

OK, I admit it. Mentioning the note to Eve had been a major blunder. I knew it the moment I opened my mouth. But let's face it, I had a good excuse. I'd been pretty upset. And worried. I'd been thrown for a loop (literally and figuratively), and so darned confused by the whole thing, I'd just naturally shared my discovery with Eve.

And Eve had just naturally blown the whole thing out of proportion.

Sure I found the note. Sure the stove went kablooey. But that didn't mean that one thing was related to the other.

Did it?

In my ordered, logical mind, I liked to think it didn't. Because I knew in my ordered, logical mind that if it did, I was still in danger.

Call me the queen of denial, but I had decided to believe that the note had nothing to do with me. That it wasn't referring to Drago's death. That the whole stove incident was nothing more than an unfortunate accident, and that I just happened to be in the wrong place at the wrong time.

The explosion was a desperate attempt by the culinary gods, that's what it was. A not-so-subtle way for the powers that be to warn me to stay away from anything that even resembled cooking.

And the note?

It had simply fallen out of somebody's purse or pocket. *You are next* in line at a doctor's office. *You are next* because whoever "you" was had a birthday coming up. *You are next* for a haircut or a nail appointment or for a tire rotation down at the garage.

Delusional? Sure. But it beat thinking that Beyla was out to get me.

While I was busy pondering all this, Jim told us to start

stripping romaine leaves off the bunch, and I did, setting them in a colander so that I could rinse them.

"Maybe the note wasn't meant for me at all," I suggested to Eve. "Maybe it has nothing to do with any of us. Or maybe someone left it there for Beyla."

"Yeah." Eve sniffed. "That's why you saw her putting a pen back in her purse."

"I didn't say anything about a pen. I said I saw her with her purse."

"I'll bet there's a pen in it."

"I'll bet there's one in yours."

"OK. Fine. If that's how you want to be." Eve tossed the last of her romaine into the colander and turned on the water. "Maybe she didn't write it. But if that's true, why—"

Eve's words stopped as if they'd been snipped in half by scissors. Her colander was still under the spigot, and water was still running over her romaine. But Eve was frozen in place. All it took was one look at the doorway to know why.

A man had just stepped into the room.

Tyler Cooper.

"My hair looks like hell." Still staring toward where her ex-fiancé was introducing himself to Jim, Eve ran one shaking hand over her ponytail. She blinked rapidly, her eyes moist with emotion. "Kaitlin must have mentioned to him that she saw me. That's got to be why he's here. He didn't know where to find me before now."

It didn't seem likely, at least not to me, but there was no use pointing it out. As her theories about Beyla proved all too clearly, once Eve got something into her head, it was nearly impossible to dislodge it.

That's why I didn't bother to mention that Tyler was a cop, and that cops can find anyone anytime they want. And that Eve hadn't moved since the days when she and Tyler were a couple, that her phone number hadn't changed, and that he'd bought her cell phone at the same time he bought his own. Her number was only one digit different from his.

"Ladies and gentlemen . . ." Jim tapped a spoon on the side of his metal colander to get our attention. He wore a serious expression, and a thread of uneasiness knotted in my stomach.

Why was Tyler Cooper at Très Bonne Cuisine?

"We've got a visitor, and I'm going to let him explain what he's doing here." Jim turned to Tyler. "This is Lieutenant Tyler Cooper of the Arlington Police Department. He's—"

"Here to see me," Eve said under her breath, standing a little straighter.

"Here to tell us some rather disturbing news," Jim finished.

Eve's shoulders drooped. She looked at me, confusion clouding an expression that only moments before was wavering between hope and disbelief. Before she could say a word, Tyler cleared his throat and stepped to the center of the room.

I have to admit, I was never quite sure what Eve saw in Tyler. Just like I couldn't quite remember what it was about him that I didn't like.

Oh, he was good-looking enough. He was a smidgen under six feet tall, with broad shoulders, sandy hair, and eyes that, in the right light, looked like they were lit with blue neon. But with Tyler . . . well, his physical appearance wasn't nearly as important as his attitude. And Tyler had attitude to spare. I suppose it was one of the things that made him a good cop. Tyler was tough, and every move he made was designed to make sure no one would ever forget it.

We knew it now, just by the way he stood there with his shoulders squared and pulled back slightly, his chin raised, his jaw tensed. He sized up each of us in turn, and I swear, he didn't even flinch when his gaze landed on Eve.

Now I remembered what I didn't like about Tyler.

He had a cold, cold heart.

"Most of you have probably heard by now that a man died in the parking lot behind the store two nights ago," Tyler said. Apparently, not everyone did know. There was a buzz around the room and I automatically looked Beyla's way.

She didn't even blink an eye.

Tyler silenced the class with a look. "His name was Drago Kravic. Did any of you know him?"

My hand twitched. Twelve years of Catholic schooling had taught me nothing if not how to be honest. Eve slapped her hand over mine to keep it in place.

Beyla didn't move a muscle.

"It doesn't matter if you did or didn't know him," Tyler went on. "What does matter . . ." Again he glanced around the room. It wasn't like I had anything to feel guilty about— well, except for fibbing to Kaitlin Sands—but just the touch of Tyler's icy blue gaze made me shift from foot to foot.

"We were sure he had a heart attack," Tyler said. "Now . . ." He shrugged. "Well, let's just put it this way. This morning, an autopsy was performed on Mr. Kravic. And now we know that he was murdered."

Murder?

The single word shivered through me, turning my blood to ice water. If Drago was the victim of a killer, *you are next* took on a whole new meaning.

I clutched the countertop to steady my suddenly wobbly legs as Tyler finished up. "Maybe you saw something," he said. "Maybe you heard something. That's what I'm here to find out. You just go about your business and do your cooking. I'll come around and talk to each of you in turn."

"Ladies room," Eve said. She turned off the water, grabbed her purse, and ducked out. I wanted nothing more than to go with her, but I knew it would be suspicious if I did, so I stayed put. While I waited, I forced myself to keep busy. I rinsed my romaine and broke it into bits, just the way Jim recommended. My bits were too bitty, and when I added what was supposed to be a drizzle of olive oil, it turned into more of a rainstorm. The salt and fresh ground pepper I sprinkled on sort of clumped in the oil and sank to the bottom of the bowl. I crumbled some blue cheese just like Jim showed us and got more on the floor than in the salad.

All the while, I was watching out of the corner of my eye as Tyler walked around the room.

Eve was back in a flash, a fresh coat of lipstick on her mouth, a little more mascara on her lashes. "Has he been by yet?" she asked, but she wasn't looking at me. Her eyes followed Tyler as he made his way from station to station, talking to my fellow students and writing in a leather-covered notebook.

When he got around to Beyla, I stopped to see what was going to happen. I couldn't hear more than the low rumble of Tyler's voice and Beyla's higher-pitched, murmured replies, but I knew he was asking questions, and she was answering them. She nodded now and then. She shook her head.

I'm no mind reader, but my guess is that she told Tyler exactly what she'd told us the night before: Drago? Drago who?

And then it was our turn.

I wasn't imagining it: there was a bit more swagger in Tyler's walk when he sauntered over. I could feel the tension that tingled through Eve's body like electricity.

"Why, if it isn't Eve DeCateur." Tyler grinned at Eve and acknowledged me with a tip of his head. "And Annie Capshaw. I might have known I'd find you two together."

"Do I know you?" Eve stepped back, her head cocked, and studied Tyler for a moment. I had to hand it to her, she could look as poised facing down an ex-fiancé as she had onstage back in her beauty pageant days. If I hadn't just spent how many hours listening to her go on and on about Kaitlin Sands, even I would have been convinced that Eve didn't care one iota about Tyler.

He was cold, but she was cooler.

I shivered.

"Why yes, I think we have met." Eve's Southern accent had never been more pronounced. Her eyes wide, she pointed one perfectly manicured finger in Tyler's direction. "Didn't you write me a ticket once on the George Washington Parkway?"

"Never worked traffic, ma'am." Tyler turned to a clean notebook page, a signal that the pleasantries, such as they were, were over. He was all business now. "I understand you two were with Drago Kravic when he died."

Eve didn't so much frown as she pouted. In a pretty sort of way, of course. "Why, that sweet little Kaitlin told you that, didn't she? I'll bet that little girl just tells you all sorts of things. Sharing. It's so important to any relationship." She finished her riff with a lift of her shoulders. "Now, what was it we were talking about?"

"Drago Kravic." Tyler was not amused. I could tell because a muscle twitched at the base of his jaw. "What can you tell me about him?"

"Not a thing, of course," Eve said, at the same time I blurted out, "We saw him with Beyla, just a little while before he died."

Eve gave me one of those looks but I wasn't about to be put off. She might have steamrolled me into keeping quiet when Kaitlin questioned us the night Drago died, but that's when we thought the man had died of a heart attack. Now that we knew it was murder . . .

Well, it was my civic duty to tell Tyler everything I knew, wasn't it?

"You saw the deceased? With her?" Tyler's laser gaze swiveled over to where Beyla was chopping parsley while she talked quietly to John. "She just told me she didn't know the man."

"Then she's lying," Eve interjected. And I had to admit, her theory about Beyla was growing more and more convincing. "They were fighting, her and Drago. Right before he keeled over."

After a year of dating her and another few months of engagement, Tyler was well aware of Eve's tendency to overstate things. He turned to me. "Is it true?"

I nodded.

"And when exactly was that?" he asked.

I thought back to everything that happened that night. "It was just after nine o'clock," I told Tyler. "I remember because Eve left her watch here. We were already on our way home, and we turned around and came back. When we got here, we saw Drago and Beyla in the parking lot. We couldn't hear everything they were saying, but it was pretty obvious that it wasn't a friendly chat. A couple minutes later, we came up here and got Eve's watch. When she slipped it on, she commented that it was exactly nine twenty-five."

"That's impossible, officer." Though we'd kept our voices down, John, the accountant, had apparently been listening. He walked over and joined in the conversation. "Beyla and I went for coffee after class that night. By nine twenty-five . . . well, I'm certain we'd already ordered and had our lattes in front of us. There's no way she could have been anywhere near here at that time, or even for a half hour or so before then."

I shook my head, certain of the facts. "Eve checked her watch. It was—"

"I'm sure I have the receipt somewhere." John patted down the pockets of his brown polyester pants and peeked in the pocket of the yellow shirt he had buttoned all the way to the neck. (After all, he is an accountant.)

"Maybe it's at home in the jacket I wore that night,"

John said. "Yeah, I'm sure that's where I stuck it. I'd be glad to stop at the police station with it when I find it. Then you'll see, officer. Beyla and I got to Starbucks just a couple minutes before nine. I know their receipts are stamped with the time. There's no way these ladies could have seen Beyla arguing with that man. At nine twenty-five, Beyla was with me."

Tyler dismissed John with an appreciative nod, then turned toward Eve and me. "You were saying?"

"We were telling you what happened!" Eve stepped toward him, her eyes snapping. "If you'd pay half the attention you need to pay, Tyler Cooper, you'd know—"

"What? That you'd like nothing better than to see me fall flat on my face when it comes to this investigation?" Tyler snorted. "Oh yeah, don't pretend it isn't true, Eve. Kaitlin told me how uncooperative you were the night she was here."

"We told her everything she needed to know." I butted in. Better fudge the truth than to watch Eve and Tyler go at each other. Even though they kept their voices low, there was no mistaking the animosity between them. The other students in class had stopped what they were doing and were watching the show. "We reported everything just as it happened."

"Except that when you talked to Officer Sands"—Tyler turned to me, automatically making the *you* plural—"you never mentioned that you saw Drago with Beyla. And Beyla says she never laid eyes on the man. Seems kind of odd, doesn't it? Plus, in case you weren't paying attention, Beyla has an alibi. You swear she and Drago were at each other's throats at a time when a witness says they couldn't have been together. You admit you didn't bother to mention any of this to Officer Sands. And now all of a sudden, you remember? I can't believe it, Eve." He looked her way, and suddenly, it was personal again. "Don't you have anything else to do but leave the scene of a man's death and go home and concoct a crazy story just so you can make my life more difficult?"

"It's not like that at all," I said. "We didn't mention Beyla to Kaitlin because—" Eve shot a dagger look in my direction, and I stopped short. I knew exactly what that look meant. I'd better not mention how jealous she was of Kaitlin, or more to the point, how jealous she was of Kaitlin's relationship with Tyler. If I did, I'd have to start looking for a new best friend.

"There is something else we should tell you," I said instead. "Drago mentioned somebody named Alba. Alba Stru. Right before he died."

"Sure he did." Tyler smiled at me the way I'd seen a mother smile at a child who was clearly making up a tall tale. "What else did he say to you?"

"Nothing." I nodded, sure of it. "He mentioned Alba, and that was it. We thought he was having a heart attack."

"Exactly what you were meant to think." Tyler nodded. "The symptoms of a heart attack and foxglove poisoning are very similar."

Foxglove. Somewhere in the back of my mind, I remembered my mother mentioning foxglove. She was an avid gardener, and she liked to tell me stories about the flowers she grew.

"Foxglove is what's used to make digitalis, the heart medicine," I said.

Tyler nodded. "And too much of it . . . well, you saw what can happen."

"We *did* see Beyla fight with Drago." Eve stepped toward Tyler, her arms close to her sides, her hands curled into fists. "Just like we saw Monsieur Lavoie arguing with Drago earlier in the evening, before class even started."

"Now you've got another cock-and-bull story to tell me?" Tyler rolled his eyes. "Give me a break, Eve. Why don't you just admit that you can't get me out of your system and you'll do anything to make my life miserable, just so you can have a little revenge? Even if it means trying to mess with my mind by introducing all this nonsense into the investigation. Let me remind you that in this case, what you're doing is called obstruction of justice. It's not cute, and I'm not going to fall for it—or for you."

Tyler's words were as sharp as a slap. If I felt their sting, I could only imagine how much they hurt Eve.

I was just about to tell him to mind his manners when Eve stopped me, one hand on my arm. "You got me there." The smile she turned on Tyler was sleek. "I was pulling your leg, Tyler, honey. And you had it all figured out. You always were as smart as they come. I should have known you'd see right through it. I *was* just trying to mess with your mind. We never saw Beyla and Drago together. We never saw that cute little ol' Frenchman argue with Drago, either. Why, we're just two little girls who are trying to add a little bit of excitement to our dull, dull lives." She batted her eyelashes at him. "Forgive me?"

Tyler didn't answer. He flipped his notebook closed and walked away.

"What was that all about?" I asked Eve as soon as he was out of earshot. "You know that's not true."

"I sure do." Watching Tyler say something to Jim, Eve smiled. It wasn't until he'd left the classroom that she turned back to me. "Don't you remember when he broke up with me, Annie? I do. Like it was yesterday. He told me he couldn't marry me because I wasn't smart enough."

"So you lied to him to prove how smart you are?"

"Don't be silly!" Eve tossed her romaine leaves into her salad bowl and reached for the olive oil. "How on earth could I prove how smart I am by lying to the man? No, I've got a better way to do it, and to make that Tyler Cooper look like the fool he is. And you're going to help me."

I didn't like the sound of that at all. "How?"

She hummed a little tune while she drizzled on her olive oil. "Why, that's simple, honey. We're going to solve Drago's murder ourselves."

I choked out a laugh. It died the moment I realized she was serious.

"You're nuts," I told her.

"Maybe, but I'm going to do it. And you're going to help me."

"No."

"Why ever not?"

"That's what the police are for."

"The police . . ." She glared at the spot where she'd last seen Tyler. "The police aren't listening to us. And Beyla is lying. So is John. Doesn't that make you want to find out what's really going on?"

"No." I wasn't kidding. There were professionals who were paid to do this kind of thing. "Eve, we don't know how . . ."

My voice trailed off as I watched Eve start to toss her salad. I might as well save my breath. She wasn't listening. She added blue cheese to her bowl, her eyes shining in a way that told me I'd never change her mind. Not about this.

That's when I knew one thing for certain: We'd just gone from Scrumptious Salads and Dazzling Dressings straight into hot water.

Seven

✖

I'VE NEVER MET A BRUSSELS SPROUT I LIKED.
Which is why when I finally got around to checking my e-mail the next afternoon and found the little buggers on Jim's list of what to bring to our fourth class, I wasn't exactly thrilled.

But there were those twelve years of Catholic education to consider, and if I'd learned nothing else at Saint Charles Borromeo Elementary and then Bishop Ireton High, it was that homework was homework. Thrilled or not, I wasn't about to argue. I dutifully wrote out my shopping list.

Brussels sprouts.

Canned chestnuts. (Canned? They came that way? And what was a chestnut, anyway? Aside from the fact that they roasted on an open fire in that Christmas song, I wasn't sure I'd ever made the acquaintance of a chestnut.)

Butter.

Salt and pepper.

Sugar. (Now there was something I knew something about.)

A quart of your favorite fruit. (I'd already decided on apples.)

I finished my shopping list, fully aware that I was spending too much time on it, but nevertheless taking care that my writing was neat and perfect, checking and double-checking the supplies I needed to purchase against the copy of Jim's e-mail that I'd printed out. All so I didn't have to think about Drago's murder, my near-death experience with the stove, and Eve's crazy idea about the two of us as Jessica Fletcher clones.

Even thinking about Brussels sprouts was better than pondering all that.

By the time I was done, I still had twenty minutes left on my lunch break. I'd just decided to take a walk and clear my head when Eve breezed into the employee lunchroom.

No, she didn't work at the bank with me. But she came to visit often enough. Everyone knew Eve and just naturally accepted her as one of the family.

She said hello to Dave and Stan, fellow tellers who were chatting near the coffee machine, then plunked down in the chair across from mine. "We have work to do," she said, and as if to prove it, she plopped a briefcase on the table between us.

Seeing Eve with a briefcase is a weird sort of thing. Like seeing a dog pull a watch out of his back pocket. Half real, half cartoon. I might have laughed if there was anything funny about it.

Instead, I weighed what I wanted to say (which was something along the lines of *What on earth are you up to now?*) against my desire not to hurt Eve's feelings.

I shilly-shallied too long.

Tired of waiting for me to respond and apparently convinced that I was going to again point out that she was off her rocker (which I was), Eve raised her beautifully arched

golden eyebrows and tapped her finger against the briefcase. "Don't tell me you've forgotten our investigation?
I've been going over my notes all morning. There are some
things we need to discuss before we continue our case."

There were so many weird miscues in her statement, I
didn't know where to begin. *Investigation? Notes? Our case?*

It was enough to boggle the mind.

Fortunately, I am not the type who stays boggled for
long. I shook myself out of my momentary stupor and decided to start with the most salient point and work my way
backwards. "Eve, *we* don't have a case. And what notes,
anyway? You haven't been taking notes. You never take
notes. You spent four years in high school not taking notes."

Eve's smile was sleek. "That was then, this is now. And
now that we've got an investigation to conduct, I figured I'd
better turn over a new leaf. I knew you'd be too busy here at
work this morning to do anything, and fortunately, I've got
the day off. I sat down and made a list." She dutifully pulled
it out of the briefcase and waved it in front of my nose. "This
is everything we know. Seems to me, all we have to do is
prove that our friend Beyla had access to the poison and—"

"You've been watching too many *Law & Order* reruns."
I pushed back from the table, making it clear that I was
putting some distance between myself and my friend's lu-
nacy. "We can't do this, Eve."

I swear, she wasn't even listening.

"Remember what that hardheaded, cold-blooded scum-
bag Tyler said?" she asked. "He said Drago was poisoned
with foxglove. I went to the library this morning, Annie,
and the nice librarian there helped me out. Did you know
that foxglove used to be called witches' gloves? And gob-
lin's gloves? And dead men's bells?"

I didn't, and I didn't see why it was important, but I was
impressed by the simple fact that Eve had done some research. I told her how much I admired her initiative.

Of course, that didn't mean I was buying into her girl-detective scenario, and I told her that, too.

She pooh-poohed my protest with a wave of one hand. "Don't you see what I'm getting at here? First that nice librarian—did I mention it was a man and that we're having drinks together tomorrow afternoon?—first, he found a picture so that I could see what foxglove looks like." This time when she reached into the briefcase, she came out holding a color-copied picture. It showed a riot of tall, spiky plants covered with drooping, bell-shaped flowers in shades from purple to white and every tint of pink in between. The colors reminded me of Monsieur Lavoie's potholder display.

"That nice librarian—his name is Tony, by the way, and he is a little nerdy, just like you'd expect a librarian to be, but in a cute sort of way—Tony, he took his break early so that we could take a little walk around the neighborhood. You'd never believe it, Annie. When you know what you're looking for, you realize that plenty of people grow foxglove. Tony pointed it out. All over the place. You see what that means, don't you? It would have been easy for Beyla to get some and give it to Drago. I'm sure she knows that it's poisonous—with names like that, it's pretty obvious that the plant can do some serious damage."

"It's only pretty obvious to someone who knows all the old names."

It seemed like a reasonable argument to me, but Eve was already way beyond it. She pulled out another printed-from-a-Web-site sheet. "Symptoms of foxglove poisoning," she said, and reached into the briefcase again. She slid out two slim volumes. The title of one said something about poisonous plants in the garden. The other was, surprisingly enough, a history of witchcraft.

I fingered the first book, flipping through it to the section Eve had marked. I scanned the pages and read a brief history of foxglove. Scientists never put a lot of credence in its medicinal properties until some time in the late eighteenth century, but it was often used in country villages before that, as an ingredient in folk medicines concocted by people known to the locals as—

My blood ran cold, and I glanced again at the second book. "You don't think—"

"That Beyla is a witch. Of course! That would explain why she wears black all the time."

"Yeah, that or the fact that she's style conscious, that she looks fabulous in black, and that it's easier to build a wardrobe around one basic color than to try and mix and match. Isn't that what you've always told me?"

There was nothing like a fashion discussion to snag Eve's interest.

Usually.

This time she ignored me, and I knew for sure that I was in trouble.

"All we have to do is prove she did it," Eve plowed ahead.

"If it was that easy," I reminded her, "the cops would have already done it."

"Yeah, if Beyla wasn't so clever. She knows better than to drop her guard. You heard her—she said she didn't even know Drago."

"And we know she did." I had to give her that one. I couldn't ignore the fact that Beyla had lied, both to us and the police. I mulled over the thought. Naturally, my brain took it one step further. "And we know Monsieur Lavoie knew Drago, too. We saw Drago storm out of the store, and we saw how upset Monsieur Lavoie was by the whole thing. And then there's John. He said he was having coffee with Beyla after class that night, but we know for a fact that—"

I heard my own words and the thread of excitement in my voice as I logically worked my way through the argument. Eve wasn't one to miss little nuances. Her eyes lit up.

"Gotcha!" she said.

I wasn't about to roll over so quickly. I tried one last objection. "Eve, we can't—"

"You want to help me get back at Tyler, don't you?" Her eyes grew sharp in a way that it was impossible for any best friend to discount. "You don't want him to spend the rest of his happily ever after with what's-her-name, talking about poor little Eve DeCateur and how she couldn't even—"

"All right already!" I threw my hands in the air, surrendering. "But I'm only going to give this a few days."

"A few days is all it's going to take."

"And I'm not going to do anything stupid."

"I wouldn't ask you to."

"And I'm not going to do anything dangerous."

"Annie! I wouldn't dream of it," Eve exclaimed. "I was thinking we could just start with a little computer research. I'm not very good at that sort of thing and . . ."

She left the rest of the sentence unspoken, but I knew just what she meant. I checked the clock that hung above the lunchroom door. "I've got ten minutes until I need to get back to work," I told her. "Let's get started."

A couple minutes later, we were logged on to the Internet on the computer that sat on a table in one corner of the lunchroom. It was supposed to be a sort of company benefit, a place where employees could play games or check e-mail while they were on their breaks. But the computer was old and even slower than the one I had at home. Most of the time, no one used it.

Luckily, today was one of those times.

Because it seemed like the most logical place to begin, I Googled "Drago Kravic." The computer went through its motions and, surprisingly, came up with a hit.

"Arta," I read the little blurb and clicked on the URL. "Looks like Drago had something to do with an art gallery."

Another wait, and then a home page popped up. "He owned it!" Eve exclaimed, reading over my shoulder and pointing to the screen. "It says here that Drago Kravic was the proprietor. Look, it's right over in Georgetown. You know what this means, don't you?"

I did, and just the thought was enough to make my stomach queasy.

It meant that after work and before Brussels Sprouts 101, Eve and I were going on a road trip.

I DIDN'T THINK DRAGO'S GALLERY WOULD BE OPEN, especially not just a few days after he died. In my mind, I pictured a black wreath on the front door and a line of sad-faced customers snaking its way around the block, waiting to pay their respects to the dearly departed owner.

Truth be told, I suppose that's why I agreed to go to Georgetown with Eve. I figured we'd be there and back in twenty minutes. The trip might even prove to Eve once and for all that there were better uses for our time than sleuthing. Particularly when the sleuths didn't know what they were doing.

And I still had to make a trip to the grocery store for those Brussels sprouts.

We stood by the curb on M Street, studying the building across the street. We could see the sleek turquoise and burnt orange Arta address sign. Much to my surprise— not to mention disappointment—the gallery lights were on, and we could see a man inside. It was raining, which seemed appropriate in a film noire sort of way. Eve shivered inside her lemon-colored tank top. Me, I was prepared; I slipped on my jacket. Just as I did, something clicked inside my brain.

I took another gander at the address.

"That's it!" I reached into my pocket, suddenly remembering the piece of paper Drago pressed into my hand right before he died. "That's what was written on the back of the restaurant receipt. The address of Arta. Look!" I pulled out the crumpled receipt and smoothed it so that Eve could read it.

She nodded, confirming my deduction, which, I will say, felt pretty darned brilliant.

"You know what it proves, don't you?" Eve asked, and when I didn't, she shook her head, amazed that I still wasn't thinking like a detective. "We're supposed to be here," she said, and before I could come up with a dozen reasons why she was wrong, she grabbed my arm and pulled me across the street.

We pushed open the gallery door and found ourselves in a huge room with track lighting on the high ceiling. The paintings that hung on the redbrick walls were too abstract for me to decipher, and the sculptures . . . well, to my untrained eyes, they looked like rocks piled one on top of another.

The man we'd seen from across the street was on the other side of the room, looking at one of the rock piles. He certainly didn't look like he worked there: he was tall, thin, and bald, and he was dressed in jeans, a dark golf shirt, and expensive sneakers. I figured him for a customer until I realized that there was no one else around. He refused to make eye contact, and I think he would have ignored us completely if Eve hadn't headed right over to where he stood.

The man turned to us sharply, and murmured an uncomfortable, "Good afternoon!"

"Hi there! We're interior designers," I blurted out. Eve turned to me, eyes wide with surprise. OK, OK, so I wasn't as good a liar as she was, but I figured I needed to take charge of the situation. "Redoing a home in

Bethesda," I continued. "We're looking for just the right painting."

"This is not possible." The man's voice was heavily accented, like Drago's. And Beyla's, for that matter. "This is a private gallery. You do not walk in without an appointment. If you will excuse me . . ." He backed away at the same time he gestured toward the front of the gallery. There was no mistaking what he meant.

Don't let the door hit you on your way out.

For all I knew about the world of art, this was how things were done. Still, to me, it seemed a funny way to do business. Or not to do business.

"I'm not sure you understand," I continued. I could tell Eve was just as baffled as I was by his attitude, and not sure what to say. "We want to look at paintings. We want to buy."

The man's smile wavered around the edges. "Yes, yes. This is very good. But you must understand. You do not come to a gallery without an appointment. How do you say this? It is not done."

Three cheers for my brain. It clicked into action again.

"But we do have an appointment. Or at least a referral." The receipt with Drago's writing on it was still in my hand, and I showed it to the man. "We met Mr. Kravic just recently at this restaurant. He told us to stop by. See, he wrote the address down for us. If you ask him—"

"This is not possible." I guess he wanted to see the proof up close and personal, because he tried to pluck the receipt out of my hand. But I was faster. After I was sure he'd seen it—and Drago's writing on it—I stuffed it back in my pocket.

He cleared his throat. "I am sorry to tell you, but Drago Kravic, he is not here."

I managed a chirpy smile. "We can wait."

"No, no. You are not understanding." The man shook

his head sadly. "My dear friend Drago, he is not coming back. He is dead."

We feigned surprise. I thought Eve's surprise was more convincing than mine, but like I said, I've never been much for prevarication. Still, I must have been convincing enough. The man turned a somber smile on me.

"I am sorry I have to tell you this distressing news," he said. "I am Yuri Grul, Drago's partner. It is a sad time for me. For all of us. If there is anything I can do—"

"Now that you mention it, you just might be able to help," Eve piped up. She glanced around the gallery, wide-eyed and with one hand on her Kate Spade to prove to Yuri that she was serious when it came to spending money.

"That nice Mr. Kravic, he talked about a painting, and I'm just dying—" How Eve could make herself blush on command was a mystery to me. Her hand flew to her mouth. "Oh! I guess that's not the best word to use, is it? You'll excuse me, won't you, sugar? What I meant to say, of course, is that the way Drago described it, why, I just know I'm gonna love that painting. We may not be able to get back here for a good, long while. So if you could just show it to me? I mean, if it isn't too much of an imposition at a time like this."

For a couple seconds, I thought Yuri was going to say it was. I almost wished he had—then we could get out of here and get back to minding our own business.

But mourning or no mourning, Yuri was obviously a man of business. He smiled in an oily sort of way that made me uncomfortable. "The name?" he asked.

"Why, it's Eve DeCateur, and this is Annie Capshaw." Eve pressed a hand to her heart and twinkled, but Yuri's blank expression said it all. "Oh, you mean the name of the painting!" She rolled her eyes as if amazed by her own foolishness. "I just know it will come to me," she said, chewing on her lower lip. "Maybe if you show us around?"

"Of course." Yuri stepped back to allow us to get closer to the displays. That was my cue—we'd discussed that much on the way over, though I never thought we'd actually do it. If Eve could keep the gallery people distracted, I could snoop around. The thought of it sent a chill up my spine, but then again, I'd already concocted a whopper of a story to get us this far. I might as well go all out.

Besides, I knew that if I didn't act fast, Eve would take matters into her own hands. And who knew what might happen then!

"If you'll excuse me for a moment." I did my best to look embarrassed. It didn't take much acting—this whole thing was beginning to feel like a scene from a bad sitcom. "Ladies' room?"

"Of course." What else could Yuri say? He waved vaguely toward the other side of the gallery, and when Eve wrapped her arm through his and started to chatter, I took off in the opposite direction.

I found myself at the back of the building in a long hallway that struck me as particularly gloomy compared to the bright lighting out on the floor. I saw the door marked *Ladies* and passed it by, glancing over my shoulder to make sure Yuri wasn't paying attention. I heard the light sounds of Eve's laughter echo against the high ceiling, and Yuri's lower, more guttural replies. Knowing she'd keep him busy for a few more minutes—and hoping a few minutes was enough time—I headed off to find the gallery office.

What was I looking for?

I really didn't know. I only knew that Eve had this crazy idea that if I could get a peek into Drago's office, I would find something that would give us a clue to the identity of his killer.

In Eve's mind, of course, that killer was Beyla.

Did I believe it?

Honestly, I still didn't know what I thought about Beyla.

At that moment, the only thing I was sure about was that I wasn't cut out to be a thief or a spy. My heart was pounding like the drum line of a high school marching band. My palms were sweaty. My blood was racing so fast and hard, it felt like it was going to spurt out of my veins.

I took a deep breath, attempting to get a grip and trying to reason through the panic cluttering my mind.

There *was* the receipt from Drago with the address of the gallery scrawled on it, I reminded myself. And there were his final words to me.

"This . . . important. You will see."

Maybe Drago was trying to lead me here all along. Maybe Eve was onto something after all. Maybe this trip to the gallery was significant. Maybe I would find something in Drago's office.

If Yuri didn't catch me snooping around first.

The thought fueled my footsteps, and I picked up my pace down the hallway. There was a brass sign hanging beside the next door on my right that said Private. The door was closed, but it wasn't shut all the way. I peeked inside.

One look in the office told me that any chance I had of finding a clue was officially gone.

All three of the file cabinets in the room were flung open, and file folders littered the blue and red rug on the floor. The desk drawers were gaping, too, and whatever had been in them was piled on the desk chair.

There was a window on one wall and a small safe under it. That had been opened, as well. It didn't appear to me that it had been broken into. I may not be much in the burglary department but I do know a mess when I see one. The door of the safe was hanging open, and what looked to be record books kicked to one side definitely qualified as a mess.

Somebody had gotten here before us, and it seemed as though that somebody had an advantage over Eve and me.

He—or she—knew exactly what he—or she—was looking for.

And it was obvious that he—or she—would do anything to find it.

Eight

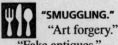 **"SMUGGLING."**

"Art forgery."

"Fake antiques."

"That's almost just like art forgery. That doesn't count."

Eve rolled her eyes. At least she remembered to keep her voice down. We were in class (Fabulous Fruits and Vivacious Vegetables), and as we had all the way from Georgetown to Arlington, we were trying to figure out what sort of shady dealings Drago could have been involved with that would have resulted in his office being trashed— and in Drago being killed.

Eve whispered to me while she opened her can of chestnuts. "Maybe it doesn't have anything to do with the gallery."

"Except that Drago said the gallery was important," I reminded her. "That's why we've got to concentrate on crimes that involve art. Unless Drago wasn't involved in anything illegal at all." Don't ask me why, but that was a new thought. I had been running on the assumption that Drago was a bad guy.

"Maybe he was an innocent bystander," I suggested. "Or a government witness. You know, like on all those TV shows."

"Of course he wasn't!" Eve practically sneered. In a beauty queen sort of way, of course. "You saw him that evening when he was coming out of here. And you saw him when he and Beyla were arguing. He was one nasty dude. Bad as bad can get."

"I hope that's not the Brussels sprouts you're talking about."

We'd been so deep in our speculations, I had no idea Jim was standing right behind us until his comment interrupted our discussion. I jumped, and the chestnuts I was just pouring out of the can landed half in the sink and half on the floor.

"Sorry." Jim sprang into action. He stooped to retrieve the chestnuts on the floor. I suppose in the great scheme of things, I should have been grateful for his gallantry.

Except that I bent to get them at the same time.

We clunked heads, and both of us came up rubbing our foreheads.

"Sorry," I said sheepishly. I was all set to bend down again when I saw that Jim was going to, too.

"Sorry." It was his turn.

We exchanged uncertain smiles, and though it was unspoken, we made the executive decision to let the chestnuts stay put for a while.

"So . . ." He concentrated on the ones that had landed in the sink. When he leaned over to scoop them out, his arm brushed mine.

I suppose I was still jittery from the whole snoop-around-the-gallery adventure, not to mention the way we made our excuses to Yuri and hurried out of there after I found Drago's office looking like a tornado had gone through it. I sucked in a breath as my arm involuntarily jumped.

"I hope I'm not that scary."

The smile Jim turned on me was as hot as his accent. And believe me, that accent was plenty hot.

I reminded myself that he was just being nice, like any cooking teacher would naturally be to any cooking student, and did my best to corral the suddenly out-of-control fantasies that threatened to leave me grinning back at him like some brainless bimbo. Or worse, like a woman whose head was too easily turned by something as simple as a man being nice to her.

Even when the man in question was the yummiest thing she'd seen since the last pint of Funky Monkey she'd gone through.

He turned off the hot-as-hell smile just as quickly as he had flashed it and backed away enough to take in both Eve and me in one quick glance.

"So, you were saying? About the Brussels sprouts?"

I was still too electrified by the brush of Jim's skin against mine to cobble together any sort of reasonable response. It occurred to me that I knew I was in trouble when I left the logical replies to Eve.

"Not Brussels sprouts," Eve said. So far, so good. That seemed sensible enough. She leaned in closer and lowered her voice even more. "We were talking about Drago."

That was not sensible!

I jumped again, this time back into the conversation before the spark of interest that lit in Jim's hazel eyes kindled into anything else. Like curiosity. Or more questions.

"Oh, Eve, you are such a kidder!" I gave her arm a playful whack and turned to Jim, my discombobulation forgotten in the face of my need to steer us clear of a subject we had no right to be discussing. Not with Beyla and John only a few feet away. "Of course she's not talking about that poor dead guy. We didn't know the dead guy. We don't know anything about the dead guy. We were just talking about the Brussels sprouts."

I flashed what I hoped was an extremely carefree smile and returned my attention to my chesnuts. Jim stood in silence for a moment, regarding us with a glimmer in his eye. Then he turned and walked away.

As I watched him go, I found myself wondering just how much he knew.

"He's cute." Eve's words cut into my thoughts.

"Not what I was thinking," I told her.

"Yeah. Right." She smiled broadly.

"I mean it. He's cute, all right. But that's not what I was thinking."

Her gaze followed Jim as he made his way to the front of the room. His back was to us. He was wearing tight jeans that stretched nicely over his butt.

Need I say more?

"Oh honey, if you weren't thinking about that . . ." Eve grinned, then eyed me, curious. "What *were* you thinking?"

"That we shouldn't say too much in front of strangers. That we don't know who to trust. That we haven't sorted things out yet and that means we don't know who the good guys are and who the bad guys are."

Eve's expression wilted. "You don't think—"

"I don't know what to think," I told her, and it was true. Deep down, I didn't believe that there was anything shady about Jim.

But if that was true, why was I more nervous than ever just thinking about him?

BY THE TIME I WAS BACK IN CLASS THE NEXT evening, I was still mulling over the questions that filled my head, as crowded and as noisy as the summer tourists out on the Clarendon streets—the ones I had to fight my way through to get to the shop.

There was the good guy/bad guy question: which people associated with Très Bonne Cuisine could we trust?

There was the Jim question, but I won't get into that. Every time I thought about Jim, my mind ping-ponged like a . . . well, like a Ping-Pong ball. Part of me was concerned with what he'd overheard the night before, what he thought of it, and the whole trust issue. But the other part of me . . .

OK, I had to admit it: I had a thing for Jim. Lately, every one of my fantasies featured him in a major way. It was playing hell with my head, not to mention my body.

Better not to go there. At least not there in class when he was standing ten feet away. I wasn't crazy: I knew he couldn't read my mind, but I couldn't risk him reading my body language, either. If he guessed at half the thoughts that flitted through my head and raised my temperature as I watched him prepare for tonight's pasta class, I'd die from embarrassment.

I decided it was a lot less dangerous to think about what Eve optimistically called "our case."

There was the Monsieur Lavoie question, and what he knew about Drago, and why they'd been arguing the night Drago was killed. I hadn't had a chance to address that one, because every evening when I arrived at the shop, the little Frenchman either wasn't around or was busy with customers.

There was the John question, too. I'd paid little attention to it so far because I figured it was just an aberration and it would go away. But it hadn't. And I wasn't imagining it, I swear.

Every time I glanced his way, John the accountant was looking back at me.

And there were more questions. Like who had trashed Drago's office? And why had his partner, Yuri, seemed unconcerned enough about it that he could chat with us out in the gallery instead of being in the office trying to get things back in order?

But then, that might have been the neatnik in me talking.

As if all that wasn't enough, as of that afternoon, I had something new to consider.

I might have felt better about the whole thing if I'd had a chance to tell Eve and get her take on things. Trouble was, I'd discovered this piece of the puzzle on my lunch hour, and by then, she was already at work behind the cosmetic counter at Hecht's. Because of her work schedule, we'd decided it was easier (logistically speaking) to meet at Très Bonne Cuisine tonight rather than drive together. And now I couldn't wait to talk to her.

I unpacked my groceries and waited semipatiently. Didn't it figure that tonight Eve was late?

I watched the minutes tick away on the clock that hung above the classroom door. If Eve didn't show up soon, Jim would start class, and we wouldn't have a chance to talk until break. Call me crazy, but if I had to hold onto this new information that long, I thought I might burst.

Lucky for me, Eve made it just under the wire. Unlike most people who at least would have made the effort to look frazzled to be arriving at the last second, she strolled into the classroom without a care in the world, every hair in place and her makeup perfect.

I waited until she was standing next to me before I turned my back to Beyla and John's cooking station and made a *psst* sound.

Eve played along.

She put her purse away and set down her grocery bag. "What?" she spoke the word out of the side of her mouth. "What's up?"

"I went to the library," I whispered back. "Today at lunch. Look what I found."

I had my purse ready on the counter. As surreptitiously as I could, I slid a single sheet of paper out of it and toward Eve. It was a copy of what I'd found on microfiche. She took one look at it and her mouth fell open.

"It's Beyla!"

So much for surreptitious. Eve's surprise was complete, and her voice was loud enough to attract attention.

All the wrong attention.

Just as I suspected, when I chanced a glance in their direction, both John and Beyla were looking our way.

I swallowed down my mortification and turned my back on them. "Keep your voice down," I hissed. Trying to be as casual as I could, I took a box of spaghetti out of my grocery bag and used it to point to the photo. It showed Drago in the foreground, a champagne flute in one hand. "It's a picture from the *Washington Post* a couple years ago. The opening of Arta."

Eve bent for a closer look. "And Beyla was there." She stood and looked me dead in the eyes. "This proves she lied. To us and to Tyler. She knew Drago. She had to know Drago—she was at the opening of the gallery!"

"Exactly. What we need to decide is what to do with the information. Do we talk to Tyler? Or do we—"

As always, Eve didn't seem to register the word *decide*. Not as much as *instinct*, anyway. Or *action*. Just as I reached to put the photo away, she slid it out from under my hand and started across the room with it. "We'll ask her to explain herself," Eve said. "Right now."

Was it a good idea?

We never had a chance to find out.

Thankfully, before Eve took two steps, Jim called our attention to the front of the room and started to talk about pasta.

Reluctantly, Eve stopped and turned back to our workstation.

At least for now, our questions about Beyla would have to remain unanswered.

JIM TOOK ONE TASTE OF EVE'S PASTA SAUCE, SMILED, and gave her the thumbs-up. "Excellent!" he purred.

Call me small-minded, but I wondered how much the comment had to do with Eve's cooking skills and how much it had to do with the peek of cleavage showing at the top of her snug white tank.

Like I said, small-minded. Not to mention flat-out, green-eyed jealous.

I hastily brought myself back to reality. What guy wouldn't appreciate Eve's good looks and her model-perfect body? And while I was at it, why would I kid myself thinking that Jim would be any different from any of the other guys Eve and I met when we were together?

You'd think by now, I'd be used to it.

Except this time, for reasons I couldn't explain, it stung a little more than usual.

Of course, there were advantages to being the wing-woman. If I were smart, I'd put any delusional thoughts of Jim as a romantic interest out of my mind once and for all, and concentrate on Jim as critic of my pasta sauce.

Somehow, that only made me more nervous.

When I spooned up a taste of my sauce for Jim, my hands shook. When I passed him the spoon, I lost control. He ended up with a splotch of tomato sauce across the front of his white cook's apron.

"Sorry!" I grabbed a towel and started dabbing at the sauce, only managing to smear it across the apron and onto his white shirt. I felt my face turn the color of a tomato. "Really sorry."

"It's OK. Honest." Jim took the towel out of my hand and did some triage on his own. "I can wash it."

"It'll stain. If we had some club soda." I made a move to go I don't know where in search of the magic liquid.

Jim stopped me with a hand on my arm. "I said it's OK, and I mean it. It's an old shirt anyway, and I'm not nearly as concerned about it as I am about you."

"Concerned? About me?" I looked down to where his hand still rested. The point of contact felt like it was going to combust. "Are you?"

For a nanosecond, I thought he was actually going to say something personal, but the second passed, and he smiled politely instead. "About your cooking, of course."

Deflated, I reached for another spoon. This time, Jim wasn't taking any chances. He slipped it out of my hand, dipped it into my sauce, and took a taste.

"It's . . ." He coughed and, bless him, tried not to make a face. "I think maybe you've added a wee bit too much sugar."

I hadn't meant to. It kind of fell in as I was measuring.

"You'll do better next time," Jim assured me. He didn't wait to hear my excuses but moved onto to Jared and Ben's station, leaving me wishing there was a remedial cooking class I could transfer to.

Of course, that was better than thinking about how the simple word *wee* snaked its way through me, leaving a thread of warmth.

"Break time," Eve said, and her voice snapped me back to reality. "I've got to duck out and call Tony."

When I gave her a blank look, she sighed.

"The librarian. Remember? We had lunch together before work today and we're meeting for a drink tonight." She glanced across the room, and her eyes narrowed. "I'll make it fast," she promised. "Then we can pin Beyla down about that picture of the gallery opening."

I nodded. As reluctant as I was to confront anybody, I

suppose talking to Beyla made sense in terms of our so-called investigation.

Beyla said she didn't know Drago, but we had proof she did. It would be interesting to see how she'd handle our questions, and if she'd lie again.

But not until Eve returned.

Suddenly, I realized the subject of my musings—Beyla—was headed my way. She had one hand cradled under a spoon of pasta sauce and a little smile on her lips that made me think of the old saying about the cat that ate the canary.

She dispensed with the niceties altogether, poking the spoon in my direction. "Here," she said. "You try."

"Oh, I don't think so." Something about a woman we had implicated in a murder suddenly offering me food made me a little uneasy. I automatically backed away. "Jim always says we shouldn't compare ourselves to the other students in the class. Everyone has their own cooking style."

"But yours . . . it is . . . How do you say this? I am thinking that yours, it is not so good."

I couldn't keep from staring at the pool of sauce on Beyla's spoon. "I'm sure my cooking isn't as good as yours," I blurted out. "At least from what you've said about how your family admires yours. And the compliments you've been getting here, and . . ."

I couldn't keep from wondering what was in Beyla's sauce, and why she was suddenly generous enough to want to share it with me.

"It's very kind of you really. But . . ."

I didn't think Beyla's sauce was poisoned, did I?

"You do not think the sauce, it is poisoned, do you?"

Beyla's question so closely reflected my thoughts that I had no choice but to protest.

"Poison! Why on earth would you want to poison me? Don't be silly." I tried for a smile that instantly wilted around the edges. "Of course I'd love to try your sauce. I'm sure it's delicious."

She held the spoon to my mouth. "Yes. It is very delicious. There is a . . . how do you say this? A secret ingredient. You will enjoy it."

I gulped, but I didn't dare open my mouth.

She moved closer. "You will enjoy it so much. If you taste this little—"

Just as Beyla was going to press the spoon to my lips, it flew out of her hands. Spoon and sauce landed in a puddle on the floor. The next thing I knew, Eve stumbled between the two of us.

"I am so sorry!" Eve offered her apologies to Beyla and a wink to me. "I must have tripped. I didn't mean to—"

"Of course you did not." Beyla's expression was icy. Without another word, she turned and walked away.

I breathed a sigh of relief, and Eve grinned. "Thought you weren't suspicious of her?"

I shrugged my answer. "I don't know what to think anymore. It's crazy to think she would try to poison me in front of the whole class. But—"

"But . . ." Eve watched Beyla get settled back at her own station.

"But maybe now that you've made another mess . . ."

Jim had a funny way of sneaking up on me. He was back from break, too, and I turned to find him surveying the flecks of tomato sauce that dotted the floor. He didn't look angry or even exasperated. He put his hands on his hips and shook his head.

"I need to talk to you," he said, turning his gaze from Eve to me. "To both of you. I'd really like to do it tonight, but I've got a committment. Tomorrow night? After class?"

Before either of us could answer, he returned to the front of the classroom. Eve and I exchanged looks, but we didn't say a thing.

We didn't have to—I could tell we were thinking the same thing.

We didn't know if we should be excited about the prospect of getting together with Jim.

Or really worried.

Nine

IN MY HEART OF HEARTS, I DIDN'T WANT JIM TO BE A bad guy.

He was too nice to be involved in a life of crime, and besides, I'd always been a big believer in lawbreakers getting their just due. Nice aside, Jim was way too cute for prison pinstripes.

But if Jim wasn't angling for information to suit his own nefarious purposes, it meant that he wanted to talk to Eve and me after class that night for some other reason.

I suspected I knew what that reason was. Jim was using this "let's all get together" excuse so that he could get to know Eve better.

Call me petty, but I was thinking I'd rather see him behind bars.

"You don't need to manhandle the dough." Speaking of Jim, he was walking by just as I gave my bread dough an extra *whap*. It was Saturday and because we were doing Scrumptious Breads, and breads (scrumptious or not) needed more time to prepare and bake, we were at Très Bonne Cuisine early in the afternoon.

"You're trying to integrate the wet and dry ingredients," he reminded me. "Not beat them into submission. Funny, I never thought of you as an aggressive sort of person," he said out of the corner of his mouth.

He'd thought of me?

Now he was being cruel.

Maybe I did want to see him in a striped jumpsuit.

I gave the bread another slap. "I'm not aggressive, I'm thorough."

"Thorough's one thing. Obsessive is something else. Here, step aside." He was already reaching into the bowl of flour I had out on the counter and dusting his hands with it, so he nudged me aside with a bump of his hip. "You're worrying too much about the right way to do this. You're so tensed up, you're not even breathing, and because your muscles are strained, you're working too hard. Think of this as Zen baking. Relax. Loosen up. Take a deep breath."

He turned to me, and I realized he wasn't just offering advice. He actually wanted me to do it, and he was going to stand there and wait until I did. Stand there, wait, and stare.

I didn't know how long I could keep my cool with him looking right at me. What's a girl to do? I inhaled.

He cocked his head.

I breathed a little deeper.

He narrowed his eyes.

I gave up and sucked in a good, long breath.

"That's it. Now let it go. Slowly. There." He inhaled and let the breath out slowly, too. I have to say, as the last of our mingled breaths faded away, I did feel a little calmer.

"Your own nature determines your style," Jim said, rolling those *r*'s like there was no tomorrow. "Don't worry about what you read in a cookbook or what I tell you up there at the front of the class. Do your own thing. Decide what feels good to you. Which way do you like it, Annie, hard or soft?"

He was talking dough kneading. And I was thinking about . . .

Well, no use getting into that.

Suffice it to say that I gave myself a mental slap.

"I've never made bread before," I said, deciding it was better to stick to the truth than give in to the fiction playing out in my head. "I don't know if I'm a hard kneader or a soft kneader. Maybe I'm not a kneader at all. Maybe bread isn't my thing."

Jim's smile was understanding—either that, or he just felt sorry for me. "Bread is everyone's thing. What do they say it is? The staff of life? Look." He buried his hands into the soft mound of dough on the counter in front of us. "You want to work this shaggy mass until it's a nice, smooth ball. See, like this." He used the heels of his hands to push the dough away, then gently brought the far edge of it forward and folded it over itself. "Lightly. Carefully. There's yeast in here, and don't forget, yeast is a living thing."

"A living thing that we're going to kill when we put it in the oven." I don't know what was wrong with me. I wasn't usually this cranky. I apologized with a quick smile. "I guess I'm just feeling a little inadequate," I confessed.

That much was true. In a black-and-white wraparound skirt and a tiny black top that showed off her store-bought tan and a whole lot more, Eve looked like a million bucks this afternoon. And even though I'd made the extra effort to look nice because I knew we'd be meeting with Jim after class, in my khakis and green tank, I felt like loose change.

Because I didn't want to think about it, I glanced around the room. My fellow classmates were all busy kneading away, their movements as graceful as if they'd been choreographed.

"Beyla and John aren't here." I don't know why it hadn't registered before but now I noticed that their workstation was empty. I threw out the comment to Eve, who was busy working her own dough on the counter beside Jim. "They've never missed class before."

Jim commented before Eve could. "They called. Each of them. John said he had to work. Some unexpected meeting. And Beyla said she wasn't feeling well."

"I'll bet." Eve pursed her lips and blew a strand of hair out of her eyes. Her hands were deep inside her dough, and she pushed it, folded it, and flipped it as expertly as if she'd been a bread baker in some past life. "I hear that killing people makes you feel not so good."

I shot her a warning glance at the same time Jim turned to her with a glimmer of interest in his eyes. "You think so?" he asked.

I knew I had to intervene before she did any more damage to our investigation. I dipped my hands in the bowl of flour. "Better get going on this," I said, my voice as sprightly as anyone's can be who isn't actually looking forward to what needs to be done. I sank my hands into the dough. "We don't have all the time in the world, and . . ."

And I forgot that Jim was already kneading the dough.

We met in a silky, glutinous sort of grasp. Our hands slid across each other's, then stuck.

Zen or no Zen, I forgot to breathe.

Jim was apparently not having the same problem. He settled his hands a little more comfortably under mine and smiled. "You finally seem to be getting the hang of this! Now decide. Hard or soft?"

"Soft." The word came out of me on the end of a little gasp, and when I felt Jim's hands twitch like he was going to pull away, I automatically held on a little tighter. "No, hard," I said. "Definitely hard."

"Hard it is then." He gave me a wink and slid his hands

out from under mine. "You go ahead and give it a try while I see how everyone else is doing."

Except that even after he walked away, I couldn't move a muscle. I was frozen there, my hands in the goo that I knew would never be decent-tasting bread, my breath trapped behind a knot in my throat, my heart ramming against my ribs like the bass line in a heavy metal rock song.

"Oh, that was good!" Eve practically purred the words, and I wondered if she was making fun of me. But when I looked at her, she was grinning.

"I didn't look like a dope?" I asked.

"Honey, you couldn't look like a dope if you tried."

My spirits were buoyed, but there was only so long they could stay afloat.

My shoulders drooped. "I looked like a dope. He thinks I'm a dope."

She clicked her tongue and flipped her dough. "If he thought you were a dope, he wouldn't have asked to meet with us tonight."

My turn to click my tongue. "You don't think he wants to see me, do you?"

Eve raised her eyebrows, but she didn't have a chance to answer. Jim was back at the front of the room, calling for our attention. He told us to finish up our kneading, and showed us how to grease the container we'd use to let our dough rise. By the time I'd flipped my globe of dough in the container to grease it on all sides and covered the whole thing with plastic wrap, I'd decided the why-did-Jim-really-want-to-talk-to-us thing wasn't worth discussing. Who was I kidding, anyway? Anytime Eve and I were in a room together, guys only had eyes for her.

Except for Peter.

The thought snuck up on me and smacked me like I'd been thwacking my dough ball. Annoyed with myself, I shook my head and tucked the container with the dough in it on the shelf under our workstation.

"It's difficult to say how long it will take for your dough to double in size," Jim told the class. "So we'll take a break now. Rising time depends on the temperature of the air and of your dough. The amount of yeast you used makes a difference, too. Drafts cause problems: they'll make your dough rise too slowly and unevenly, so make sure you've got it wrapped good and tight."

I did all that and washed my hands. I was just about to ask Eve if she wanted to head over to the natural foods store for a yogurt when she informed me that she had other things to do.

"Tony." She held up her cell phone. "You remember? The librarian? I'll run outside and do that and pick you up a sandwich. You want ham or roast beef?" she asked, but before I even had a chance to answer, she was already out the door.

The other members of the class scattered. Jim disappeared into the kitchen area where we washed up our pots and pans, and I didn't want to risk going after him and looking pathetic.

I drummed my fingers against the countertop, considering my options. I decided I might as well keep playing detective.

I took a deep breath and strolled over to Beyla and John's workstation. It was as clean as a whistle. I checked out Jim's workstation at the front of the classroom, too. I suppose if I really wanted to find something, I would have given it more than a quick once-over. But I wasn't a real detective, and as I mentioned before, I didn't want Jim to be a bad guy. Besides, I didn't see anything out of the ordinary, and certainly nothing suspicious.

That took care of our suspects here at Très Bonne Cuisine—all except one.

I gathered up my purse and went off in search of Monsieur Lavoie.

HE WASN'T DOWNSTAIRS IN THE SHOP. HE WASN'T IN the back storeroom, either, or in the tiny, neat-as-a-pin office I could see through a doorway behind the front counter where jars of Vavoom! were lined up in tidy, come-and-get-me rows.

In fact, Monsieur Lavoie was nowhere to be found.

A real detective would have been suspicious. After all, it was Saturday afternoon, and though the store was empty at the moment, the streets outside were chock-full of summer tourists. The man had a business to run. How could he do that when he wasn't even in the store?

Of course, I wasn't a real detective, even though I was pretending to be one. Though Monsieur's absence offended my sense of order and challenged my concept of customer service, I didn't see how it affected our case.

I was just about to chalk the whole thing up as a big ol' nothing and head out for that yogurt when I heard a noise outside the back door.

Like the sound of glass breaking.

Maybe I was getting into the whole girl-detective schtick after all, because before I even realized it, I was heading to the back door, curious to know exactly what was going on.

Don't get me wrong: I still wasn't a fly-by-the-seat-of-your-pants sort of person like Eve. Before I got to the door, I grabbed one of the wooden meat tenderizing mallets on display with the other cooking utensils. After all, Drago had been murdered in that parking lot. I wasn't going to take any chances.

I leaned my ear to the door and heard another piece of glass shatter. Carefully, I turned the knob and just as cautiously, I opened the door just a crack. Nothing could have surprised me more than what I saw: Monsieur Lavoie. He was standing at least fifteen feet away from the Dumpster. One by one, he was chucking glass bottles into it. Just like he'd been doing the night Drago died.

"Monsieur?"

He spun around when he heard my voice and tucked his hands behind his back. Though he tried for a smile, his complexion was ashen.

"So, you are . . . how do you say it? Breaking, yes?" Monsieur shifted uncomfortably from foot to foot. He looked over my shoulder toward the door. "Your classmates, they are coming out here, too?"

"No. Just me." Before the little Frenchman could see that I was using his stock as a potential weapon, I set the meat tenderizer down on the nearest counter and stepped into the parking lot. I closed the door behind me. "Speaking of breaking, I heard some noise. I thought maybe something was wrong."

"Wrong?" He laughed in that Gallic way that made me think of Pepe LePew. "What could be wrong on a day like today? It is beautiful, yes?"

It was, and I wasn't about to argue the fact. I stepped toward the street, poking my thumb over my shoulder in the general direction of the whole foods store. "I'm just heading out for a yogurt. Can I bring you back something?"

"No, no." Monsieur's smile jiggled around the edges like a poorly set Jell-O mold. "I am fine. Really. You can just run along, yes?"

"Yes," I said. "Well . . . good-bye." I set off across the parking lot and over to the sidewalk where just a few days before, Eve and I had stood and watched Beyla and Drago have a knock-down-drag-out. As I did, I noticed Monsieur Lavoie turned completely around to watch me leave. It might have been the most natural thing in the world, but I couldn't help but notice that by doing so, he made sure I couldn't get a look at what he was holding behind his back.

Was I finally thinking like a detective?

Maybe, because as I walked away, I had already decided I knew two things.

Number one: He didn't want me to see whatever he was holding.

And number two?

That was pretty much a no-brainer. Monsieur Lavoie could have disposed of the whatever-it-was simply by tossing it over the side of the Dumpster. But he didn't.

Whatever he was getting rid of, Monsieur wanted to make sure it was gone for good. As in smashed to smithereens.

Apparently whatever it was, he wanted to make sure no one else found it, either.

"I'VE GOT SOMETHING FOR YOU."

Eve was waiting for me at our cooking station when I got back from our lunch break. I half laughed, wondering how a roast beef or a ham sandwich could cause the shimmer of excitement in her eyes. But then I noticed that she wasn't holding either. Suddenly, I was glad that I'd had that yogurt after all.

"Bread dough?" I put away my purse and pulled out my own bowl. The dough inside was as flat as a pancake. "Looks like I could use some."

"No, silly." Eve made a face and looked around to make sure no one was listening.

I looked around, too, and just like my dough, my spirits fell. All around us, our fellow students were returning from lunch and checking on their creations. I could hear their murmurs of amazement when they saw how what had been heavy, dense balls of water and flour had magically transformed into light and airy clouds of yeasty-smelling wonder.

"I've got something better than bread dough."

Eve's word yanked me away from my thoughts, and I remembered that she wasn't the only one who'd accomplished something on our lunch hour.

"I've got something, too," I told her. "Information. About Monsieur Lavoie. He's up to something. He was out in the back parking lot smashing glass."

Eve dismissed my findings with a shake of her shoulders. "This is better," she said.

"But it could mean something. Whatever he was breaking into a million little pieces, it was obvious he didn't want anyone to find it. Or identify it. What if it was—"

"Foxglove?" Eve stuck something so close to my nose, I had to back up so that my eyes could focus and see what it was. It was a thin glass vial stopped with a cork, filled with what looked like a dried herb.

"Foxglove?" I parroted the word and automatically grabbed for the vial. Not that I knew what I was looking for, but I turned it in my fingers, studying the dark green leaves from every angle. "How do you know?"

"Well, what else could it be?" Eve rolled her eyes. "That's what Drago died from, wasn't it? Foxglove poisoning."

"And you're thinking of using it yourself now?"

Eve wasn't in the mood for jokes. "She left it here," she said, with a meaningful look at Beyla's empty workstation. "That's where I found it."

"You did?" I thought back to the inspection I'd done before I headed downstairs. "No way. I looked."

"In the drawers?"

Of course not. I never would have dared.

I didn't need to explain that to Eve. That's the thing

with a best friend—she knew more about me than I did about myself. Including that I'd never do anything that rash, that sneaky, or that borderline dishonest.

Now she also knew that I could have cracked our case wide open and didn't. Because I was too cautious to take a chance.

My gaze traveled to Beyla's station. Like ours, it was complete with a cupboard for pots and pans, a shelf (where we'd left our bread dough to rise), and two drawers. I knew one of my drawers had knives and graters and meat thermometers and such in it. I kept my purse in the other. "You mean—"

"Did I snoop? You betcha!" Eve grinned. "It was worth it, too, wasn't it? Look at it, Annie. Isn't it amazing?"

I took another gander at the vial of dried herbs in my hand.

"But how do you know—"

"Come on, what else could it be? I'd bet anything this is the stuff she used to try to poison you in class last night."

The very thought made my stomach a little queasy. I pushed the vial back into Eve's hands. "No way."

"Why not?"

"She wouldn't be so dumb as to leave it here."

"She didn't think anyone would find it. I mean, not without a warrant or subpoena or whatever. Besides, Beyla didn't know she wasn't going to be here today—she couldn't have known she was going to get sick. She was probably going to take another shot at killing you."

"Oh, that's a pleasant thought!" I angled a look at the vial before Eve tucked it in her purse. "How are we going to find out for sure?"

"What it is?" Eve wrinkled her nose. In her mind, she'd already made up her mind that the vial was filled with foxglove. She wasn't anticipating my scepticism. "We can't taste it."

"No shit, Sherlock."

"Somebody here might know."

"And we can't take the chance of asking."

Eve's golden brows dipped low over her eyes like they always did when she was thinking hard. "I know!" Her eyes lit. "I've got just the person who can help us. We'll go see her tonight. After class."

"Not tonight we can't," I reminded her, just as Jim stepped out of the kitchen and toward the front of the room.

Eve took a look at him, and her excited expression melted. "I forgot."

Honestly, I didn't know how it was possible.

I'd been trying to forget. And between playing detective, trying to deduce what Monsieur Lavoie was up to, going to get that yogurt for lunch, and stopping for that double scoop of chocolate raspberry from the ice cream place I passed on my way back from the whole foods store—just to settle my nerves—I'd nearly done it, too.

Nearly.

Because just thinking of spending time with Jim after class made me feel as light as a cloud and as airy as my bread dough wasn't. And just thinking that I'd been invited along only because he was being polite . . .

I imagined myself smiling and waving good-bye as he headed up the river.

"Get a grip, Annie," I muttered to myself. I had to keep it together long enough to find out how much Jim knew. He was getting uncomfortably interested in our investigation, and Eve and I couldn't afford to take any chances.

Besides, it was just a couple of drinks.

I glanced over at Eve, who was busy applying a fresh coat of lip gloss.

It was going to be a long night.

Ten

✕

 "SIT STILL! RELAX! YOU'RE DOING FINE."

I wasn't.

For the umpteenth time since we arrived at Whitlow's On Wilson, I shifted my position in the vinyl booth. "I just can't get comfortable," I told Eve.

She glanced over to the bar where Jim had gone to get our drinks. "Stop worrying, will you. He's not looking at you under a microscope."

"No, he's looking at *you* under a microscope." I sighed.

Eve stuck out her tongue.

I did the Zen thing again, drawing in a breath through my nose and letting it out through my mouth. By the time Jim sidestepped his way through the crowd between the bar and our table and showed up with Eve's lite beer and a glass of Chardonnay for me, I was almost human again.

Almost.

He went back to the bar for his own drink, and I leaned over to Eve.

"What if he wants to talk about cooking?"

I cringed at the memory of the loaf of bread I'd produced earlier that day. If NASA ever needed a substitute for moon rocks, something told me they'd give me a call.

"Don't worry about it!" Eve laughed. She could afford to; her bread was light and airy and delicious. "You heard what Jim said back in class. He said good bread takes practice. I was just lucky, that's all."

"And I'm a disaster." I pretended to sip my Chardonnay, but I was really watching Jim over the rim of my glass.

"Honestly, Annie, Peter needs to be drawn and quartered. No, that's too good a fate for that no-good, lying cheat." Eve's lips thinned, her eyes narrowed. I'd seen that look before, and I knew she was imagining some kind of bizarre revenge that she'd talk about with glee but never carry out. "What that man did to your self-esteem is criminal."

The word snapped me back to reality.

"Speaking of criminal . . ." It wasn't easy to see past the groups of people standing between us and the bar—I had to sit up and crane my neck. If I leaned just the right way, I could look between a tall, bald guy with his back to me and a woman in a red sequined top and too-big hair to see Jim paying for the drinks. I needed a moment to talk to Eve before he got back to the table. "You don't think he's involved, do you?"

"Jim?" Eve's eyebrows shot up. It was clear this was one piece of the puzzle she hadn't considered before. "No." She shook her head, convinced. "He's too much of a hottie."

"Hot has nothing to do with it."

"He's too friendly."

"Maybe because he wants to find out how much we know."

"He's too—"

"Talking about cooking, are you?"

The way Jim said *cooking* made my knees weak. He pronounced it like *kook*.

Kooking.

It was adorable.

Maybe he wasn't a bad guy after all.

"Actually, we were talking about crime."

Eve always was one to lay her cards on the table. Jim, it seemed, was more into the poker-faced approach. He settled himself in the booth across from us. His beer was the color of chocolate and the foam on top was as thick as whipped cream. He took a sip and grabbed a pretzel from the bowl in the center of the table.

After another sip of beer and a bite of pretzel, he cleared his throat. "So you think Beyla killed Drago?"

"Nobody said that. Not exactly." I felt like somebody had to give the amateur detectives' version of the surgeon general's warning. Before we said something we might regret later, we had to make sure all our bases were covered. "We're not accusing Beyla of anything."

"Sure we are!" So much for subtlety. Eve waved away my attempts at being impartial. "She hated the man. Pure and simple. She couldn't stand his guts."

Jim cocked his head. "And you know this, how?"

"We don't know it," I interjected before Eve could get us in any deeper. Somebody had to retain some sort of standards. "We don't know anything about Beyla and Drago's relationship, except that she says she didn't know him, and we know that's not true. We saw them fighting in the parking lot the night Drago was killed. And even though she says she didn't, we know she met him even before that night."

Jim didn't have to ask—I knew what he was thinking.

"I did some research," I confessed, and I wondered if Jessica Fletcher ever felt as foolish as I did at that moment. Did anyone in Cabot's Cove ever come right out and say that she was nothing but a busybody? At least now Jim knew there was more to me than just bad cooking—he knew I was nosy, too.

"I went to the library," I continued, because there didn't seem to be much point in not explaining myself. "I went through the microfiche and checked the local news stories. I found one about the opening of Drago's art gallery."

"Beyla was there," Eve interrupted. "She was in a picture with Drago."

"That's very good." Jim took another sip of his beer. "Did you think of doing that bit of research on your own?" He aimed the question at me, not at Eve, and for a couple seconds, I hesitated. What was it called when you told lies about people, libel or slander? Could Jim be angling for a piece of the pie when he turned around and reported what I'd said to Beyla, and then Beyla turned around and sued me for it?

My cautious side urged me to keep my mouth shut, but another part of me told me that I didn't have to worry. Not about Jim.

It was the part of me that I usually didn't listen to. As usual, I was tempted to tell it to shut up. Except, there was something about this guy. There was warmth in his hazel eyes. There was understanding in his smile. There was his I'm-so-smokin'-I-might-start-a-fire smile, but I ignored that part for now.

I told my cautious side to get lost and took a leap of faith.

"We Googled Drago," I explained. "That's how we found out about the gallery in the first place."

"And then we went there," Eve said.

A muscle tensed at the base of Jim's jaw. "Not a good idea. If Drago was up to no good, it's probably not safe to go poking around into his business."

At the time Eve and I visited Arta, I didn't think it was a good idea either, but hearing Jim challenge what we'd done brought out a strange defensiveness in me. "No one got hurt," I told him. "And nothing much happened at the gallery, except that we met Drago's partner."

"And we found his office trashed," Eve reminded me.

"Drago's office? Vandalized?" Jim cocked his head, thinking. "You've really been hard at work at this. You've gotten a lot farther than I have."

"You?" For reasons I can't explain, the thought of Jim spending any time thinking about Drago's murder struck me as extraordinary. He was a chef, not a detective.

I reminded myself that I wasn't a detective, either. I was a bank teller, and if I was smart, I wouldn't forget it.

"You don't mean you're investigating Drago's murder, too?" I asked hesitantly.

Jim laughed. "I wouldn't exactly call it investigating," he said. "But I admit, I'm curious. It's not every day a man is murdered in the parking lot of the place you work. As a matter of fact . . ." He sat back, his right arm thrown casually across the back of the booth. "I've been wondering if you two had anything to do with the murder."

I would have laughed if it was funny.

And if I hadn't picked that exact moment to take a sip of my wine.

I choked and coughed, and felt along the bench for my purse so that I could pull out a handkerchief. Of course, I couldn't put my hands on it—at least not right away—so I settled for pulling in a few calming breaths. "Us? You think we—"

"I didn't say that." Just like I had, Jim distanced himself from anything that sounded even remotely like an accusation. "But you have to admit, you two have been acting mighty suspicious. There was that bit with Beyla and the pasta sauce."

Eve shot up in her seat. "She tried to poison Annie!"

"And the part about how you told the police one thing and now you're telling me something else," Jim added.

"That's because in this case, *the police*," Eve gave the words a sour emphasis, "is Tyler Cooper, and Tyler Cooper is the biggest horse's patootie this side of the Chesapeake. He said I wasn't smart enough. Smart!" She snorted. "Like that Kaitlin what's her name is any smarter than me. And another thing—"

I knew I had to do something before what had been a conversation about murder turned into one about Eve's love life.

"We didn't exactly lie to the police," I explained to Jim. "We tried to tell the truth. Tyler wouldn't listen."

"So we decided to investigate on our own." Eve pulled back her shoulders, her body language saying that it was all her idea and she was mighty proud of it.

"You certainly did." Jim turned in his seat, just enough to put me fully in his sights. "And you're certainly having some success."

It might have been a warning, but I chose to think of it as a compliment. I felt my spirits lift in a way that my yeast had never raised my bread dough.

"You've found out a great deal. I've wondered about it all, too, but I didn't know where to begin. You've done a great job."

That *was* a compliment, pure and simple, and it warmed me down to the tips of my toes.

Jim pinned me with a look. "And here I just thought you were sticking your nose where it didn't belong because you were guilty. I never dreamed you were actually investigating."

I wasn't sure what he was talking about until I remembered how I'd looked through Beyla's workstation that afternoon before lunch. And Jim's, too.

My cheeks got hot. "You saw me."

"I was on my way back into the classroom. You weren't exactly being subtle."

My hot cheeks got hotter. "You must think I'm awful."

"As a matter of fact, I think you're—"

Whatever Jim thought of me, I didn't have a chance to find out. Eve's cell phone rang. She checked the caller ID and answered.

"Sure," she said. "Ten minutes. See you there."

"Got to go," she said. "Meeting Tony." She gave me a meaningful look, and I snapped to. Eve was sitting nearest to the wall, and in order for her to leave, I had to slide out of the bench. I made a grab for my purse, and this time, I found it exactly where it should have been the first time I looked. I stood. She shimmied out and I sat back down.

"Thanks for the drink," Eve told Jim.

Jim nodded. "Don't forget, tomorrow's Sunday. No class."

"No school tomorrow! That means I can stay out as late as I want," Eve said with a laugh and a brilliant smile. Before I could say anything back, she was gone.

"Well . . ." I took another sip of my wine, at a loss for words. I wasn't sure how to make it clear that I understood how these things worked. Eve was gone. Sooner rather than later, Jim would find an excuse to leave, too.

The easiest thing to do was beat him to the punch. "I guess you'll be going now, too."

Jim looked at his beer, which wasn't even half gone. "There isn't a Scotsman alive who would let this precious liquid go to waste. Not one who's worth his salt."

"Then you don't want to leave?"

"What do you think?"

"I think now that Eve's gone—"

"You think that I asked the two of you out so that I could be with Eve?"

"It's what always happens."

"Really?" He took a sip of beer. "And why do you suppose that is?"

I shrugged. That would have been the only explanation any other guy needed, but Jim waited for more. "She's beautiful," I said. "Anyone can see that."

He waved away my assessment with one hand. "She's flashy."

"She's funny."

"So are you, in your own way."

"She's spontaneous."

"Spontaneity is overrated, and besides . . ." Jim leaned forward, his elbows on the table. "I have a hunch you could be spontaneous as well. At the right time. With the right person."

I wanted to tell him I could. I tried to tell him I wanted to.

Which doesn't explain why the words that came out were, "My husband left me for the girl at the dry cleaner's."

"Aye, I thought it must have been something like that." Jim nodded and called a waiter over. "Let's order dinner, why don't we. Then you can tell me all about it."

I DIDN'T TELL HIM *ALL* ABOUT IT—NOT IN DETAIL, anyway. I mean, what would that have accomplished, aside from making me look pathetic?

Instead, I munched a burger and gave Jim the Reader's Digest Condensed version of my marriage. Happily ever after until Dry Cleaner Girl came along.

"And since?"

Jim's question came just as I was putting a French fry in my mouth. I held up a finger, chewed, and swallowed before I answered. "And since, what? That's all there is to it."

"And you don't want to get married again?"

I'd considered the question myself a time or two. Honest, I had. I just never expected to hear it from Jim. "I'm not ready," I told him. "I'm not even ready to think about being ready."

"But it's been more than a year."

I shrugged and took a sip of wine. My second glass. "I thought it would last forever." A new thought occured to me. "Are you—"

"Married?" Jim wrinkled his nose. "No, and never have been. Not that lucky." From most guys, the answer would have been nothing short of facetious. But Jim meant it. Don't ask me how I knew—I just did. "Never have met the right woman. And besides, what they call the hospitality services industry . . . well, it doesn't leave much time for a social life."

"You're lucky when it comes to your job, though," I told him. "You're a great teacher, and I can tell that you really love what you do for a living."

"And you don't?"

He had a way of asking open-ended questions. From anyone else, I would have considered it prying. From Jim it was honest concern.

"I work at a bank," I told him. "I'm a teller. I've been a teller since I graduated from high school. It's a good job, but—"

"But you're not happy."

"I didn't say that." I dabbed some ketchup from my mouth with a napkin. "I'm very good at what I do."

"I have no doubt of that."

"It's a good place to work. I've got benefits and a dependable paycheck."

"And you like that."

"It's secure."

"But it's boring."

I stared at my burger for a moment. Were my words telegraphing thoughts I'd never allowed myself to even consider?

Being a bank teller was what I did, end of story. Until now, I'd never entertained the thought of doing anything else.

"I admit that I've been feeling a little restless," I told Jim. "But I don't really like to talk about it—bad luck, or bad karma, or whatever you call it. And I don't know why I'm talking about it now. It's not like I'm dissatisfied."

"But there has to be more."

"Are you looking for more, too?"

He sat back, obviously surprised that I'd turned the tables on him. He toasted me with his beer glass. "If I don't get away from whacky Monsieur Lavoie sometime very soon, there may be another homicide at Très Bonne Cuisine."

I couldn't help it, I had to laugh. "He's odd."

"Tell me about it." His sigh was nothing short of dramatic. "It's a good job. Like yours." He grinned. "But it isn't what I want to do. Not really. What I really want . . ."

He pulled in a breath and let it out slowly. "I want my own place. My own restaurant. I have an uncle with a place over in Alexandria. Mum's oldest brother, Angus. It's not exactly the kind of place I'd like for my own, but he has been an inspiration to me. In my place . . ." Jim tipped his head back, and from the smile on his face, I could tell he was picturing every little detail of his dream. "Something upscale, but not so expensive that it's out of reach of folks who want a special experience for special occasions. Something trendy, but not so trendy that once the newness wears off, the place empties out. I want to showcase really fine cooking using all the best, freshest ingredients."

I nodded, taking a moment to think about the idea. I'd heard restaurant work was brutal. I suspected it cost a fortune to open a place, too.

Jim must have been reading my mind. "I've been saving," he said. "And working on a solid business plan so I can get a bank loan. Every time I think I'm finally close, real estate prices skyrocket. It's always out of reach."

"Which explains Très Bonne Cuisine."

He nodded. "But it doesn't explain . . ." He paused, and I could tell he was wondering if he should say any more. "Have you noticed anything odd about Lavoie?"

"Anything?" It was my turn to laugh. "Where do you want to start?"

"I think he's up to something." Jim took the last bite of his roast beef sandwich and brushed crumbs from his hands. "I don't know what it is, but it makes me wonder about the man."

"Maybe he's the one who killed Drago?"

I thought Jim would meet the suggestion with laughter. Instead, he looked at me hard. "I've considered the possibility," he said. "After all, Lavoie was still in the shop when I left that evening. That means he must have been there around the time that Drago was killed."

"That gives him opportunity but not motive. At least not any motive that we know about." As if it could help order my thoughts, I shook my head. "Of course, if Beyla has motive, we haven't found that, either. We know she's lying, though. That seems pretty important. And we know she's carrying around some kind of herb that might be foxglove. Maybe we need to make another trip over to Arta and see if Yuri can tell us anything useful."

"Are you listening to yourself?" Jim's question stopped me cold. "I mean, it's fun to sit here and speculate. It's a fine game to play with friends over a couple drinks. But you and Eve, you've taken it to another level. It worries me that you sound as if you're actually enjoying it."

"No, not enjoying. But it's a puzzle, and all the pieces aren't in place. I'd like to get them sorted out, that's all. I'd like to figure out how everything fits together."

"I can understand that. Only, Annie . . ." Jim reached across the table and covered my hand with his. "I don't think it's a good idea. A man has already died."

"And you think—"

"I don't think it, I know it. Remember, your stove exploded. I thought it was an accident until right this very moment. Now I'm not so sure. In light of everything you've told me, I can't help but think you're onto something. And somebody doesn't like it."

"Really?" Honestly, I hadn't thought we were that close to solving the murder. Now, thinking that we might be close, I felt a rush of adrenaline "Maybe I'm a pretty good detective after all." I couldn't keep a smile from spreading across my face.

But why didn't Jim look as excited as I felt?

He slid out of the booth. The next thing I knew, he was sitting next to me. He grabbed both my hands and looked me in the eye. "You must promise me something, Annie," he said.

Promise?

At that point, I would have promised anything. The sun. The moon. The stars. When Jim looked at me that way, no way I could refuse him anything.

I swallowed hard, schooling my voice and forcing another smile. "What is it you want?"

"Promise me you'll stop investigating. Right now. It's too dangerous."

"But—"

"No. That's not good enough. No excuses. Annie, there are professionals who take care of these things. You do your job and you let them do theirs. It's too dangerous."

The cautious part of me knew he was right. But I couldn't get something he said out of my head.

My job.

Do my job.

My boring, go-to-the-bank-every-day job.

Suddenly, it didn't seem like enough anymore.

"You're right," I told Jim. I slid my hand out from his so that I could take a drink of my wine. But when I was done, I didn't put my hand back on the table. I placed it on my lap.   .

"It is too dangerous. And we're not being careful enough. I promise," I said. "No more investigating."

Jim smiled.

Good thing he didn't see that in my lap, my fingers were crossed.

Eleven

◼

THOUGH IT ISN'T FAR FROM ARLINGTON, OLD TOWN
Alexandria is one of the places I hardly ever went
to. Not that it isn't interesting, and picturesque, and wonderful. The narrow streets and side-by-side town houses
evoke the time when Alexandria was the thriving port city
and George Washington lived just up the river at Mount
Vernon. The shops are charming (and charmingly pricey).
The restaurants are some of the best in the D.C. metro area.
I ought to know—Peter loved seafood, and back when we
were a couple, he used to love to impress me, too. We cele-
brated many a special occasion watching the boats out on
the Potomac while we ate lobster. I still remember it
fondly.

The lobster, not Peter.

Of course, all that ambiance has a price. Old Town at-
tracts hundreds of thousands of tourists a year. Maybe
millions.

I swear, that Sunday afternoon when Eve and I arrived,
every single one of them was there.

And we were all looking for a parking space.

"There's one!" I nudged Eve and pointed down North Patrick to an empty spot on the street. But by the time we mauevered our way to it, up a one-way street and down another, the spot was taken.

I collapsed against the passenger seat and sighed. "Are you sure this is worth it? We could just go home."

"And miss this opportunity to do a little more investigating?" Eve's gaze swiveled from one side of the street to the other, her parking-spot radar on maximum. "Not on your life. Besides, when we talked on the phone this morning, I thought you were all for this."

"I was. I am." It was true. I may have lied to Jim the night before, but at least I wasn't trying to fool myself anymore. I *did* want to investigate. Not to prove I was smart, and certainly not to get back at Tyler Cooper like Eve was trying to do. Not so people would look at Eve and me and think we were some sort of whiz kids when it came to solving crimes, either. And not to show up the professionals. I had all the respect in the world for the men and women who did this sort of thing for a living, and I had no doubt that even as we cruised the streets of Old Town in vain, they were out doing some investigating of their own and probably having more success than we were.

But the time I'd spent with Jim the night before had done more than just stir up my hormones. (And believe me, being with Jim really stirred up my hormones!)

As crazy as it seemed, our conversation had pulled something out of me. Something that had been hidden so deep, even I didn't know it was there.

Maybe it was because he was such an honest guy, and I couldn't be anything less than 100 percent aboveboard when I was with him. Maybe these thoughts and feelings had been there all along and were just waiting for the right moment to emerge.

Maybe . . .

Maybe I couldn't explain it, and maybe I didn't want to. Maybe I didn't even have to try.

Maybe it was just time for me to accept the facts: I really wanted to figure out who killed Drago. Not for anything or for anybody, but for me, so that I could prove to myself that I could do it, and more importantly, that there was life beyond the walls of my bank branch. I had to go out on a limb for once. I wanted to take a chance to do something different and exciting. Somewhere along the line, I'd forgotten that there was a big world out there, and for the first time since Peter descended into heavy-on-the-starch madness, I realized I wanted a little piece of it.

Of course for now, I'd settle for a parking space.

"There!" Eve hit the accelerator, and we shot toward a black Volvo that was just pulling away from the curb.

I dug my fingers into the upholstery. "Parallel parking makes me nervous."

Eve laughed. "Parallel parking is a challenge. Like love. And speaking of that . . ." She poked the car into reverse, turned the wheel, and slid into the parking space as if it was made for her three-year-old red Mazda. "What's up with you and Jim?"

My cheeks got warm. "Nothing. He just wanted to talk. About Drago."

"Uh-huh." Eve punched the car into park and reached in the backseat for her purse. "You're lying to yourself if you think that's true."

"You think so?" Even though a relationship with Jim was all I'd thought about all night long, I couldn't allow myself to consider the possibility in the cold light of day. Not without getting all fizzy. I twitched away the sensation that tickled up my back like champagne bubbles in a crystal glass. "I'm not so sure," I said.

Eve squealed out a laugh and slapped me on the knee.

"Oh, honey, you are blinder than a one-eyed jack! Come on." She got out of the car, and I followed. Her legs were longer than mine, plus she knew where she was headed. I had to scramble to catch up.

"You think he really is . . ." I felt myself blushing as I tried to get the words out. "Attracted to me?"

"Like bees to honey." She gave me a sidelong look and grinned. "Didn't you know that? Right from the start? Haven't you seen the way he's been looking at you since day one?"

"No." Maybe. Was I that unconscious?

We were just walking past a town house where geraniums and petunias overflowed from boxes on every window, and I paused, taking in the riotous color. "You think so?" I asked Eve. "You really think Jim is—"

"Oh, Annie!" Eve looped her purse over one shoulder and hooked her other arm through mine. Laughing, she steered me toward King Street. "You've been asleep ever since that lowlife Peter up and left you. It's time to wake up, honey! Welcome back to the world."

Welcome back to the world.

I liked the sound of that.

As I walked along toward wherever Eve was headed—and the next phase of our investigation—I realized that I was smiling from ear to ear.

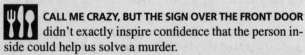 CALL ME CRAZY, BUT THE SIGN OVER THE FRONT DOOR didn't exactly inspire confidence that the person inside could help us solve a murder.

It was purple and silver. There was a cute-as-a-button, smiling angel in one corner and loopy cursive across the rest.

Angel Emporium.

When Eve reached for the brass doorknob, I tugged her back. "I don't know," I said. "It doesn't look—"

"What?" She wrinkled her nose the way she always did when she was impatient. "I thought you said you wanted to investigate. I told you, Annie, this lady can help us."

I pressed my nose to the front window, but it was hard to see anything beyond the crystals that hung just beyond it, catching the afternoon light and shooting it back at us in a million, colorful pieces.

"We need a poison expert to figure out what's in that vial you stole from Beyla," I reminded Eve. "Not someone to put us in touch with our higher selves."

Her shoulders stiffened. "I didn't steal it. I borrowed it," she said, firmly ignoring my objection. "And besides, it was all in the line of duty. This vial . . ." She reached into her purse and pulled it out for me to see. "This vial is a major breakthrough in our case. We would have been crazy to ignore the opportunity to appropriate it."

I didn't point out that her use of the word *we* wasn't exactly accurate. I also didn't mention that the simple fact that Eve had even used a word like *appropriate* meant that she had been spending far too many hours in front of *Court TV*. One of us had to stay levelheaded. And even though I'd made the decision to continue with our sleuthing, I knew that one—now and always—had to be me.

"Major breakthrough or not, we have to find out what's in the vial before we move forward," I reminded her. "Maybe a doctor would be able to help us. Or the police. I'll bet the police know plenty about poison."

Eve's upper lip curled. "You want us to go to Tyler and ask him for help? You'll have to boil me in oil before I'll do that. Or make me wear polyester. It's not going to happen, Annie. Not in this lifetime."

"OK, I get it. I agree, no police. But the Angel Emporium?" I could just about feel *cute* ooze out of the shop and wrap around us where we stood at the front door. "Are you sure?"

Eve nodded. "You said we needed an expert, right? That's why we're here. I know Rainbow can help us."

If I was going to buy into this scenario—and at this point, *if* was a pretty crucial word—my confidence evaporated right then and there. "Rainbow? That's not her name, is it? You haven't brought us all the way here and made us parallel park just so we can talk to someone named Rainbow?"

Bless Eve for not knowing sarcasm when she heard it. As always, she took my questions at face value. "Rainbow DayGlow. Is that a great name or what? You'll really like her. Come on."

Because she knew I wasn't going to budge without a little more urging, she opened the door and stepped into the Angel Emporium. I followed her inside.

No sooner had the door closed behind me and the little angel-topped wind chime above us announced our presence than I was overwhelmed by the mingled smells of incense and scented candles. There was a fountain to our right, and the sounds of trickling water provided a liquid counterpoint to the New Age music playing softly in the background.

"Blessed be!" a woman's voice called to us from somewhere beyond the beaded curtain that partitioned the main part of the store from what was probably a storeroom or office. "I'll be there in just a moment. Look around, why don't you."

She didn't have to tell me twice. I was already checking out the place.

The wall next to the gurgling fountain was stacked floor to ceiling with candles that had names like Morning Prayer and Angel's Kiss. The counter to my left was filled with beaded jewelry, incense that made my nose itch, and angels of all shapes and sizes. Angels graced everything from buttons to brooches. Angels perched on scrunchies and were emblazoned across the fronts of T-shirts and night-gowns and tank tops. Straight ahead was a huge quilt filled with brightly colored fabric angels, all of them pink-cheeked, bright-eyed, and as cute as . . . well . . . as cute as little angels.

Did I mention that I was losing confidence in Eve's plan?

My level of trust dipped a little more when the owner of the chirpy voice that had greeted us stepped out from behind the brightly colored beaded curtain. Rainbow Day-Glow was middle-aged, as short as I am, and twice as round. She had a head of springy red curls and wore a flowing tie-dyed skirt that touched her ankles. Her matching top, though it was loose and wide, did not disguise the fact that she wasn't wearing a bra. She smelled like patchouli (or was it sandalwood?). Her feet were bare; her toenails were painted purple.

"Blessed be!" She caught sight of me and smiled in an angelic sort of way. What else had I expected? "Can I help you with—" Rainbow's gaze moved past me to where Eve was checking out the display of books with titles like *Getting in Touch with Your Angel Guides* and *Talk to Your Angels and They'll Talk Back.* "Eve! Hey, girlfriend, what's shakin'?"

Eve stepped forward. She was still holding the vial of herbs, and she used it to point my way. "This is my friend, Annie," she said. "We need your help."

"Help?" Rainbow looked around the shop. Outside, Old Town was wall to wall with tourists, but right now, it appeared that none of them was in need of heavenly guidance; we were the only ones in the shop. "You mean—"

"You got that right." Eve hurried toward the beaded curtain, and because I wasn't sure what else I was supposed to do, I marched after her. Rainbow got there before either of us. She held the curtain and stepped aside to allow us into the back room ahead of her.

Did I say *room*?

OK, let me correct that right here and now. The place we walked into was less like a room and more like a cave. Dark walls. Dark ceiling. Dark floor.

In fact, the only light in the place was the single black candle burning in the center of a pentagram painted on the floor in the same silver paint that had been used on the smiling angel on the sign up front.

I screeched to a stop just inside the doorway and plucked at Eve's sleeve. "Are you sure you—"

Rainbow was right behind me, and she prodded me forward, one hand on the small of my back. "The only magic going on here is the white kind. You don't have a thing to worry about."

"But how—?" I gathered my thoughts and my composure. Whatever I had expected when I looked inside the Angel Emporium, it sure wasn't this. "Eve, how do you know about this place?"

It was too dark in there to be certain, but I swear Eve blushed. Since it's not something she does often, I was more curious than ever. Rainbow spared her the effort of an explanation.

"I've known Eve for years," she said. "We took belly dancing classes together back in '95. Remember that, Eve?" Rainbow laughed and did a couple of quick moves that made her hips sway in dizzying ways. Even after she stopped, they kept shaking. "Since then, I've been able to help her a time or two. As a matter of fact, Eve, I've been wondering how that latest spell worked out for you."

The color in Eve's cheeks deepened. She gave me a sheepish grin, and I knew right then and there that I didn't have to ask what kind of spell Rainbow was talking about. Or who that spell was intended to bewitch.

"You've used love spells? On Tyler?" My voice cracked over the words. "Eve, I can't believe you. Why didn't I know about this? How could you even begin to think that this kind of nonsense—"

"Now, now, don't knock it until you try it." Rainbow moved past me and flicked on a light, and for the first time, I saw that the room wasn't as bare as I thought. The wall just behind where she stood was covered with shelves. Each shelf held glass containers on it, and each and every container was filled with some kind of dried herb or powder. Rainbow gave me a knowing grin. "If I'm not mistaken, you look like you might be in the market for a love spell yourself." She reached for one of the jars and held it out to me. "Eye of newt?"

When I went pale, she laughed.

"Just kidding, kiddo!" She replaced the jar and stepped around to the other side of the long counter that was parallel to the wall. "So tell me what you two are up to. You're wearing that serious face of yours, Eve. The one you showed up with the day that son of a bitch Tyler broke up with you. Don't tell me my spell didn't work. Are you sure you did what you were supposed to? Did you sprinkle that powder I gave you all around his house? Every nook and cranny?"

Eve's silence was answer enough. And that was OK with me—I really didn't want to know the details.

She put Beyla's vial on the counter. "We need to know what this is," she told Rainbow. "It's important."

There was another light nearby, the kind that clamps onto the corner of a desk. Rainbow snapped it on and held the vial up to it. She twirled it around in her fingers, looking at its contents from every angle. "Where'd you get it?" she asked as she popped the cork and took a sniff. "Do you know what you're dealing with here?"

"Is it—?" I swore I was going to keep out of it, but I couldn't help myself. The suspense was killing me. I swallowed down the tight ball in my throat. "Is it foxglove?"

"Oh, you're good!" Rainbow looked at me with something like admiration, but in a second, that expression dissolved into concern. "*Digitalis purpurea.* You're not messing with this stuff, are you?"

"We're not," Eve said. "But we think someone else is."

"Then I'm glad I don't know that someone else." Rainbow took another whiff. "Foxglove is not something to fool with. Fresh or cooked in with food, just a smidgen of this stuff can kill a man."

"We think maybe it already has," I told her.

Rainbow's eyes went wide. She put the cork back in the vial and handed the foxglove to me. "I won't have anything to do with that kind of thing. It's nasty, and it works quick, twenty to thirty minutes tops. Did you know that to a person who's been poisoned with foxglove, everything looks blue? Weird, huh?"

Plenty weird.

I tucked the foxglove in my purse. "So where would a person get foxglove?" I asked Rainbow.

She shrugged, a motion that caused her breasts to settle on the counter like tie-dye-draped pillows. "Lots of places. Plenty of people grow it and don't have a clue how dangerous it is."

I glanced at the shelves behind her. "And you sell it, here, too. Right?"

It was just a guess, but I knew I was spot-on when Rainbow backed away from me, her hands out like she was a cop stopping traffic. "I'd never sell it to anybody if I thought—"

"That's not what we're saying. Honest." I did my best to relieve her fears. "We're just trying to get a handle on things."

She looked at my purse as if she could see beyond the faux leather to the little glass vial inside. "It could be mine," she said.

"And the woman who bought it?"

Just as Eve asked the question, the little wind chime at the front door jingled.

"Blessed be!" Rainbow called out, and she headed back out into the shop.

Eve went out after her, and I brought up the rear. But not before I stopped to blow out the candle. I may have been a new woman with a new outlook on life, but there was no use taking foolish chances.

I brushed aside the beaded curtain, stepped into the shop, and stopped dead in my tracks.

The customer who'd just walked in was Beyla.

She looked at Eve. She looked at me. And she took off out the front door like a bat out of hell.

Twelve

HAVE I MENTIONED THAT I'M NOT EXACTLY ATHLETIC?

Eve is, of course. Or at least with her slim body and long legs, she could be, if she made the effort. And if she thought that physical fitness was about more than Botox injections and electrolysis. Of course, all things considered, no matter how heart-healthy she was, it probably wouldn't have done a whole lot to overcome the issues that are bound to arise from trying to run in three-inch heels.

I scrambled around a display of angel greeting cards, trying to reach the front door before it slammed behind Beyla. Eve high-stepped after me. I ducked under a mobile, but she smacked right into it and sent the shimmering heavenly messengers that hung from it dancing. I darted out the front door, leaving her behind me grumbling words that never should have been used in a store full of angels. By the time we were both outside, we were breathing hard.

And Beyla was nowhere in sight.

"Now what do we do?" Eve asked. But I'd already formulated a plan.

I pointed to the right. "You head that way," I told her. "I'll go the other way. At least maybe if we can find her, we can talk to her. Ask her what she's doing here and why she ran when she saw us."

"Got it," Eve said. I would like to say that she took off running but . . . well, remember those three-inch heels. Eve took off striding gracefully in one direction. In my sensible sneakers, I hurried off in the other.

Of course, *hurried* is a relative word.

The sidewalks were packed, and I sidestepped a lady with a stroller, a man walking a sickly looking poodle, and a Japanese family taking pictures outside the pub and brew house next door to the Angel Emporium. Even before I got swallowed up by the crowd patiently waiting for the light to change at the next cross street, I knew I was getting nowhere fast.

I stood on tiptoe and craned my neck, attempting to see over the heads of the people all around me. Across the street and three stores up, I thought I saw a flash of black. I didn't know if it was Beyla's clothing, Beyla's hair, or if it was Beyla at all, but I knew that I had to find out. I excused my way through the crowd, looked both ways at the corner, and took off running across the street just steps ahead of a Dash About bus.

I had no sooner leapt onto the opposite sidewalk than a man stepped out of an alley right in front of me. We were outside a little sidewalk café, and with tables on one side of me, the building on the other, and the man blocking my path, I was trapped like the proverbial dirty rat.

And Beyla—if it really was Beyla—was putting more distance between us with every second that passed.

"Excuse me!" The man blocking my way was tall, thin, and bald. His back was to me, and he seemed to be busy looking at something down the street. I raised my voice so he could hear me above the sounds of traffic. "Excuse me," I said again when he didn't respond. "I need to get by."

Still nothing. I tapped him on the back.

He turned, startled, and I let out a little gasp. I was face-to-face with Yuri Grul, Drago's former partner.

If Yuri was surprised to see me, he didn't stay that way for long. He took one look over his shoulder, another at me, and one more at the crowd that was coming our way like a wave, now that the light had changed.

Without a word, he grabbed my arm and pulled me into the alley he'd just stepped out of.

We were sandwiched between the café and the boutique next door. It was shady and damp, and after the press of the crowd and the summer heat that rippled off the sidewalk, I felt suddenly chilled. I hugged my arms around my chest and wondered if I should listen to the cautious voice inside my head—the one that reminded me that I shouldn't be alone with a man I barely knew, out of sight of the crowd. The one that whispered the word *murder* and told me not to forget that whether or not I was playing detective, I might be playing with fire.

But Yuri was blocking the mouth of the alley. And one step in the other direction put me even farther into the shadows.

I had only one option: I stood my ground and raised my chin. "What are you doing here?" I asked him in my most challenging tone.

Yuri stared at me, his expression unreadable. He'd been puffing on a long, thin cigarette, and after he took the last drag, he tossed the butt on the ground and crunched it under the sole of his expensive sneaker. When he blew out a long stream of smoke, I leaned downwind.

"You are Miss Capshaw. From the gallery. You are following her?"

It took me a couple seconds to figure out what—and who—he was talking about.

Yuri could obviously read the surprise on my face. A slow smile lifted the corners of his mouth. "You are police?" he asked.

I knew I had to regain my composure, and fast. I shook my head. "No. Not police. I'm . . ." What was I? And how could I even begin to explain it to Yuri?

I decided on the truth. Or at least part of the truth.

"I'm a bank teller at Pioneer Savings and Loan. But I go to school with Beyla. We take a cooking class together at Très Bonne Cuisine. I was in a store over there . . ." I poked my thumb over my shoulder roughly in the direction of the Angel Emporium. "And I thought I saw her walk by. I wanted to catch up with her. To say hello."

"You do not try to arrest her?"

OK, so maybe I'm a little slow. Chalk it up to the heat or to the fact that I was a novice when it came to this whole detective game. It took me a while to process what Yuri was saying. When I finally did, it hit me like the smell of the men's locker room at the gym where Peter and I used to take couples aerobics.

I staggered back against the brick wall behind me. "You sound like you expect the police to be following her. That means you think she's guilty. Are you saying . . ." Eve and I discussing our theory of the crime was one thing. But hearing our theory echoed by an almost stranger . . . well, I suddenly knew how Chris Columbus must have felt the first time someone slapped him on the back and told him that he'd been right about that whole the-world-is-round thing all along.

I sucked in a breath to steady my voice. "Are you telling me you think she's guilty? You are, aren't you? You think Beyla killed Drago. Or do you know it for a fact?"

This time, Yuri's smile was quicker. And grimmer.

"So, this is why you follow her." He nodded, and somehow that one gesture said it all. Yuri and I were in agreement: he thought Beyla was guilty, too.

Yuri's thin fingers fidgeted with the big metal buckle on his belt. "What is it you see?" he asked.

"See? Nothing." That was the truth, too. Listening to myself say it, I realized how totally lame it sounded. I decided to stick with my original half truth. "She walked by the store where I was shopping," I said. "I told you, I just wanted to say hello. But she saw me and she ran away."

"This is so?" But he didn't wait for me to respond. He lit another cigarette and took two long, slow drags. His eyes narrowed as if he was thinking very hard. "You saw from where she came?" he asked.

I hadn't. At least I didn't need to lie about that part of the story.

"You know where she is going?"

I didn't, except for the Angel Emporium part of the equation. But right about now, that didn't seem to matter as much as the fact that Yuri had put the kibosh on this part of my investigation. "How was I supposed to figure out where she's going when you stopped me from following her?" I asked him. "And what are you doing here, anyway? Why are you following Beyla? Are you investigating, too?"

Yuri's eyes were small and dark. His gaze darted away from me as if he was uncomfortable with what he had to say. "Drago Kravic, he was like a brother to me. And you said it, yes? You said that Beyla killed him."

"You know this for certain? For real?" I took a step closer to him, intrigued and eager to know more. "Can you prove it? Should we go to the police?"

"No, no. No police. Not yet. It might be . . . how would you say this . . . bad luck, yes? It would ruin everything. First, we must have proof."

"We do. Or at least a little bit of proof." I reached in my

purse and pulled out the vial. "It's foxglove. It belongs to Beyla. I even know where she bought it."

I swear, at that moment, Yuri looked as beatific as one of the angels over in the Emporium. When he reached toward the vial, his hand quivered. "And this, it is Beyla's? You are certain of this?"

I nodded, but when I tried to give the vial to him, he pulled his hand back to his side.

"You must keep it safe," he said. "If the police are looking for evidence, this is perfect, yes? With this and the disc—" As if he was afraid he'd said too much, he stopped abruptly and gave me another long, careful look. If we were in the bank, and I was on one side of the teller station and he was on the other, I might have thought he was going to rob the place. That's how intense that look was. He must have known it, too, because he erased the expression and gave me what was almost a smile of apology.

"I am sorry. My mind is busy. Preoccupied. I am thinking, perhaps, that you might be able to help me."

"Help you prove Beyla is the killer? It's exactly what Eve and I have been trying to do all along. Or at least what Eve's been trying to do. I haven't been so sure—until now. Now that I know this is foxglove . . ." Suddenly, the herb in the vial made me queasier than ever. I tucked it back in my purse. "I'll have to turn it over to the police," I told Yuri and reminded myself. "I suppose it's pretty compelling evidence."

This time, Yuri's smile was wide and broad. He breathed a sigh of relief. "I am so glad. So glad you have found such a thing. And so glad that I do not have to search for the truth by myself any longer. I have an ally, yes? And a pretty one at that."

I was so ingrained with the Eve-is-gorgeous-and-then-there's-Annie frame of mind, I almost didn't realize Yuri was talking about me. Until I realized he was looking at my chest.

He took a step forward.

I took a step back and smiled in a way that was friendly. But not too friendly. "An ally when it comes to investigating and nothing else," I said. It was best to get that straight right there and then. "Tell me, how do you know Beyla is guilty? And what's this about a disc?"

Lucky for me, Yuri knew when to back off. He refocused his eyes on mine. "Drago and Beyla . . ." He shook his head, like he was trying to find the right words. "There has been bad blood between them for many years. They were lovers once, you know. Back in Romania. Now, they feel nothing but hate for each other. As only former lovers can."

Yeah, I understood that.

"But why kill him?" I asked. "Why now?"

Yuri scraped a hand over his head. "It is complicated. And I, I am not certain. Otherwise I would have gone to the police with this story. But I think that Beyla, she has stolen money from Drago. From the gallery. I think Drago had proof that she took the money. The day he died, he told me there was something we needed to talk about. Something serious. I believe . . ." He paused. Though he wasn't an attractive man, there was a sort of straightforwardness about Yuri, a frankness that made me feel sorry for him. He had to relay all this painful information, and in a language he wasn't comfortable with.

"You think the disc contains proof that Beyla took Drago's money and killed him because of it."

Yuri smiled, relieved that I'd helped him out. "That is it. Just so. It is a disc. You know, like for computer. Like for DVD. It was Drago's. Ours. It was in the gallery."

"And now you can't find it." One by one, every fact Eve and I had discovered was falling into place. I smiled, pretty pleased with myself. "Beyla's the one who trashed the office at the gallery. She was looking for the disc. And you think she found it."

Yuri nodded. "This is why I follow her, thinking she will lead me to it. Hoping she will show me where she has hidden it. This is why we must keep our eyes on her. We must find the disc. Maybe she has already destroyed it. I do not know. But I know I must try to find it. You will help me? You will make sure that Drago's killer is brought to justice?"

I nodded, and he smiled. As we prepared to part ways, Yuri and I exchanged phone numbers and promised to keep in touch. He slipped out of the alley into the street; after he was out of sight, I turned the corner in the other direction.

A thought struck me when I reached the crosswalk: today's trip to Old Town Alexandria had been a lot more successful than I ever expected. We knew that the herb in Beyla's vial was foxglove. We knew she had a connection to the Angel Emporium and that she was plenty worried that Eve and I were closing in on her—otherwise, she never would have run when she saw us. And now, we had Yuri's input and support.

Most importantly, we knew about the disc. We now had something concrete to focus on and search for.

All in all, things were looking good. Our investigation was cooking along just right.

OUR INVESTIGATION WAS GOING ALL WRONG.
    I knew this for a fact because no sooner did we walk into class that night than Eve insisted we confront Beyla.

And no sooner did we confront Beyla about her relationship with Drago and her attendance at the opening of Arta and her quick trip into and out of the Angel Emporium than she gave us a blank look and an elegant little shrug that pretty much told us we were being absurd.

"You are mixed up. Crazy in the head." Apparently, Beyla

wasn't very worried about either our mental states or our accusations. She went right on getting set up for class as if she didn't have a care in the world. "You say you see me at Alexandria yesterday, but I tell you, I have never been there."

"Then you have a twin sister." Eve tossed out the comment, then slapped the counter with one hand. "Hey, that's it! Do you have a twin sister? That's something we never thought about. If you do—"

"Eve." I knew I had to keep Eve in check. Better me than Beyla—I could just about see the words that were about to leave her lips. They weren't going to be any prettier than the fierce glare that hardened her beautiful, exotic features. "I don't think Beyla has a twin sister. Do you?"

The rumbling noise Beyla made from deep in her throat was all the answer we needed.

"Look, we've got proof," I told Beyla, keeping my voice down and my stance casual so that our fellow students wouldn't think we were talking about anything more important than tonight's Poultry and Game menu. "We've got an old newspaper picture that shows you at Drago's gallery."

Beyla's hands stilled over her grocery sack. Her hesitation lasted only the blink of an eye, then she went right on emptying her bag. She pulled out a container of cream and set it on the counter.

"And we're not the only ones who saw you in Old Town," I added without mentioning Yuri's name. There was no use tipping our hand that much. "You can deny it all you want, but we know that you were there."

"And that's not all." Eve moved in close. "We've got the foxglove."

"What?" Beyla's face turned as white as the flour she was just pulling out of the bag. She dropped it back into the sack and yanked open the top drawer in her workstation. It was empty. Of course it was. I still had the vial of foxglove in my purse.

"You!" As if she knew which one of us was holding onto the purloined herb, Beyla's gaze shifted from me to Eve and back to me, and I couldn't help but think of that expression that starts out, "If looks could kill . . ."

Because if looks could kill, I would have fallen down dead right then and there.

Her temper so close to snapping that her entire body quivered, Beyla slammed the empty drawer closed and leaned in close, her voice low, her eyes on me. They were as steely as the blade of the knife that lay near her right hand. "You have no idea what you are dealing with," she whispered. "Who you are dealing with. There are dangers, ones you do not understand. If you are not careful . . ."

When she grabbed for the knife, I automatically jumped back.

Beyla's smile was sleek. She raised the blade to only an inch or so from her neck and made a slashing movement. "If you are not careful," she said, "you might get hurt."

I'm pretty sure I didn't answer her. What can you say when somebody just about comes right out and threatens to slit your throat? I don't remember walking away, either. That's probably because I was frozen on the spot. Too scared to move.

The next thing I knew, Eve's hand was on my arm and she was tugging me back across the room to our cooking station. When we got there, she let go of me, drew in a breath, and smiled.

"I think that went really well," she said. "We got a rise out of her. That means we're making real progress."

 WERE WE?

Making progress, that is.

It sure didn't feel like it to me.

I knew that I, for one, was definitely not making progress

when it came to my cooking. Maybe it was because every time Jim came around, gave me a smile, and asked how I was doing, my stomach got fluttery, my temperature shot up, and my mind wandered about as far from cooking as it was possible to get.

Maybe it was because every time I chanced a look her way, Beyla was glaring back at me, fingering that big ol' knife with the big ol' blade.

Good excuses?

Not really, but I liked to think that if I wasn't so distracted—both by Jim and by the thought of a gruesome act of violence being committed on me—I might have produced something better than the dry-as-dust Cornish hen I pulled out of the oven. And the duck with orange sauce . . . well, it's best not to even go there.

Of course, the whole time I was busy with the poultry from hell, my mind was racing.

"Maybe she really is innocent." I halfheartedly made the comment to Eve as she was finishing the last bits of her duck. She'd given me a taste, and it was as delicious as it looked. "Maybe she's just pissed because we keep bothering her."

"Beyla?" As if I could be talking about anyone else. Eve shook her head. "No way. And besides, it's not like we have any other suspects."

I set down the fork I was using to poke my duck to see if there was any scrap of meat on its bones that wasn't shriveled. "Except that we do," I murmured. Before she could say what I knew she was going to say—that we still had one more recipe to try, and that I was literally throwing in the towel by not sticking around for the venison stew—I threw in my pot holder, took off my apron, and headed downstairs to find Monsieur Lavoie.

This time, I promised myself, I wasn't going to let him weasel out of a heart-to-heart talk.

"You're hiding something."

Even I was surprised at the words that popped out of my mouth when I got downstairs and found him behind the front counter. But my instincts told me I was on the right track when Monsieur took one look at me and went as white as a ghost.

He forced out a laugh. Below the counter, his hands moved nervously. Even his smile was anxious—it came and went, limp around the edges. "You are talking crazy."

It was the second time that night that I'd been called crazy. For all I knew, both Beyla and Monsieur Lavoie were right. But that wasn't enough to stop me.

"Every time I try to talk to you, you avoid me. And what was that bit with the Dumpster? You weren't just throwing something away, you were destroying it first. You're up to something."

"Up to?" Monsieur's stare was blank, but I wasn't buying any of it.

"Don't pretend you don't understand what I'm talking about. You've been as jumpy as a June bug ever since the first day of class, and just in case that doesn't translate into French, June bugs are very jumpy. You're jumpy now."

Monsieur backed away from the counter. "No."

"Yes, you are. Nobody hops around from foot to foot like that unless they're uncomfortable about something. Nobody moves things around under the counter unless he's trying to . . .

"You're hiding something!" I never knew I could move so fast. I leaned over the counter as far as I could and snatched at whatever it was that Monsieur had tucked away under there.

Which was a great big container of seasoned salt.

The cheap, generic kind I'd seen at the local market: sixteen ounces for one ninety-nine.

I stared at the glass container of salt. I looked back to Monsieur, who was looking at me, his expression teetering on the brink of tears, as if he thought I'd just exposed some national security secret.

And the truth hit like a two-ton truck.

"You're kidding me, right?" But I didn't wait for him to answer. Instead, I reached under the counter again and found exactly what I feared I'd find.

A big spoon.

A funnel.

And empty Vavoom! jars.

How many different ways are there to say *Feeling like a fool*?

For thinking that Monsieur ever had anything to do with Drago's death. And for every single one of the jars of Vavoom! that had ever taken up residence in my kitchen cupboard.

I dropped back to the soles of my shoes, my mouth hanging open with disappointment and surprise.

"You're repacking cheap seasoned salt! You're marketing it as magical seasoning!"

"Magic is where you find it, yes?" I was surprised to hear a calm—almost resigned—tone to Monsieur's voice. I guess now that he realized I was more let down than angry, he figured he could come out of the culinary closet. Or maybe he just knew he was trapped, and no amount of lying was going to convince me otherwise.

He shrugged. "Customers, they believe Vavoom! is special. A special thing, it needs a special price. Do you not think so?"

"Not when I'm the one paying that special price!" I thought of all the jars of Vavoom! I'd stockpiled, just in case there was ever a shortage and I was in danger of going without. I propped my elbows on the counter and dropped my head into my hands. "All this time, all you've been doing is trying to cover up your little shell game."

"This is true. Yes." He had the nerve to look repentant. "I must smash the glass containers that the salt comes in. So no one will see and discover what I have been doing."

"Then it's not a secret recipe?" I should have gotten that part through my head by now, but some legends die a hard death. "There's nothing rare and exceptional about Vavoom!?"

Monsieur's shrug was answer enough.

"And you didn't have anything to do with Drago's death?"

This time, he didn't shrug. He jumped as if he'd touched a finger to an electrical line. "Me?" Monsieur's cheeks got red. "You thought I—?"

"You have been acting mighty suspicious."

Another shrug. He glanced at the seasoned salt. "And now you see why."

"And you *were* having an argument with Drago that first night of cooking class."

Monsieur nodded. "This is true. He came into the shop. He demanded that I let him upstairs. I did not think it would hurt until he said something about one of the students. The beautiful woman, Beyla. He said he must talk to her. And when I saw the fire in his eyes . . ." Lavoie shivered. "I did not think this was a wise thing. I told him no. I sent him away."

"And he was so mad that you didn't cooperate, he almost mowed me down at the front door." I nodded, too. It all made sense. "And the Vavoom!?"

Monsieur held a jar out to me. "Lifetime supply," he said. "If you do not breathe a word."

I didn't take the jar. I had enough at home to last at least a half a lifetime. Besides, now that I knew what it really was, how much I'd overpaid and for how long, the bloom was off the spice.

My illusions shattered, my faith in human nature (at least Monsieur Lavoie's human nature) shaken, I headed back to class.

I didn't say a word to Eve about what I'd discovered, partly because I was embarrassed and partly because I didn't have a chance. Luckily, we weren't actually making the venison stew, just talking about it. I'd missed the beginning of the discussion, but at the end, just as we began our cleanup, I managed to tell Eve that I'd eliminated Monsieur as a suspect. Fueled by the thought and the realization that it left us with only one viable culprit, I watched Beyla work at the other end of the big sink where we washed up the pots and pans and dishes that we'd dirtied in class.

"She's in an awfully big hurry," I told Eve, and it was true. Beyla had whisked through her dishes and her pots and pans in no time at all. (Then again, from the praise I'd heard her get from our classmates and from Jim, I don't think she had scorched orange sauce to deal with.)

Eve's gaze followed mine. "Suppose she has a hot date?"

I wiped up the sink and tossed my sponge. "Suppose we should find out?"

"You mean . . ." Eve's eyes lit up. She always was up for an adventure, but she was blown away by the thought that for once, maybe I was, too. "Annie, are you talking about following her?"

Was I?

The new bold and daring Annie Capshaw warred with the person I used to be, the play-it-safe woman who didn't have a thing to show for thirty-five years of doing just that. Except an ex who'd left her for greener pastures, a bank account that would never support a house payment, and a job that was safe, dependable—and completely boring. Oh yeah, and a whole lot of jars of seasoned salt that she'd been conned into buying because the roly-poly Frenchman on the label had seduced her with promises of culinary wonder.

I threw back my shoulders and stood as straight and tall as a short person can.

"You're darned right I'm talking about following her," I told Eve. Right after Beyla walked out of the classroom and headed downstairs, I grabbed Eve's hand.

"Let's go."

Thirteen

✖

THEY MAKE IT LOOK REALLY EASY ON TV BUT IN reality, the whole following-the-bad-guy thing is about as tricky as cooking and as sticky as my failed orange sauce.

It also takes a whole lot of logistical coordination.

Lucky for us and for our investigation, I might have been a disaster when it came to cooking, and I was definitely a chicken when parallel parking was the name of the game, but I was a crackerjack organizer.

I was also quickly becoming a pretty good liar.

Remembering my promise to Jim—the one about how I wasn't going to investigate anymore—I made up a convincing (if I do say so myself) excuse about how I had to get home quickly because I was expecting a phone call from my folks in Florida. With that taken care of, we were out of the cooking school and downstairs in the shop in a flash.

By then, I already had a plan. And the moment we stepped out the door and into the humid evening air, I put it into action.

First, I sent Eve to follow Beyla so we could find out where she was parked and what kind of car she was driving. Then, because I'd driven that night, I hurried to get my car, leaving Eve with specific instructions to keep an eye on Beyla so she could point the way if Beyla up and left before I returned.

Of course, thanks to a parking lot tight on spaces, a series of one-way streets, and traffic that was as dense as peanut butter, Beyla up and left before I returned.

Was that going to stop me? No way! The excitement of the chase pumped through my veins like fire. I was hot in pursuit and on top of my game.

I knew Eve was feeling the exhilaration, too. When I finally cruised by the front of Très Bonne Cuisine where she was waiting, she jumped into the car before I had a chance to come to a complete stop. Breathless, she pointed directly at my windshield. "That way! She went that way!"

I flicked on my signal and turned back into traffic with far more daring and far less civility than I usually displayed. I claimed my patch of street right between a dark sports car and a light-colored SUV, the driver of which had a few choice words to describe both me and my driving skills. Any other time, I would have been appalled, not to mention upset. But tonight, I didn't care one bit. I was on a mission, one the SUV driver couldn't possibly understand. And I wasn't about to let a little thing like traffic stand in my way.

Up ahead, the traffic light turned from red to green, and I scanned the cars in the line in front of us. "What kind of car?" I asked Eve.

She buckled her seat belt. She was as jazzed as I was, and her eyes sparkled when they met mine. She gulped in a breath, so proud of her part in the hunt, she looked like she would burst. "Green."

Good thing traffic was moving like molasses. We didn't jerk (at least not too much) when I slammed on my brakes.

"Green? As in green sports car? Or green minivan? Or green sedan? What make of car is it? What year? Did you get a look at the license plate?"

Eve shrugged, and her smile wilted. "Green. It was green. You know, the same color as that winter coat I bought a couple years ago. The one I never wore because it made me look fat."

The way I remembered it (and I knew I remembered it correctly), the coat in question never made Eve look anywhere near fat. But there was no use getting into that discussion again. We'd gone a few rounds at the time she bought the damn thing. What mattered now was that I remembered the coat. I knew exactly the color she was talking about. It was green, all right. Dark green. Like a Christmas tree.

Which was great, and actually might have been helpful if the traffic in front of us wasn't as thick as flies at a church picnic, if it wasn't just past sunset, and if, between the glow of the streetlights and the glare of the headlights from the cars headed toward us from the other direction, every car in the sea of cars didn't look the exact same dark color.

I scrambled to come up with a plan B.

"Which lane did she get into?" I asked Eve.

She closed her eyes, thinking hard. "Right," she said. "No. Left. Definitely left. She pulled away from the curb and angled her way across a couple lanes. Like she was going to turn."

She imparted this piece of information just as we cruised under the light. I didn't have time to wonder if it was right or wrong. I didn't bother with a signal, either. I turned left.

Traffic wasn't quite as heavy in this direction. I glanced over the cars up ahead. The bright lights of a bar washed over the sidewalk and out into the street; in the glow, I saw a green car.

"There!" I didn't wait for Eve to confirm my hunch. I stepped on the accelerator, and we took off as fast as a four-year-old Saturn can. When the green car made a right at the next cross street, we did, too.

I hung back a little. Just in case it was Beyla. Just in case she looked in her rearview mirror and saw that we were following.

"What do you think?" I asked Eve.

She leaned forward and squinted to get a better look at the car twenty feet or so in front of us. "It looks like the right one. Maybe. I dunno. It could be. Yeah!" Her expression cleared, and she sat up straight and grinned. "It has one of those magnetic signs. One of those yellow ribbons on the back of the trunk. Beyla's car had that. I remembered because I thought the yellow looked good against the green. Definitely. Yeah, it's her."

"Good. Let's not lose her again." I waved toward where I'd tossed my purse on the floor of the front seat. "Open the front zipper pocket," I told Eve. "There's a notepad in there, and a pen. Write down the license plate number, and that it's a green Taurus. I don't know the year; do you?"

I didn't know why it mattered, either; I only knew I wanted all my ducks in a row. And I wasn't talking ducks with orange sauce.

The traffic light up ahead was yellow, but when Beyla cruised through the intersection, I followed. When she turned, I turned. When she headed across the Potomac toward Georgetown, I glanced at Eve.

"What are the chances she's heading for Arta?"

"The gallery?" Eve was skeptical. I was too busy concentrating on the road and on my quarry up ahead to spare her a look, but I could tell from the tone of her voice. "That doesn't make any sense. If she's got the computer disc and she's trying to keep Yuri from finding it, she wouldn't be taking it back to where she stole it from in the first place. Besides, just because we're headed across the river doesn't mean anything. There are a million other places in this direction."

It was true; there were. But Beyla was headed to only one of them.

When we turned onto M Street, I knew I was right; that one place was Arta.

OK, so my smile was a little on the smug side when I turned it on Eve. But who could blame me? I was starting to get the hang of this Sherlock Holmes thing. And truth be told, I suspected—or should I say deduced?—that I was getting pretty good at it.

I stepped on the brakes and pulled up next to the curb in an area clearly marked No Parking, Bus Stop, watching as Beyla slowed just before she got to the gallery, then rounded the corner onto the nearest street. Though I couldn't see her car, I knew from the faint red glow of brake lights that she'd stopped. I knew we had to act fast. If we were going to keep her in our sights, we needed a parking place, too.

Have I mentioned that finding a parking place in the D.C. Metro area is like trying to get out of the seventh circle of hell?

Except this time.

Like a gift from heaven, a spot opened up twenty feet ahead, across the street from and just a little ways past Arta. Before I had a chance to remind myself that I was scared to death by the very thought of parallel parking, I shot ahead, poked the gearshift into reverse, manuevered my car into place, and cut the engine and lights.

"Now what?" Eve whispered.

"I don't know," I whispered back. Not that there was a chance Beyla was going to hear us; she was across the street and around the block. But I guess there's something about a stakeout that demands secrecy. "We're going to have to check it out." I paused, the wheels in my head turning a mile a minute.

"I'll head over to the gallery," I told Eve. "There's got to be a back door. Maybe I can see if it's open, see if she went in that way. Why don't you—"

"Oh, no!" Eve shook her head so hard and so fast, it mussed her hair. Always conscious of appearances, she smoothed it back into place. "No way are you sending me off on my own. Not in the middle of the night in a strange part of town. I'm sticking with you. You're in charge, fearless leader! Just tell me what to do—as long as it involves doing whatever I'm doing at the same time you're doing it."

There was no use even trying to argue with logic like that.

With a nod that told Eve I was ready, I slung my purse over my shoulder, opened my car door, and pointed across to the gallery. "Let's take a look. Only we're going to need to be quick. And quiet." I mouthed the words and hoped that in the dark, Eve could see enough to know what I was saying.

I didn't have to worry. Eve stuck to me like a limpet on a rock. Together, we crossed the street and closed in on Arta.

There was a spotlight trained on the burnt orange and turquoise Arta sign. Instinctively, I skirted its glow, keeping to the shadows. Maybe it was instinct, too, that told me to keep my back up against the wall. When we got as far as the front window of the gallery, I signaled Eve to stay put and pivoted to take a look.

There was no one in the gallery. Most of the interior lights were off. Here and there an overhead light shone on some objet d'art: a blue glass vase artfully displayed on one shelf, a hammered copper bowl on another, an abstract painting on the far wall that looked like water lilies. Or was it a New York City taxicab?

Before I had time to give it any more thought, Beyla walked into the gallery.

I dropped to my knees below the window and the window box in front of it, pointing inside as I did. "She's in there," I whispered just loud enough for Eve to hear me. "I wonder what she's doing."

There was only one way I was ever going to find out.

With a signal to Eve to stay put and keep quiet, I rose to my feet. The window box was overflowing, and I positioned myself behind a spicy geranium and parted the red impatiens, trying for a better look. I was just in time to see Beyla peering into the copper bowl.

That might not be a weird thing for a customer to do, but it struck me as an odd way for a burglar to act.

So did the fact that when she'd satisfied herself that the bowl was empty, Beyla lifted it, looked underneath it, and ran her hand over the shelf where it was displayed. When she was done, she took what looked to be a man's big, white handkerchief out of her pocket and wiped every surface she'd touched.

"She's not looking to hide anything," I told Eve while I shifted positions from the cover of a geranium to a curtain of marigolds. "She's searching for something."

"You think?" I saw Eve's muscles tense and stopped her with one hand on her arm before she could move. It was dangerous enough for me to be risking exposure. There was no use taking the chance of Beyla seeing the two of us watching her through the flowers.

When she was done with the copper bowl, Beyla moved on to the blue glass vase. It was big and obviously heavy and she used two hands to lift it. She studied the vase and the shelf where it was displayed carefully before she put it back into place. She gave the same kind of attention to each of the paintings on the wall. When she walked over to the counter where purchases were written up and wrapped, I figured I'd better provide Eve with some kind of narrative.

"Whatever she's looking for, she hasn't found it yet,"

I told her, partly to relieve the I'm-dying-to-know-what's-going-on look on her face, and partly because I was trying to work through the thing in my head, and I found it easier to think out loud.

I also found out the hard way that keeping still while half crouched and hunched over did ugly things to my calf muscles.

I winced and dropped onto the sidewalk, rubbing the back of my right leg with one hand. "Something tells me Yuri got his info wrong," I said. "If she already has the disc, why would she be here looking for it?"

"Unless she's looking for something else."

It was a possibility. Still, something about Eve's theory just didn't feel right to me. Neither did Yuri's take on the situation.

"I don't think so," I said, convinced, though I didn't know why. "She's being too careful. And she doesn't want anyone to know she's been here, either. She's wiping away her fingerprints."

"Really? This I've got to see!" Eve moved too fast for me. Before I could stop her, she slid away from the wall and turned to look in the front window. Let's face it, tall and beautiful is great when it comes to most things, but it's not much of an asset when you're trying to be sneaky.

I made a grab for Eve to tug her down next to me, but she waved me aside.

"She not there," she said. I guess I must have looked like I didn't believe her. "Take a look for yourself." She pointed into the gallery. "She may have been in there before, but I don't see hide nor hair of Beyla now."

Eve was right; Beyla was gone. And the way I read the situation, that meant that there were two possibilities: either she was in one of the back rooms, or she'd already left.

Two possibilities, and only one way to find out which one was right.

"Come on." I grabbed Eve's arm and tugged her toward the street where Beyla had parked her car. "Let's go around back and find out what she's up to."

We crept around the corner. When I saw that Beyla's car was still parked at the curb, I breathed a sigh of relief. "She's still in there," I whispered and pointed. There were no windows on that side of the building, but there were three stairs that led up to a small, rectangular porch and a door. Obviously, that was the way Beyla had gotten in, and for a moment, I considered checking to see if the door was still open and going in after her.

For a moment.

Logic prevailed, as did my desire not to be caught doing anything that looked even a little like breaking and entering. I continued down the sidewalk toward an alley behind the building. "Maybe there's a window."

"Back there?" Eve hissed. She glanced to where the sidewalk met the back alley and gulped, as if she expected something to jump out of there and bite her.

Which, for all I knew, it could have.

"It's the only way we're going to find out what she's up to," I reminded Eve, fishing in my purse for the mini flashlight I kept there. I might have been a new woman, but I hadn't lost all my common sense.

"There's the Annie Capshaw I know and love," Eve said, relieved now that we had a little bit of light. "Always prepared. Always on the ball. Always sure of herself."

I hated to burst her bubble. Because I was about to make a very un–Annie Capshaw–like move. I pulled back my shoulders, lifted my chin, and trained the beam of my flashlight into the pitch-dark alley. Before I could talk myself out of it, I followed the trail of light inside.

My self-confidence lasted for exactly three steps.

That's when I slammed my knee into the corner of a

wooden packing crate. I stopped to rub it, arcing the ray of light all around.

From what I could see, the alleyway ran along the back of Arta as well as behind the two buildings beside it on M Street. My flashlight beam only penetrated so far, and beyond its soft yellow glow, everything was dark and quiet. At our backs was another row of buildings, their shapes tall and hulking in the dark. Right next to us were the packing crates I'd already gotten too up close and personal with. They were stacked one on top of the other in a neat pile, probably awaiting a trash hauler to cart them away. There was no back door, but there was a window that looked out over the alley. From what I remembered from our reconnaissance trip, the window was in Drago's office. Unfortunately, it was also at least ten feet off the ground, and there were no lights on inside the office. From here, all I could see was a black square a little less dark than the building around it.

Until a light came on inside.

"She's in there. In the office." I flicked off my flashlight and backed up as far as I could, but because of how high up the window was on the wall, I still couldn't see anything. Even Eve standing on tiptoe couldn't catch a glimpse of the person inside. I shook my head in frustration. "We've got to see what she's doing. We might be missing something important."

Before I could remind myself that sensible women didn't do unsensible things, I maneuvered the first packing crate into place.

"You're not—" Eve began, but one look at the set of my chin told her I was.

It didn't take more than a couple minutes to place three crates one on top of the other like stepping-stones.

Using Eve's hand for support, I carefully made my way

to the top of the stack. From my vantage point, I could just see over the ledge of the window.

As I expected, Beyla was in the office. What I didn't expect, though, was that it would still be as much of a mess as it was the last time I'd looked inside. Why hadn't Yuri cleaned? How could he work in such chaos?

I recognized the questions for what they were, the workings of a mind too obsessed with cleanliness, and snapped myself back in focus. I watched Beyla kick her way through the flurry of paper on the floor. She hurried across the room.

"What's happening?" From the darkness below, I heard Eve's anxious question. "What's she doing?"

I shushed her with a wave of my hand and kept watching. From what I remembered from my peek into Drago's office, there was a small safe right under the window. Sure enough, Beyla headed that way.

Trouble was, the closer she got to the window, the less I could see of her.

I stood on my toes, and caught a glimpse of the top of Beyla's head.

I craned my neck, but I couldn't see much of anything except the occasional glimpse of her black clothing.

She moved a little farther to her right, and suddenly, I couldn't see anything at all.

Now it was frustration fueling my every move. I braced my hands against the window ledge and pulled myself up off the packing crates.

Success!

Suspended like a gymnast, my feet dangling and my arm muscles screaming in protest, I watched Beyla grab the corner of the red and blue area rug nearest to the safe. She yanked back the carpet.

I couldn't tell what she found there; I only knew it was something important. Beyla breathed a sigh of relief. When she looked up, she was smiling.

She was also looking right at the window.

Instinct took over—and instinct told me to run for cover. Not exactly an easy thing when you're hanging like a salami in a deli window. I lowered myself back to the packing crate, feeling for a foothold. When my sneakers touched, I settled myself and squatted down, out of range of the window and Beyla's gaze. I breathed a sigh of relief.

Until I scooted forward and my knee hit an exposed nail.

I felt a sharp pain and the warm trickle of blood, and though I knew it wasn't serious, I reacted like anyone would have: I jerked away.

Unfortunately, I moved too quickly.

The stack of packing crates shifted and tilted. From somewhere down in the darkness, I heard Eve gasp with horror.

Then the crates went out from under me, and a noise exploded inside my head. In perfect rhythm to its wailing, pulsing sounds, I sailed through the air and tumbled into the darkness.

Fourteen

✖

I MAY HAVE MENTIONED A TIME OR TWO THAT I'M quite possibly the most logical person on the planet.

Logically, when I woke up, I expected to find my arms and legs twisted like pretzels and my head cracked open against the pavement.

So naturally, I was amazed when I came around a few minutes (hours?) later, and the first sensation I had was that of being cradled in warmth.

The second thing I realized was that the noise I'd heard right before I fell—a shrill, whiny sound that made my nerve endings tense like the grating sound of nails on a blackboard—still throbbed inside my head.

I ignored the wailing and concentrated on the warmth, trying to forget the sensation of spiraling through the darkness. I smiled and let myself sink farther into what I assumed was some sort of concussion-induced delusion.

I was snug.

I was comfortable.

I sighed and turned my head, settling further into my

daydream and wondering if instead of delusional, I might actually be dead. Maybe I already had my wings and was perched up on a cloud, like one of Rainbow DayGlow's adorable cherubs. No, it didn't account for the noise, but it went a long way toward explaining my contentment. And the gentle warmth that pervaded every cell in my body, like sunshine after a storm.

I rubbed my cheek against the smooth something next to my skin and let myself drift back into oblivion. Until I realized the softness against my cheek felt like fabric. More specifically, like denim. Way more specifically, like blue jeans.

My eyes popped open, and at that moment I knew for sure that I must be delusional, dreaming, or dead.

Because Jim was looking back at me.

"It's about time!" My head was on his lap, and it jostled slightly when he spoke. The light was pretty much nonexistent, and my thoughts were soft and hazy, but still, I could see the relief that washed over his expression as he peered down at me. I heard it in his voice, too, right there next to a note of urgency. "I was beginning to think I should really be worried. Are you all right? Can you move?"

Did dreams speak with Scottish accents? Did they roll their *r*'s? Were their thighs lean and muscular, and when they moved—just a little so that I could get more comfortable— was a thrill supposed to tingle through my body?

I wasn't about to take any chances. I didn't want the answer to any of those questions to be *no*. I closed my eyes so that I could go back to sleep and keep on dreaming.

"Oh, no you don't!" Jim nudged me. "I may know more about cooking than I do about medicine, but I do know that going to sleep probably isn't a good idea right now. And medicine aside . . ." He glanced toward the street, and when I followed his gaze, I didn't see Eve. "We've got to get out of here."

"But . . ." I tried to sit up, but I was either too weak or just unwilling to leave what undoubtedly was the best lap I'd reclined on in years. I sank back down. "What happened?" I asked him. "Where's Eve? Why are you here? You weren't. Not when we got here. Not when I climbed on the crates."

"Aye, the crates." Funny how an accent that's so scrumptious one moment can sound so ominous the next. Especially when the person wielding it is annoyed. "Have you no sense at all, woman?" he asked. I decided it was a question I didn't have to answer. Besides, Jim didn't exactly give me time to get a word in edgewise. He made a sound of disgust as he slipped an arm around my shoulders and helped me sit up. When I wobbled, he propped a hand behind my back. "You might have been seriously hurt. You might have been killed. Why on earth would you take the chance of doing something so daft?"

"Why?" I brushed a hand over my ear. When that didn't make the noise stop, I gritted my teeth and braced my hands against the rough pavement on either side of me. "We followed her," I said with as much indignation as I could muster. And if Jim couldn't see the importance of that, well, I'd just have to explain it to him another time. Maybe when I was capable of stringing together more than three words into a coherent sentence. "She was looking. For something. I had to see. What it was. There was no way. Except the crates."

"So you risked your life because of this goofy investigation."

Goofy? I'd take that up with Jim another time, too. Like when he wasn't trying to help me to my feet, and when my head wasn't spinning, and my legs didn't feel as if the bones hadn't been yanked out of them and replaced with rubber bands.

"Didn't risk life," I told him, even though the fact suggested otherwise. "And even if . . . It doesn't matter. I'm fine." They were brave words, but now I knew I had to put some oomph behind them. I pulled myself out of the circle of Jim's arm. The world wobbled a little more, and as casually as I could—so Jim wouldn't see and accuse me of covering up, even though that was exactly what I was doing—I propped a hand against the brick back wall of Arta.

"Good as new. Better! I know more, much more than when I got here."

While I was busy justifying the new, daredevil me, Jim grabbed my hand and tugged me toward the mouth of the alley. I suppose being a new woman, I should have stood my ground and refused to budge, at least until I had the full story about what was really going on. But new woman or not, there was something about the feel of his skin against mine that made it impossible to resist. When he moved, I moved.

Except for my head whirling and the pavement rising up at me in waves, I think I did a pretty good job of it, too.

"But . . . Eve . . ." I looked back into the alley, hoping to penetrate the darkness. "We can't leave—"

"She's gone on ahead," Jim told me. "I'll tell you later. When we're away from here." We were just about to step from the alley onto the sidewalk when a car turned into the street. With no warning, Jim grabbed me, pushed me back into the shadows, and pressed himself against me to shield my body with his.

"What on earth?" I exclaimed. OK, it's true, any woman who brushes Jim off needs to have her head examined, but there were extenuating circumstances here. Like the fact that things were moving too fast for me. I slid away from him and did my best to sound like the new, self-assured woman I was.

Which would have been easier if I didn't find myself pushing away from him one moment and gripping his arm the next to keep from toppling over.

"Why are you in such a big hurry?" I demanded. "And where's Eve? And what—?"

The car that had turned into the street passed by, and Jim let go the breath he'd been holding. He tugged me onto the sidewalk. "You hear that noise?" he asked.

I shook my head, trying to clear my thoughts. "You mean you hear it, too?"

"Aye, I hear it right enough. Do you know what it means? The window you were looking in must have been wired, and when you fell, you knocked against it and tripped the alarm. If we don't get out of here—"

I got the message.

And even if I hadn't, the sounds of a police car racing down M Street . . . well, that pretty much sealed the deal.

Jim led the way. With one arm around my shoulders to steady me, he hurried me as quickly as he could in the opposite direction from M Street. We stagger-stepped into a parking lot just out of range of the pulsing red and blue lights from the police car that screeched to a stop in front of Arta.

"Time to get out of here," Jim told me.

I was all set to agree until I saw our mode of transportation.

When Jim stepped up to a big, black motorcyle, I hung back. "Oh, no." I shook my head. Not a good idea for a woman who was dizzy to begin with. "I can't ride on that. It's too dangerous. And you'll drive too fast. And there are no airbags, or seat belts, or—"

"Would you rather be arrested, then?" Jim held out a helmet.

It was a damn good question.

I plunked the helmet onto my head and buckled the straps under my chin. When Jim patted the seat behind where he was already perched, I gulped down a breath for courage and climbed on.

He didn't have to tell me to wrap my arms around his waist. He didn't have to tell me to hold on tight. I figured out the part about squeezing my knees against his thighs all on my own, too, and wondered if he knew that when he expertly threaded his way through traffic and we headed as far away from Arta as fast as we could, I slipped back into the dream I'd been having back in the alley.

The one that was all about warmth, security, and the all new but surprisingly not so bad combined sensations of speed, danger, and excitement.

BEING A DAREDEVIL TAKES YOU ONLY SO FAR. THEN reality closes in, and all the things that are really important in life push the speed, the danger, and the excitment into the background.

Things like how I hoped I didn't leave any unwashed dishes in the sink.

And how I prayed that there weren't magazines scattered around the living room.

And how I had to make sure that the bathroom was clean, because if Jim needed to use it and if there was a pair of panty hose hanging from the shower curtain rod, I'd die of embarrassment.

My hands were unsteady when I unlocked my apartment door, but a little thing like vertigo wasn't going to stop me. When Jim pushed the door open, I strode in ahead of him and took a quick look around.

Magazines? Dirty dishes? Of course there weren't any anywhere. I never would have left the apartment without everything being in place. At least, I hoped I wouldn't have.

Of course, that didn't explain why the books on the living room shelf looked as if they'd been shuffled around. Or why the china in my dining room buffet (it was a wedding gift from my parents, which is the only reason I didn't let Peter get his grubby hands on it) was out of place.

Wasn't it?

I shook my head, trying to line up my memories with the reality in front of my eyes. When that didn't work, I decided the bump on my head was worse than I realized.

I'd obviously done some rearranging that morning and just didn't remember.

With no time to worry about it, I darted (relatively speaking) into the bathroom. Just as I suspected, there was a pair of panty hose on the shower curtain rod, and I ripped them down.

"You're not fussing about how things look, are you?" Jim was right behind me, just outside the bathroom door. I tucked the panty hose behind my back. "You've nearly broken your neck this evening. You've nearly been arrested. Something tells me you should have better things to worry about than panty hose."

He was right, of course.

But that didn't make me feel any more comfortable about airing my dirty linen. So to speak.

I ducked into the bedroom to deposit the pantyhose on my dresser. When I came out, Jim was still waiting in the hallway. I barely had time to get my bearings before he grabbed me by the arm and tugged me into the living room.

"Stop with the clean-freak routine, will you? You need to sit and rest," he said. "Here." He desposited me on the blessedly magazine-free couch. "Do you want a pillow? An aspirin? Cold water?" He leaned over and peered at my face, concern darkening his features.

I wasn't used to being spoiled like this. It was certainly not something Peter had ever done. Not one to complain himself (except, apparently, to Dry Cleaning Girl, who I'd heard knew more about my shortcomings than I knew myself), he didn't tolerate any show of weakness from others.

Even if the weakness in question was something as mundane as a headache. Having someone worry about my welfare felt different. And good.

"Yes," I said in answer to all of Jim's questions. "Aspirin's in the medicine cabinet in the bathroom. Cold water's in the kitchen along with glasses. Pillow—"

"In your bedroom. Aye, I figured that part out," he said. And right before he went in search of all those things, he smiled in a way that made me wonder if me and my bedroom were something Jim had spent some time thinking about.

I was still tingling at the prospect when he returned.

"There you go." He propped the pillow behind me and nudged me back against it, handing me the water and the aspirin. "Not that I'm an expert, but you seem to be in good enough shape. I don't think we need a visit to the ER, though if you're feeling you need it . . ."

I shook my head.

"Very well then," he said. "I imagine you'll be as right as rain by morning."

I had no doubt of it. I was already feeling better. Except . . .

"But I don't understand." It's not a good idea to try and talk while gulping water and swallowing aspirin. I coughed and waited for everything to settle before I tried again. "What were you doing at Arta?"

Jim got a chair from the dining room and pulled it up next to me. He swung my legs onto the couch and grabbed the black-and-white granny square afghan (actually made by my granny) folded neatly on the back. He draped it over me.

I sank into the warmth of the couch and the afghan and of Jim's concern. I might have kept on sinking and gone right back to sleep if he hadn't spoken.

"I might ask you the same question," he said. "Annie, you promised you were done investigating."

I had promised. And no sooner had I made the promise than I broke it. It was bad enough I felt like a turkey. But what made it worse was that I didn't want Jim to be disappointed in me.

Then again, maybe it was too late for that.

I shook away my stupor. For all Jim had done for me, the least I could do is offer some sort of explanation. The truth this time. Besides, I needed to start sorting the facts in my own mind. No better way to do that than to talk them through. "We decided to follow Beyla. After class. She went to Arta, Drago's gallery. She was looking for something, and she found it, too. Only I couldn't tell what it was. I think maybe it was a computer disc, because Yuri—"

Jim's eyebrows rose.

"Yuri was Drago's partner in the gallery," I continued. "He's been following Beyla, too. He thinks she's guilty because Beyla, she stole money from the gallery and—"

Jim stopped me with a look. "How do you—"

"Know all this? Because I've been investigating, of course. And because Yuri told me. He suspected Beyla was stealing, and Drago was all set to confirm everything. Only Drago got killed. And Yuri, he thinks there's a computer disc that proves everything. Because in spite of how much Beyla says she didn't know Drago, she's lying. Yuri thinks there's a disc that proves it. Yuri thought Beyla already had the computer disc—at least that's what he told me when I ran into him in Old Town Alexandria, when we went to visit Rainbow, the witch with the angels. Only she couldn't have had the disc—Beyla, that is, not Rainbow—because if she did, she wouldn't have been at the gallery looking for it, would she? Which she was, because she was checking out every little thing in the place. Obviously, she was looking for something, and like I said, I think she found whatever it was because I saw the way she smiled, and then I wanted to tell Eve about it and—" I dragged in a breath. "What happened to her, anyway? Where's Eve?"

"Not to worry." When the afghan fell off my shoulder, Jim gently put it back into place. "Eve is fine. She left when I arrived."

It was an explanation of sorts. But not enough of one.

"But why—"

Jim stood up. "Is it true, do you suppose, what they say about a person in shock needing sugar? I'm going to get you something to eat."

"But I'm not in shock." I struggled to sit up; I would have done it, too, but for the flash of stars behind my eyelids. That, and Jim pushing me back against the pillow.

"I'm getting you something to eat," he said. "Besides, I'm starving. Rescuing a damsel in distress has a way of making a fellow hungry."

"Rescuing?"

The single word slipped out of me at the end of a sigh, but by the time it did, Jim was out of earshot, already in my kitchen. I heard him rustling through the cupboards.

Rescue.

I turned the thought over in my head while I waited for him to return.

When he did, he was holding a container of Monsieur Lavoie's Vavoom! He shook it to get my attention. "How much of this bloody stuff do you have?"

I pictured the bottles of Vavoom! lined up in my cupboard in neat, soldierly lines. I pictured Lavoie with his funnel, filling the little jars and adding that over-the-moon price. My cheeks got hot, and I started picking at a corner of the afghan. Did Jim know about the Vavoom! scheme? No way. He never would have put up with it. I decided to wait for a better time to tell him. He already knew I was a liar when it came to making promises. And now he knew how shallow I was when it came to fine cuisine. There was no use bursting the bubble when it came to Monsieur Lavoie's reputation, at least not tonight.

"I like Vavoom!," I said, "and it was on sale a couple months ago, and—"

"All well and good, but I suspect the sodium content of this stuff is out the roof."

If only he knew! I looked away. "That's why it tastes so good."

"Aye." Jim agreed, but he didn't look happy about it. He disappeared back into the kitchen. "Lavoie makes a fortune off this stuff, you know," he said, his voice raised so that I could hear him from where I lay. The sound of his voice was a nice counterpoint to the clanking of pots and pans on the stove and the swish of the refrigerator opening and closing. "It's a gold mine. And do you know you don't have any pot holders?"

"You don't sound so happy about that." I wasn't talking about pot holders, and Jim knew it.

He poked his head out the kitchen door. "I'm not unhappy, if that's what you mean. Lavoie is as nutty as a fruitcake, but the shop is a good one, and I don't mind having my name associated with it. He gives me a free hand in running the school as well, and there aren't many chefs who would do that. Temperamental lot, don't you know. Besides, I'm not about to complain. The man pays my salary."

I remembered what he'd said the night we had a drink together. "But you'd like to own your own restaurant."

He stepped back into the kitchen. "And when I do, I won't waste my resources on swill like Vavoom! Fresh foods, pure ingredients. None of that commercial hocus-pocus that makes people feel like they're expert chefs when they really don't know a saucepan from their arse."

Jim stepped out of the kitchen, a plate in each hand. "Excuse my French."

My laughter told him no apologies were necessary.

Besides, when he handed me my food, I couldn't have said anything, even if I wanted to. There on the plate was a mound of buttery yellow scrambled eggs, cooked to perfection and sprinkled lightly with Vavoom! Next to it was a little pile of ham, cut in ribbony lengths, and next to that, strawberries, hulled and sliced to look like flowers.

Talk about hocus-pocus!

My amazement was complete. "You found this stuff?" I asked Jim. "In my refrigerator?"

It was his turn to laugh. "All it takes is a little imagination. You'll see, once you do a bit more cooking."

I wasn't so sure of that. I took a bite of the eggs and smiled my approval. (Of Jim's cooking, not of the prospects of me expanding my culinary knowledge.)

"OK," I said, nibbling a strawberry. "I'm having my sugar fix. Now explain. Everything. How did you end up at Arta? And where did Eve go?"

"Eve went after Beyla."

It was brilliant! I liked to think if my mind wasn't so muddled, I would have thought of that myself. "Then Beyla *did* find something in that office."

"And took off hell-bent-for-leather when that alarm went off." Jim nodded and scooped up a forkful of scrambled eggs from his plate. "I arrived on the scene just in time to see you take a tumble. That's when I told Eve to keep an eye on Beyla and that I'd take care of you."

"And you did. Just like you said you would." I took another drink of water, which helped wash down the sudden lump in my throat. "So Eve has my car and is headed . . . where?"

Jim shrugged. "Wherever Beyla leads." He touched a hand to the cell phone clipped to his belt. "I knew you'd be worried about her, and I admit, I am, too. She may be sweet, but Eve isn't the most sensible girl in the world. I made her promise to keep in touch."

"That means wherever they're headed, they're not there yet. Otherwise, Eve would have let us know what's going on."

Call it fate or one of those strange coincidences that happens once in a while, but just as I spoke, Jim's phone rang. He answered, and the conversation was quick.

He flipped his phone closed. "Eve's home. She says she'll bring your car to class tomorrow. I'll stop by the bank and take you to the shop. You can get your car there and drive Eve home."

"And—?"

"And she says she knows where Beyla went. She said to tell you she wrote it down, so you don't have to worry that she'll forget."

"And—?"

"And that's all she said. Honest." Jim finished the last of the ham on his plate. "She knows you well enough to know that if she told you where she'd been, you'd go chasing over there this very minute, and she didna' want you to do that, because she knows you need your rest."

Call me skeptical, but I wasn't sure if that was Eve or Jim talking. But I didn't care. I was enjoying delicious food prepared by a delicious chef, as content as I'd ever been, and suddenly so tired, I couldn't have gone racing off anywhere, even if I wanted to.

I finished the last of the eggs on my plate and watched while Jim carted everything back into the kitchen.

"That still doesn't explain everything, though," I said, leaning back into the pillow and relishing the comfort that came from having someone else care for me. About me. "You still haven't told me how you knew where we were."

Jim walked out of the kitchen, wiping his hands on one of my kitchen towels. "I heard something you said to Eve before you raced out the door tonight. Something about Beyla. I thought you might get it into your head to follow her."

"So you followed us."

He nodded.

That much of the story made sense. "But why?" I continued. "You said yourself that our investigation was goofy. You said we should leave it to the real professionals. If you don't care, why did you bother to follow us?"

He tossed the towel aside and sat down next to me. "Who said I didn't care?"

Between the touch of his hand against mine and the way my head suddenly started twirling all over again, I could barely get the words out. "You mean—"

"Look, there's something you should know about me right now," Jim said. "I've got some ideas that might be considered old-fashioned. About things like watching out for people I care about and keeping my eye on a woman who's special to me, just to be certain nothing bad happens to her. That's also the reason I'm staying here tonight."

So it wasn't the most romantic declaration I'd ever heard. Was I complaining?

I guess the fact that I practically leaped off the couch and headed for the bedroom pretty much told Jim everything he needed to know.

But I didn't expect him to laugh about it.

"Hold on there!" Jim exclaimed, keeping me in my place with one hand on my arm. "I'll admit, this isn't how I imagined we'd spend our first night together, but you're staying put. And I'm staying right here." He pointed to his chair. "That way, I can wake you now and again just to be sure you're all right, and keep an eye on you all night long."

It sure wasn't what I had in mind, but as I sank back onto the couch and my eyes drifted closed, I realized that in the great scheme of things, it was a pretty good trade-off.

I'm pretty sure I was still smiling when Jim kissed me good night.

Fifteen

✖

"ALBA STRU."

I was staring down at Drago, clasping his clammy hand in mine. His face was contorted with pain as he choked out his last words.

"Alba Stru . . ."

I sat up with a start.

"What's that you said?" Jim poked his head out of the kitchen door. He was still dressed in the clothes he'd worn the night before. Of course. Since he'd slept sitting up—if he slept at all—he wasn't too wrinkled or mussed. Except for his hair. A thick lock of it hung over his forehead. It made him look younger and a little sleepy in an incredibly sexy way.

He was making French toast, and it smelled divine. "It sounded as if you were talking another language."

"Not a language, a name." I stretched and swung my legs off the couch. When I sat up, my head didn't hurt, and the world didn't wobble. Both good signs. "It was one of the things Drago said to me before he died."

"And this Alba person . . ." Jim called over his shoulder, as I made my way into the dining room. As much as I would have liked breakfast in bed (or more accurately, breakfast on couch), I knew it was time to stop being coddled and get back to reality. I had to be at work in a little over an hour. There was no time for spoiling or shilly-shallying.

Jim brought two plates in, smiling when he saw me up and around. He pulled a chair away from the table for me and chuckled softy when he saw my eyes widen. In front of me was the most incredible breakfast I'd ever seen.

The French toast was made with cinnamon bread that I knew for certain Jim hadn't found in my kitchen. He must have been up and out early, then back before I even knew he was gone. Each slice of bread was at least an inch thick, coated with a thin glaze that made syrup extraneous.

"It's a sugar lover's dream." I dug in and was rewarded with a taste as heavenly as the aroma. "But wait a minute . . . what's that you said about Alba?"

Jim was taking a sip of coffee, enjoying watching me enjoy my breakfast. "That's right, Alba." He set his cup on a saucer. "When I heard you say the name, I wondered. Do you know who she is?"

"Not a clue," I admitted. "I've checked the phone book, traditional and the Internet white pages. No one named Stru listed anywhere. And it's a weird name, anyway, isn't it?"

"Foreign." Jim sliced his French toast into neat pieces. He held his knife and fork oddly, the way the British do, fork upside down in his left hand, knife in his right. "Like I said, when I heard you say it, I thought you were speaking a different language."

I held my own fork the regular old American way. It was halfway to my mouth when an idea hit out of the blue.

"You don't like it." Jim mistook the frozen fork and the look on my face for displeasure. He frowned. "The French toast. It's too sweet, isn't it?"

"There's no such thing as too sweet. And I love it, honest." He might have been more inclined to believe me if I didn't push back my chair and race away from the table.

When he found me again, I was in my bedroom, at the computer that sat on a desk in the corner by the window.

"Looking for a new French toast recipe?"

I like the way he said *looking*. It was like *cooking* with that scrumptious, long *oooo* sound.

"Not looking for a recipe," I told him, unconsciously adding the same long *oooo*. I clicked my way around the Internet. "Looking for Romanian."

He braced his hands on the desk and leaned over me for a better look. "Because . . . ?"

"Because I've been a moron!" I would have slapped my forehead if I wasn't afraid it would make my head start hurting all over again. "Look!" I pointed at the screen. "Romanian translations. *Albastru*. It's not a name, it's a word. It means *blue*."

"Blue?" Confused, Jim stared squint-eyed at the Web page. I remembered that though he knew most of the details of our investigation, there were some things I hadn't had a chance to fill him in on yet. Like our visit to the Angel Emporium.

"I should have known the moment Rainbow DayGlow mentioned it," I said. When he looked as if he was about to ask who I was talking about, I waved away the question. It would take a while to even begin to explain Rainbow, and I still needed to shower and get dressed for work. We'd have to save the explanation for another time. "She said that one of the symptoms of foxglove poisoning is that everything looks blue."

"And Drago told you. About the blue part, at least."

"Yup. He said it. *Albastru*. Blue. The poison was working in his system, and he was close to death. Everything must have looked blue to him by that time. Which means

I must have looked like a perfect idiot, telling Tyler that he needed to track down someone named Alba Stru. Darn!" I slapped my hand against the desk and hit my mouse pad. The cursor jumped on the screen. "I don't care about me, but the whole point of this investigation was so that Eve could look good in Tyler's eyes. He must think we're amateurs."

"You are." Jim's smile was wry. Still, something in his words stung.

"Think he's figured it out yet?"

"You mean Tyler? Is he smart?"

"He thinks he is." I drummed my fingers against the desk. "How much do you think he knows that we don't?"

Jim could only shrug in response. I sighed as I turned back to the monitor and clicked off-line.

Little did I know that soon enough, we'd find out just what Tyler knew—and more.

 SEAFOOD IS A FUNNY THING. ACCORDING TO JIM, how it ends up tasting depends an awful lot on how fresh it is, how it's cooked, and for how long.

Who was I to argue?

The good news was that the first recipe we tried in class that night was for steamed mussels, and surprisingly, mine were pretty tasty. Even Jim said so.

The bad news was . . . well, there were really two bad things. The first was that Eve was late for class. She got there just as we were sopping up the last of the mussel broth with thick slices of crisp-crusted Vienna bread. I'd worked all day. She'd worked all day. We'd taken our breaks at different times.

In other words, I hadn't had a chance to find out where she'd ended up when she followed Beyla from the gallery the night before, and I was dying to know.

The other bad thing wasn't related to our investigation. It was all about cooking. No big surprise there.

I hated to burst Jim's bubble, especially when he saw the mussels as a sign from the cooking gods that I had turned a corner. But throwing mussels in a pot, dumping water on them along with a little chopped garlic and a bit of lemon juice and turning on the heat, that was one thing.

Grouper was the second item on the menu. Sauteeing a fillet after it had been soaked in milk, seasoned with salt and pepper, dredged in flour mixed with parlsey, then encrusted with thinly sliced potatoes . . . that was a whole different ball game.

I struck out.

Not to worry. Every cloud has a silver lining, and Fabulous Fish and Shellfish night was no exception. When Jim sampled my mussles and told me how much he enjoyed them, he leaned in close and whispered that he'd let me make him a batch of the yummy mollusks for dinner one evening very soon. Silver lining number one: a night dozing on my dining room chair hadn't made him change his mind. He wanted to see me again.

And number two? Well, I'm not one to toot my own horn. Usually. But the minute Jim said that we were going to try an experiment in class and adjust standard recipes for larger and smaller quantities, I knew I was home free.

I am, to put it bluntly, smarter than the average bear when it comes to numbers.

He asked us to double recipes.

No problem.

He asked us to halve recipes.

Piece of cake.

He told us to pretend that we were hosting a dinner party and that at the last minute, Aunt Margaret decided to bring Cousin Henry and the kids. We'd need to triple, then add a wee bit more (I loved when he said that!), and just before dinnertime when Henry called to say the kids had the flu, we were forced to cut back again.

I sailed through the exercise as easily as I cruised through the legion of numbers I faced at work each day.

"Aunt Margaret plus Cousin Henry, plus how many kids?" Eve wrote a long line of numbers on a legal pad, scratched them out, and started again. She pulled at her hair with one hand. "And how many ounces in a cup?"

I was way past that. "Sixteen cups of chicken broth," I whispered the answer to her, feeling like I was cheating on a math test. I shot up a hand to give my answer to the class.

"Sixteen cups of chicken broth." Beyla answered before I could.

"Very good." Jim went over the calculations for those who weren't as quick. "And how many pounds of chicken?"

I'd figured that out already, too.

Beyla's hand went up before mine. "Ten," she said, as confident as I would have been if I had a chance to answer.

"And the whipping cream?" Jim glanced my way to give me the perfect opening, but Beyla was on a roll.

"Four and three-quarters," she called out, and from the way she did, I could tell she was feeling mighty satisfied with herself. "Four and three-quarters cups."

Considering that she came from a country that used the metric system, I should have been impressed. I would have been if I wasn't so busy being envious at being shown up at my own game. Not only had the woman outsmarted us enough to stymie our investigation, not only could she cook to beat the band, she was also as much of a math whiz as I was.

I tamped down the jealousy that reared its ugly head. It was unworthy of me, and besides, maybe that painful fact was really silver lining number three in disguise.

"I think we know more about Beyla than we used to," I told Eve, who gave me a blank stare in return.

"She's good with numbers. Really good with numbers. I wonder what that means."

AS IT TURNED OUT, WE NEVER HAD A CHANCE TO discuss Beyla's mathmatical talents. We had more important things to think about.

Eve was as anxious to talk to me about her adventure the night before as I was to pump her for information about where she'd gone and what she'd seen. There was no use doing it in class, and we both knew it. Every time we looked at her, Beyla was talking quietly with her cooking partner, John. We couldn't take the chance of them over-hearing anything we said. Besides, there was nothing we could do about our own mystery while we were busy trying to solve the mysteries of cooking fish.

The moment we got out of class, though, was another story.

Jim had agreed to come with us, wherever we were headed, but unfortunately, Monsieur Lavoie waylaid him on our way out the door. From the looks of the list of things the little Frenchman had to discuss with him, I knew Jim would be detained for hours. He gave us a reluctant wave as Eve and I continued out the door.

I had my extra set of car keys in my hand as soon as we hit the sidewalk. I looked around to see if my car was parked anywhere in sight. "Let's get moving."

"Not that way." Eve headed in the other direction. "And you won't need your keys."

"Because you have the other set."

She waited for the light to change, and when it did, we crossed the street. "Because we're not driving," she said.

"You mean . . ." Eve's strides were long, and I hurried to catch up. "She came here? To Clarendon? Within walking distance of the school? That's bizarre."

"You have no idea! Wait until you see where we're going."

She turned the corner and continued three blocks up from Très Bonne Cuisine.

At this point, I should probably say a little more about the geography around here. Most folks hear *Arlington*, and they think that it's a city in Virginia. Not true. Arlington is a county. There is no city of Arlington. But the neighborhoods within the county all have names. And the one we were in, as I've mentioned before, is called Clarendon.

The Clarendon neighborhood is nice. Really nice. It's also a little quirky. That, and the fact that there's a Metro station for the commute into D.C., are what give it its charm. And its sky-high real estate prices.

Million-dollar condos stand side by side with neighborhood bars. Trendy eateries that attract the movers and the shakers from across the river are next door to everyday places, like hardware stores and tanning salons.

The entire area is a jumble of old and new, chichi and downright odd. The farther we got from the bright lights and action of the fashionable spots, the quieter and quainter the neighborhood became. I would like to say *seamier*, because that would add a dash of adventure to our investigation, but I won't get carried away. If the neighborhood had been seamy, I wouldn't have let Eve set foot in it. And I wouldn't have been there, either.

I'll go with colorful, instead. Just like the wash from the pink neon sign glowing from the nearest storefront.

Miss Magda's Tea Room: Fortunes Told, Secrets Revealed.

Eve stopped right outside the front door.

I don't know what I expected, but it wasn't this. "You mean Beyla came here? To a fortune-teller?" I stood on the sidewalk, staring at the picture of the giant hand in the window that showed the life line, the love line, and something

called the mound of Venus. "Why?" I asked Eve and myself. "Of all the places she could have gone, why here?"

Eve shrugged and pointed across the street. "She parked
over there. I know for sure it was her because I watched her
like a hawk all the way from Georgetown. I saw her go inside this place. A couple minutes later, she was back in her
car. I followed her after that, too, but the only place she
went was an apartment building over on Ballston. I checked
the class list Jim gave us the first day of school. That's where
she lives."

I chewed on my lower lip and stared at the neon sign in
the window as if just concentrating hard enough would
force Miss Magda to reveal all her secrets right then and
there. "So Beyla was here, but she didn't stay long. When
she left, was it with or without what she'd found at Arta?"

Eve shrugged. "Beyla wasn't carrying anything. Going
into the tea room or coming out of it. Maybe the alarm
went off too soon. Maybe she didn't find anything at the
gallery after all."

I remembered the flash of Beyla's smile that I'd seen
before I took that misstep and landed in a heap on the pavement in the alley. "No. I know she found what she was
looking for. Maybe it was just something small enough to
tuck in her pocket. Like a computer disc."

"And maybe there's only one way to find out."

I eyed the hand in the window suspiciously. "You don't
think I'm going to have my fortune told, do you?"

Eve tugged my arm. "It says Secrets Revealed. What
have we got to lose?"

Did my pride count?

I swallowed it down and went inside.

Pink neon sign aside, Miss Magda's Tea Room was a
bare-bones kind of place. The room we stepped into was a
nine-by-nine square, with walls painted a particularly un-
appealing shade of pumpkin. There was a faded rug in the

center of the floor with a table set in the middle of it, two chairs facing each other on either side. The window with the hand and the neon sign was at our backs, and to one side of us was a battered wicker settee. On our right was a long, low table where mountains of flyers and out-there newspapers extolled everything from the study of alien landings to the latest techniques in mediumship.

There was no sign of tea. Or of Miss Magda, for that matter.

In the center of the table was a crystal ball and a small brass bell. I rang it.

No answer.

"Maybe we need to make an appointment," Eve whispered.

I didn't have that much respect for the paranormal. In fact, I didn't have any at all. "The sign on the front door says Open, Come In," I pointed out, not whispering just to prove how unintimidated I was. "Miss Magda must be communing with the spirits somewhere."

"Don't make fun." Though Eve had started out in front of me, she hadn't ventured as far into the room as I had. She leaned over my shoulder. "Some people have gifts we can't possibly understand."

"Yeah, the gift of talking people out of their hard-earned money." A door on the far wall caught my eye. Ignoring Eve's protests, I walked over and rapped on it.

Nobody responded, but the door hadn't been shut all the way. It swung open.

The light was off in the back room, but even so, I knew right away that something was wrong. There was a window on the far wall, and the bit of light that seeped through it outlined something lying on the floor. Something bulky and as big as a—

I felt for a light switch, and the when I found it, my worst fears were confirmed.

Miss Magda was communing with the spirits, all right. Firsthand.

She was lying on her back, her eyes bulging and her mouth open in a silent scream of horror. She'd been strangled with her silk head scarf.

Sixteen

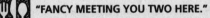

"FANCY MEETING YOU TWO HERE."

The way Tyler Cooper said it, it didn't sound fancy or refined. It sounded downright obnoxious.

He closed in on us, and the uniformed officer who'd arrived when I called 911 got out of his way.

Didn't that just figure. Tyler's ego was so big, there wasn't room for anybody else's. Especially in a place as small as Miss Magda's Tea Room.

When he got to where Eve and I were waiting, Tyler put one hand on his hip, brushing aside the jacket of his four-hundred-dollar suit just enough for us to see the gun he wore in his shoulder holster. I told myself it was an ingrained gesture learned from years of dealing with bad guys. That was better than thinking he considered us some sort of threat.

"You want to explain what's going on here?"

Was it an accident that Tyler looked at me when he asked the question? I didn't think so. Call me a cynic, but I think the fact that Eve wasn't gazing adoringly at him was his first and only clue that if he was going to get answers, he'd need to get them from me. He completely missed Eve's pale cheeks and rapid breathing. The young uniformed cop didn't—he saw that Eve was looking a little shaken. I don't know where he got it, but before he went back out to his patrol car, he brought her a can of Pepsi.

I knew the sugar would bring her around. With Eve taken care of, I turned my attention back to Tyler.

"We walked in and found her," I told him, cutting to the chase. I hated to look inept, but let's face it, there really was nothing more I could tell the man. "End of story."

"Really?" Tyler perched himself on the edge of Miss Magda's fortune-telling table. I suppressed the nasty comment bubbling inside me. I didn't know Miss Magda, and even if I did, I sure wouldn't believe in any sort of hocus-pocus nonsense. But honestly, the woman was lying dead in the next room. Tyler could have shown a little more respect.

He pulled a small notebook from his pocket. "So, for the second time in . . . what is it . . . ?" He flipped through the notebook pages. "A couple days? For the second time in a couple days, you two call in a report of a dead body, and you expect me to believe that you just strolled in here and found her?"

"That's what happened." I crossed my arms over my chest, lifted my chin, and met Tyler's icy blue gaze head-on. "Why would we want to hurt Miss Magda? We didn't even know her."

"Miss Magda . . ." Tyler leaned over just enough to see into the back room where a woman from the crime scene unit was dusting for fingerprints, while another tech, a man, checked the fortune-teller's body for clues. "Her real name is Tammy Jo Boykin. Bet you didn't know that. Or that she's got a sheet. Been arrested a couple times here in the D.C. area, and a few more times down in Atlanta where she's from originally. Fraud."

I managed the sort of gosh-gee wide-eyed look that macho men like Tyler expect from women. "Guess we should have known better than to come here to get our fortunes told."

"Guess you should have." Tyler took a pen out of his breast pocket and clicked it open. "What did you see?"

There was no use lying, just as there wasn't any use stalling. The sooner we got this over with, the sooner we could leave. Then maybe we could start to put together the pieces of what had happened here.

"What did we see? Nothing," I told Tyler, and I didn't even need to feel guilty about it because it was the absolute truth. "The door was open and we walked in. No one answered when we rang the bell. That's when we found her."

"And she was already dead?"

"Just like you found her."

"At least twenty-four hours." The tech who'd been checking the body walked out of the back room, stripping off a pair of latex gloves as he supplied the information. "As near as I can tell, she was killed last night, somewhere between nine and midnight. We'll know more after the autopsy."

"And let me guess . . ." Tyler's chilly gaze swiveled from the tech to me. "You have an ironclad alibi."

"If being with the instructor from my cooking class counts." I knew it did, and that Jim would verify it if he needed to. "As for tonight, the time of our 911 call confirms that we arrived just a little while ago."

Tyler knew it. He knew it before he ever walked into Miss Magda's and started treating me like public enemy number one. I could tell because he didn't look happy about being shown up.

With a scowl, he slapped his notebook closed. "You two aren't involved in anything stupid, are you? You're not playing detective?"

This time, he knew he wouldn't get an answer from me.

Not a straight one, anyway. He turned to Eve, but I spoke up before she could.

"What makes you think that?" I asked Tyler.

"I dunno." He shrugged. The gesture would have made anyone else look uncertain. Coming from Tyler, it sent a whole different message: he might have been saying one thing, but he believed something else. And he didn't care if we knew it. "Seems funny to me, is all. You think what happened here has some connection to Drago Kravic's murder?"

Was he asking for my opinion? My input?

And was I supposed to be flattered?

For a second, the prospect cheered me right up. I *was* a private detective, and Tyler knew it.

Or was this my official notification that if I knew what was best for me, I'd back off?

Before I had a chance to decide what Tyler meant and how to respond to it, Eve popped off the settee.

"That's exactly what we think," she told Tyler, and emphasized her point by stabbing a finger in his direction. "If you weren't so blind, you'd see it, too. Who's the smart one, now?"

"Who's the one who still seems to care so much?" Tyler got up, too. He turned to Eve, both fists on his hips.

He moved so fast, the table bucked. Miss Magda's crystal ball tipped. Eve and Tyler were so busy facing off, neither of them noticed.

I darted forward just in time to catch the crystal ball before it rolled over the edge of the table and landed on the floor. Bracing the hefty item in my hands, I stood next to the table, wondering what to look at. The floor? The ceiling? The Eve vs Tyler heavyweight match being slugged out right in front of my eyes?

It seemed like a safe bet, so I decided on the table. But what I saw there nearly blew me away.

A computer disc.

It had been hidden under the crystal ball. Because of the curvature of the glass and the reflection of the light, nobody ever could have seen it when the ball was in place.

My mind raced. This was the disc Yuri talked about. It had to be. Beyla must have found it at the gallery and brought it here. But why? And why would she kill the fortune-teller and leave the disc behind?

I would have loved to think my way through the puzzle, but it was a little hard to concentrate with the sounds of Eve and Tyler going at each other echoing through my head.

"You think I care?" Eve snorted her opinion. "Honestly, Tyler, you have grits for brains."

"At least I have brains," he shot back.

"And what a pity you never use them. If you did, you'd know the two murders are connected. Beyla came here last night. I know because I followed her from the gallery that Drago owned. You want to know why, Tyler? My goodness, I'm surprised you haven't figured all that out for yourself by now."

"Oh, I've figured out the Beyla part. But you apparently haven't." The noise Tyler made from deep in his throat was more of a growl than a laugh. "Your imagination is running away with you, Eve. You've been reading too many books, if you read at all. You've concocted something straight out of a James Bond novel. Do you think that life really works that way? So what if Beyla went to the gallery? That's not all that surprising, is it? After all, she was Kravic's bookkeeper. Or didn't you know that? As to why she went to the gallery last night . . . why would she bother? The place has been locked up tight since Drago's death. What would she want there?"

"What would she want? How about a—"

Before Eve could blow our entire investigation with two little words, I opened my hands and let the crystal ball slip.

It hit just where I inteded, right where the rug ended and the hardwood floor began. The crash made both Eve and Tyler shut their mouths and brought the crime scene techs running.

I didn't stop to think about right or wrong. I didn't debate the ethics of the situation or my obligation—moral or otherwise—to authority.

Who knew I could be so downright underhanded?

While Eve, Tyler, and the crime scene techs were all busy staring at the thousands of glass shards that littered the floor like fallen stars, I whisked the disc off the table and tucked it into my purse.

"YOU'RE KIDDING ME, RIGHT? YOU TOOK IT? RIGHT out from under Tyler's nose?" Eve practically crowed. "Annie Capshaw, you are the bravest and the coolest thing on two feet!"

I wasn't so sure.

As we drove away from Clarendon, my hands were shaking against the steering wheel.

Eve chuckled. "When Tyler finds out, he'll have a cow."

"He'd better not find out!" I flicked on my blinker and waited for the opportunity to turn left, slanting Eve a look as I did. "You're not going to tell him. Not ever. If you do, I could be arrested. Tampering with evidence is a crime, isn't it?"

Eve gulped down her horror. "I guess it is. I never thought of that." She crossed her heart with one finger. "I swear, I'll never breathe a word. Not to Tyler or anybody else. Besides, once we give the disc to Yuri, it won't matter. You won't have the disc, and Tyler will never be able to prove where Yuri got it. You'll be home free."

I liked the sound of that. A life of crime, it seemed, did not agree with me.

By the time we got to my apartment building, parked the car, and got upstairs, I was lightheaded and my knees felt as if they were made of jelly. I needed chocolate, and I needed it bad.

If only I hadn't eaten my emergency Hershey bar the night we found Drago's body.

I peeked in the pantry and saw the Nesquik jar was empty. Apparently I'd forgotten to restock the last time I was at the store.

I checked the stash I kept in the freezer for those times when I absolutely, positively needed chocolate and none was to be had anywhere else, but even the cache of chocolate chips I usually kept squirreled away was gone, too.

It had been a stressful summer.

I settled for salt and vinegar potato chips. I ripped open the bag and plunked down in one of the kitchen chairs.

"My nerves are shot," I said, tipping the bag toward Eve.

She reached in for a handful. When that first, tangy taste of vinegar hit her tongue, she made a face. "Mine aren't." She grinned. "I'm still too jazzed thinking about what you did to Tyler. That no-good slimeball. Did you hear him? 'If you read at all.'" She echoed Tyler's words from back at Magda's in a singsong voice. "He's got a lot of nerve. If he only knew how smart we both are! And he will, too, won't he? As soon as we get this case cleared up."

She crunched into another handful of chips. "We can do it, don't you think? Now that we have the disc, we can prove that Beyla stole money from the gallery. That will give us the motive we've been looking for. Then we can prove that Beyla killed Drago and probably Magda, too. My gosh, Annie!" Eve blanched. She stopped dead just as she was reaching back into the potato chip bag.

"Do you suppose Beyla was inside the tea room strangling Magda while I was outside waiting for her to come out?" she asked.

"Looks that way." There was no use denying it, but I knew I had to get Eve's mind off poor, dead Magda, or she'd end up convincing herself that there was something she could have done to stop the murder. There wasn't. Not without her risking herself and her own safety. I had to change the subject, and fast.

"I absolutely think we can solve the case," I said loudly, heartened to see her smile in response. "We're close. We've got exactly what we need now." I glanced toward my purse and the disc inside it. Suddenly, the thought of how it got there washed over me.

The salt stung my tongue. The vinegar soured in my stomach. My throat tightened.

"If I don't get arrested and thrown in prison for the rest of my life first!" I murmured.

"There, there." Eve reached over and patted my shoulder. She left a trail of crumbs and salt in her wake, and when she moved back, I brushed it away. "That's not going to happen. Remember? Vow of silence. Nobody's ever going to know where that disc came from. And if Yuri ever says we gave it to him . . . well, we'll just deny it. Why shouldn't we? Everything we've done, we've done to help the authorities. I don't see them solving Drago's murder."

"Except Tyler said something about that, didn't he?" I reached for another handful of chips, the better to smother my doubts. "He said he'd figured out Beyla's part in the whole thing."

"Yeah, just like we have. But he hasn't been able to prove it. If he could, he would have arrested her by now." Eve brushed crumbs from her hands and went to the fridge to get two bottles of water. She set one down in front of me. "He can't prove anything because he doesn't have the disc. We do. Which makes us way smarter than him. Take that, Tyler Cooper!" She twisted the cap off the bottle, and

I couldn't help but think that as she did, she pictured herself wringing Tyler's neck.

Eve took a long swallow before she spoke again. "Let's get this disc over to Yuri and be done with it. What do you say, Annie? Let's call Yuri." She reached for the phone. "Where's his number?"

I dug it out of my purse along with the disc. "Maybe we'd better take a look at the disc before we hand it over to him," I suggested. "Maybe it wouldn't hurt to make a copy, either. You know, in case something happens to this one. Beyla might try to steal it back."

"Or kill Yuri for it!" Eve gulped a too-big swallow of water and coughed.

I hadn't thought of that scenario, but after what happened first to Drago and then to Magda, I wouldn't be surprised. I went into the bedroom and dug through the desk drawer for an extra disc. Eve joined me a moment later.

"I want a look first," I told her, inserting the disc we'd found at Magda's into the proper drive. We waited for the disc to boot. When it did, my anticipation melted like an ice cube in the summer sun.

"It's not in English." Her nose wrinkled, Eve pointed at the screen. "How are we supposed to know what it says when it's not in English?"

"Somebody will be able to read it." I consoled myself with the thought while I clicked through a couple pages of what I guessed was Romanian. "Yuri can probably translate it. He never came right out and said he was Romanian, but I'll bet he is. He knew that Beyla and Drago were lovers back in Romania. That means maybe he knew them back then. He'll for sure know what this says."

"All the more reason to tell him what we found." Eve had brought the scrap of paper with Yuri's phone number on it into the bedroom with her. She reached for the bedside phone.

"Not so fast." I waved to her to relax as I started paging through another couple screens full of incomprehensible writing. "Let's at least make the copy first," I said. I had every intention of doing it, except that I was too fascinated by everything on the screen to stop.

"It's funny, isn't it," I said, so engrossed, I was only vaguely aware of Eve standing behind me. "Yuri says that Beyla stole money from the gallery, and that the proof of her scheme is on this disc. But you'd think if this had anything to do with stolen money, there would be numbers. Lots of numbers. Like a ledger or an account book. There's nothing like that here. There's just writing. Page after page of it."

The phone still in her hand, Eve leaned over my shoulder. "Maybe she's explaining how she did it."

"I don't think she's that stupid." The little bar at the right side of the screen showed that there were more pages I hadn't seen. I scrolled down.

"You're not going to learn Romanian just by looking at it." Eve clicked her tongue. "I'm calling him," she said. In the screen, I saw the reflection of Eve with the phone to her ear. "There's no way we're going to find out what it says otherwise. And I'll tell you what, I'm just dying to know."

I was only half listening.

Something on the screen had caught my eye.

There in the middle of all the Romanian were bits and pieces of things I recognized. Not words, exactly, but letters and numbers. I pointed at the screen, even though I didn't know if Eve was looking or not.

"It's a list," I said, and I scrolled down some more.

That's when the pieces clicked.

"Yuri? Hi, it's me, Eve. Eve DeCateur. Sorry you're not there and I have to leave this message. I really wanted to talk to you."

I heard Eve's voice as if it came from a million miles away. It bumped around inside my head, smacking against the realization that hit me like a freight train.

"You met me at your gallery," she was saying in her sweetest Southern belle voice. "And you know my friend Annie. Annie Capshaw? She's the one I've been working with on the you-know-what. You know, the case we're trying to solve. The one that involves you-know-who and the art gallery."

I jolted out of my daze and turned in my chair. "Eve, hang up the phone."

She waved aside my protest. "Listen, Yuri, I'm calling because—"

"Eve, hang up the phone."

She rolled her eyes. "I just wanted you to know that we've got what you were looking for. The—"

I didn't know I could move that fast. Not until I snatched the phone out of Eve's hand and hit the Off button.

"Annie Capshaw! What on earth has gotten into you?" Eve tried to take the phone back, but I threw it over to the other side of the room. "Do you know how rude that was? I didn't even finish leaving my message."

"Good."

"Good?" She tipped her head, trying to work through the thing. "I just don't understand you. First you want Yuri's help. Then you don't. How are we going to know what that disc is all about until we get him to tell us?"

"We don't need his help." I grabbed Eve's arm and tugged her closer to the computer. "Look!"

"At what?" She bent at the waist and narrowed her eyes. "It's a list. Big deal. It's—"

"AK-47. HK MP5. M16." I read over the list. "It's guns, that's what it is."

"What?" She sprang back and looked at me as if I'd suddenly started talking Romanian.

I pointed to the screen. "AK-47. M16. I'm no expert, and I don't know jack about weapons, but I recognize these names. This has nothing to do with the art gallery, Eve. It has nothing to do with stealing money. At least not gallery money. I don't know what the rest of the pages mean, but I'd bet anything that Beyla . . . She's not cooking the books. She's smuggling guns into the country."

Seventeen

✖

 WE WERE IN OVER OUR HEADS. WAY OVER OUR heads.

I knew it the moment I saw the names of those guns pop up on my computer screen. It took a little convincing and a little more explaining, but Eve (who before my minilecture on global politics and federal crimes was inclined to think that lawbreaking was lawbreaking whether we were talking guns or art gallery money) finally understood, too.

The trick now, of course, was to figure out what to do about it.

Did I go to the police and admit that I'd stolen vital evidence from the scene of a crime?

Did I hope that Yuri returned Eve's phone call, and that he'd pick up the disc and we'd be rid of it?

Or did I stick where I had been stuck since I put that disc I my computer: my brain in a loop, my mind so muddled I'd actually given out the wrong change to a bank customer that day? Since it was something I'd never done before, I guess the loop and the muddle were winning.

By next evening's Marvelous Meats class, I still hadn't worked things through. Which of course didn't explain the mess that was my cheeseburger pizza. I liked to think so, but I wasn't kidding myself. Not anymore. As much as I tried to concentrate on the advice Jim tossed out to the class as easily as he flung ketchup, mustard, and other traditional burger ingredients onto pizza dough with the skill of a magician and the flair of an artist, I couldn't turn my mind off.

Guns.

Smuggling.

Murder.

The words whirled around like the pickles, wine, and secret spices Jim tossed in a blender to make his own relish.

It was one thing playing detective to try to help Eve get back at Tyler. It was another to really consider the international implications of what Beyla was doing. And I wasn't kidding myself: I knew I didn't know the half of it.

It was that half that scared me half to death.

I was just scraping the burnt remnants of cheddar cheese off my pizza pan when Monsieur Lavoie stuck his head into the classroom and wagged one finger in Jim's direction, calling him out into the hallway. "There is a phone call for you. They say it is important."

It must have been. Jim was back in less than a minute.

"Have to skedaddle," he told the class, but he was looking right at me while he said it. "Sorry to leave you high and dry. Going to need to cancel tomorrow night's class, too. You've got your recipe for the pork loin marinated in orange juice and soy sauce. Try it at home. It's fabulous. In the meantime . . ." He consulted his class syllabus. "I'll see you all back here on Friday for Delightful Desserts. Can you believe it's our last class?"

He headed into the back kitchen and came out carrying a motorcylce helmet and a jacket, mouthing the words *I'll call* as he walked by.

And just like that, class was over.

"Well, that's weird," Eve chirped. If I wasn't so busy being preoccupied, I might have rejoiced that for once, Eve's culinary results were just as bad as mine. Her pizza crust was the color of the toffee twin set she wore with her black capris. "What do you suppose has gotten into Jim?"

"Obviously, it's something important. He'll let me know."

"You're very trusting."

"Shouldn't I be?" Until that very moment, it had never crossed my mind not to be. Not with Jim. "You don't think—" My thought was interupped by the ring of a cell phone. It was Beyla's. She grabbed her purse and headed out the door.

"I'll bet she's up to no good," Eve whispered.

It seemed like a pretty sure bet.

I tossed down the towel I'd used to dry my pizza pan. "You up for tailing her again?"

"Are you sure you want to?" Eve's voice was anxious.

I wasn't. But I still hadn't made up my mind about what to do with the disc and the information on it. Whatever we saw Beyla do, wherever she went, whoever she met with . . . maybe it would help me come to a decision.

I held onto that thought as we went outside. I clung to it as we dodged raindrops, following Beyla as she walked away from the parking lot, across the street, and a couple blocks up from Très Bonne Cuisine. By the time she got to a placed called Bucharest, I was hanging on to my hopes by my fingernails.

We'd played it safe and smart, staying far enough back so that Beyla didn't see us, but when she went inside the restaurant, we dared to get closer. We huddled under the awning above the front door and watched her through the rain-spotted window. She said something to the hostess, who nodded and led her away from the door.

"Nothing." Eve's shoulders drooped. She spun around

and leaned against the building. Her hair was as wet as mine. On Eve, slick and wet looked good. On me . . . well, my hair was so curly, rain almost never penetrated. And humidity only made it curlier. I suspected that right about now, I looked like I had a head full of rotini noodles, and one glance at my reflection in the window confirmed my worst fears.

"She's going to dinner, that's all." Eve was disappointed. "She's not going to lead us anywhere interesting."

"Who schedules a dinner on the night of a cooking class?" I took the chance of peeking in the window again, but by now, the hostess was back at her station, and Beyla was nowhere in sight. "Beyla didn't know Jim was going to cancel class. Jim didn't even know that. He would have mentioned it to me if he did. And Bucharest . . ." I studied the lighted sign above the door. "That sounds mighty familiar. It might be—" I fished in my pocket for the piece of paper Drago had given me the night he died.

"Bucharest!" I exclaimed and held the paper up for Eve to see, my mind already spinning with the possibilities. "He wrote the address of the gallery on the back of a receipt from this place. That means he'd been here. I wonder if he ever met Beyla here. Maybe she's meeting somebody again."

Eve didn't look convinced. "Maybe she's just hungry."

"Maybe we should find out."

Just as I was about to head inside, she plucked at my sleeve. "Are you sure you want to do this?" she asked. "I've already gotten you into enough trouble. If it wasn't for me, we would never have started this investigation. You never would have lied to the police. You never would have concealed evidence. You never would have stolen anything, either, because you're the most honest person I know."

"And I would have never stopped being such a sissy, would I? Come on, Eve. Let's finish what we started."

The grin Eve gave me in return was all the response I needed. We headed inside.

I guess I was hungry, but then, that was no surprise—I hadn't been able to eat my cheeseburger pizza. It smelled really good inside Bucharest. Directly in front of the door was a desk, where the hostess was busy on the phone taking a reservation. To her right was a doorway into a dark, wood-panelled bar, and behind her was a long, narrow hallway. I'd seen the same setup in restaurants in other old buildings in the area, and I suspected the hallway led into a room in the back that was the main dining area. With a smile at the hostess, I pointed in that direction, like I knew where I was going and who I was looking for.

Actually, I did.

I just didn't know who I'd find her with when I got there.

The hallway opened into exactly the kind of room I expected, but unfortunately, when it did, there was no place to stand back and stay out of sight. Eve was eager to get wherever we were going, and when I stopped to peek around the corner, she kept going. She bumped me from behind and, like it or not, I was catapulted out of the shelter of the hallway and into the room.

Even in the dim lighting that passed for ambiance, I saw Beyla immediately.

And she saw me.

She was seated at a table for two, her back to the windows that ran along that entire side of the restaurant. Though I could tell she struggled to keep her expression impassive and her eyes on the man seated across from her, one look at me and she went as white as the tablecloth she was clutching in her hands.

Naturally, the man seated with his back to me turned to see the cause of her alarm.

"It's Yuri!" I grabbed Eve's arm and pushed her back the other way before she even had a chance to peek into the dining area. "She's with Yuri. Damn it! Something tells me we shouldn't have come. He might be trying to get information out of her. Or—" I stopped dead. "Or they might be in this thing together!"

The very thought was enough to get me going again. With Eve leading the way, we raced toward the front of the restaurant. The hostess was nice enough to ask if we needed assistance finding the party we were looking for, but we didn't stop to return the pleasantry. In fact, we didn't stop at all. We had just made it to the front door and Eve was already outside under the awning when a hand clamped down on my shoulder.

I wasn't surprised when I turned and saw that the hand belonged to Yuri.

"Ah, Miss Capshaw!" He smiled in a way that would make anyone watching us think we were old friends. "So good of you to take the time to stop by. You will join us for dinner?" He backed up a step and made a broad gesture, like a waiter showing a guest to table.

"No, thanks. I'm not very hungry."

"But surely that is why you are here?" Yuri motioned toward the dining room again. I stayed put. "What else would bring you to Bucharest on such a rainy night?"

I peeked around Yuri's shoulder toward the back dining room, picturing Beyla there.

"I might ask you the same thing," I said.

Surprise flickered across his face. I couldn't tell if it was because he didn't expect me to come right out and ask why he was consorting with the enemy, or because of the nasty tone in my voice.

He lit a cigarette. Apparently the No Smoking sign above our heads (in English and Romanian) did not apply to him. As he slowly dragged in and let out a lungful of smoke, he narrowed his eyes just a bit, as if he'd never seen me clearly before and wanted to get a better look.

"What is that saying about the bees and the honey? You can catch more by being sweet, yes? You see what I mean? I am being sweet to Beyla so she does not think that I know what she has done. In the meantime, I try to find out what she knows. And what she doesn't know."

"Is it working?"

Yuri's shrug was noncommittal. "It would be working better if I had all the evidence I need." He raised his eyebrows. "Or perhaps that is why you are here? Perhaps you have been following me, and you saw me come into this place. You are here to give me the disc?"

I didn't answer. I couldn't. Not until I had the good guys and the bad guys straight on my scorecard. If Beyla and Yuri were in cahoots, it changed everything. Especially when it came to handing over the disc.

Yuri dragged in another lungful of smoke and blew it out in a stream in my direction. I held my breath. "I am sorry that I have not had a chance to return your kind phone call," he said. "I should say, the call from your friend." He peered out the front door to where Eve was looking at us, wide-eyed and curious. When she waved (ever the beauty pageant contestant), he waved back. "Miss DeCateur, she is very beautiful, but not very smart. I think you are not happy that she made that phone call. You are not thinking that you can get money for the disc, are you? That you will hold onto it until I pay you? That is your plan? I must tell you, that would not be smart. Not at all. Please, tell me you brought it with you. Then we can put an end to this business."

I didn't have the disc—I'd left it at home. In fact, before I left the apartment that morning, I'd switched the disc with a CD of Sinatra's greatest hits that Ed Downing at the bank had once burned for me to thank me for saving him from the royal screwup that was his cash drawer.

Paranoid?

Maybe. But I wasn't taking any chances.

I'm not sure exactly how I managed to return Yuri's smile with one of my own. I sidestepped away from his grip.

"Eve was mistaken." I backed up a step. Toward the door and away from Yuri. "You don't know her. She gets a little carried away sometimes. We were talking about looking for the disc, I will admit that much. We talked about following Beyla, too, to see where she might lead us. And before you know it . . ." I snapped my fingers. "There's Eve, jumping to conclusions."

Yuri's smile never faded. "I do not think so. I saved the message. Please, you will come to my home with me and I will replay it for you. Then you can hear for yourself what she said. She said you had it, not that you were looking for it. And I must tell you, I was so relieved to hear it. To hear that finally, we had proof of all that Beyla has done. Come. If you would come with me, you will hear the message for yourself. Then you will remember."

He reached for my arm, but I wasn't going to let him latch onto me. And I wasn't going anywhere with him, either.

"I think I'll stay right where I am."

Yuri pulled his hand back to his side. Was it a trick of the light that made his eyes look hard? It must have been, because he was back to his old self in a moment. Suave and gracious in a very European sort of way. "But you never have said what you are doing here."

Didn't I? My mind raced, and I blurted out the first word that popped in my head. "Dinner."

Yuri laughed. "But you said you were not hungry!"

"Hungry? Not yet. But cooking class was cut short. This seemed like a logical spot to stop. And I'll tell you what . . ." I pulled in a long breath. "The more I smell the delicous aromas here, the hungrier I get."

Yuri wasn't convinced. "You will forgive me, but I do

not think Romanian food is something a young American woman can appreciate and enjoy. But . . ." His eyes lit. "But perhaps I underestimate you. Perhaps your tastes are more sophisticated than most of the women I have met here in this country. You have been here before, yes? That is right." He nodded, clearly satisfied with himself.

"If I am not mistaken, you showed me a receipt from this place. The one Drago wrote on the back of. You met him here, and this is where he gave you the address of the gallery, yes?"

The receipt was in my pocket, and I pulled it out. "That's right," I said, thanking my lucky stars. How often is there actual evidence to support a totally outrageous lie? I turned the receipt over, not to the side Drago had written on, but to the one that showed that there had been two for dinner that night, and what they ordered. "I have been here before. And it was the night I bumped into Drago and he told me to stop by the gallery. See, right here. My friend and I stopped by. We had *bors de*—"

"*Bors de berbec.*" Yuri moved too quickly for me. Before I could pull my hand back, he plucked the receipt out of my fingers. "Who would think you would enjoy this sour soup with mutton. Such a pronounced flavor! Too strong for a girl like you. But Drago, he liked this soup very much. You knew he would order it that night, as he always did. You knew it has a strong taste, and that it would be easy to disguise the flavor of foxglove in it."

I heard what Yuri said, but honestly, it was so outrageous, I was too shocked to respond. All I could manage was a couple of weak laughs.

Was Yuri really suggesting that I was the one who—

My laughter faded. The blood drained out of my face. I stared at him, stunned. "You don't actually believe that, do you?"

Yuri took another drag on his cigarette.

"Have you taken the time to look carefully at this receipt?" Yuri held it up, careful to keep it far enough away that I couldn't get it back from him. "Do you realize Drago was here? That night?"

"*That* night?" I didn't like the way Yuri said it, and it only took me a couple seconds to work out why. "You mean the night he was killed?"

"Look." Yuri pointed to the date on the receipt, confirming my worst fears. He held the receipt toward the light to see it better. "I think it is just about right, don't you? Twenty to thirty minutes, that is how long it takes for foxglove to take effect. You will know this, I think, because you carry that vial of foxglove with you. And if I am not mistaken . . ." He took another look at the receipt, drawing out the suspense. "This receipt proves that you and Drago paid for your dinners just about thirty minutes before he died."

"That's ridiculous." I made a grab for the receipt, but I wasn't quick enough. Yuri had already tucked it into the breast pocket of his polo shirt. "I didn't have dinner with Drago that night. I'd never met Drago before that night. I've never been here before."

Yuri patted his pocket. "That is not what you told me just a moment ago. You are confused, yes? We will ask Constanta, the hostess. I am sure she will verify the fact that she has seen you here before."

"That's impossible." I spun away from Yuri, ready to head out the door. But he grabbed me so hard and so fast, I was facing him again before I even knew it.

"Nothing is impossible," he said, his words quiet, like the hiss of a snake. "Not if I say so."

"But you know I didn't kill Drago." Was that my own voice I heard? The one that wavered over the words? It sounded small and afraid. I didn't like it one bit.

I raised my chin and looked Yuri in the eye. "Quit playing

games. You know Beyla's the one who killed Drago. What do you want?"

I didn't really need to ask.

"The disc, you stupid woman." His eyes flashed. But a moment later, he let go of my arm.

"But of course . . . You cannot realize how important it is." His gaze whipped back to mine. "That is, unless you have looked at it?"

"I haven't." I was getting to be a skilled liar—I never even blinked. "Now here's the deal: the disc in exchange for the receipt."

Yuri didn't expect me to drive a hard bargain. His lips curled into something between a sneer and a smile. "I hate to give up the receipt so easily, when I worked so hard to get it in the first place."

"Worked?" I rolled my eyes. "You snatched it right out of my hand. Like a bully on a playground. You—"

Suddenly, I felt cold settle in the pit of my stomach. "You've been trying to get that receipt from me for weeks. That's why I couldn't find my purse that night I went to Whitlow's with Jim. You snatched my purse and looked through it and put it back when you didn't find the receipt inside. And my apartment—" The cold solidified into ice. "You were there. When Jim and I got there the night I followed Beyla, I thought my things had been moved around. You were in my apartment!"

Yuri shrugged. "I am not a dishonest man," he said. "But you see how desperate I am. You see how very important this is to me."

"OK, you wanted the receipt. But why? At the time, you didn't know—"

"Does it matter?" he snapped. As he fought to calm himself, his teeth clenched and his jaw tensed. "We will make a trade," he said more quietly this time. "The disc for the receipt."

Try as I might, I couldn't wrap my brain around the bits and pieces of everything Yuri had said. If he knew about the receipt, but he didn't know if I'd ever find the disc . . .

I shoved the thoughts aside. Better to stick to one subject than to let Yuri know I was baffled. "So if the disc is that important, why not just let me take it to the police?"

"You will not do that." The steel in Yuri's voice made it clear that the subject was not open for discussion. "You will bring it to me. I will call to tell you when and where. And once I have it, I will deal with Beyla." He turned to walk back into the dining room. "Me. Not the police."

It simply didn't make sense. At least not in my mind. "But why?"

When Yuri turned, the smile on his face was so icy, it sent a chill through my body. "Why? The best reason of all . . . Revenge."

Eighteen

 I DECIDED TO FACE THE MUSIC AND TAKE THE DISC TO the police.

Was it smart?

I honestly didn't know, especially with Yuri's threat hanging over my head.

Yuri knew I didn't kill Drago. I knew I didn't kill Drago. But the police . . . well, I liked to think that if Yuri came forward and produced the receipt from Bucharest, the police would need a little more evidence before they locked me up and threw away the key.

Besides, I had bigger things to worry about than a restaurant receipt.

I had to admit that as a detective, I was a failure. Somehow, everything had turned into a gigantic mess. The worst of it was, I was confused about exactly what had happened and where our investigation had gone wrong. If all Yuri needed to establish that Beyla killed Drago was the disc now residing in my Sinatra jewel case, why wasn't it enough for me to prove that she was guilty? Except for the fact that it was all in Romanian, of course.

But now the stakes were higher. No matter what Yuri said, there was something about him I just couldn't trust. Something dangerous. Which is why, at some point in the day after I'd run into Yuri at the restaurant—a day in which my stomach was tied in knots and my head pounded like a brass band—I'd decided to let the professionals sort it all out.

As for me . . . well, I'd probably have enough time to work things through for myself.

Like the three to ten years I'd get for stealing evidence from a crime scene.

That evening after work when I stopped home to collect the disc, I packed a small overnight bag. I wasn't going to take the chance that they wouldn't give me a toothbrush when they threw me in the slammer. I stashed my fuzzy slippers in the bag, too, then gave myself a mental slap and pulled them out again. Something told me pink faux fur was not de rigueur in lockdown.

As I zipped up my bag, I noticed my hands were trembling. For about the hundredth time that day, I looked longingly at the phone, wishing I could call Jim. Jim would understand. I couldn't explain how I knew it, but I was certain in a way that I had never been certain about anything before. Jim would support me. Jim would come to the police station with me, and stand by my side. He'd hold my hand if I asked him.

But I couldn't ask him, not for any of it.

Not without involving him—and there was no way I was going to do that.

After everything that had happened with Peter, I knew enough not to fall head over heels for any guy. Not too quickly, anyway. But I couldn't deny that I liked Jim— more than just a little. It wouldn't be fair to tangle him up in this mess. After all, Jim had plans, and he had ambitions of his own. Someday, he was going to own that upscale restaurant he'd always dreamed about. I wasn't about to risk embroiling him in my problems.

I set my bag down by the door and went to the living room where I kept my CD player, and what was left of my collection of music after Peter had gotten through raiding it. I grabbed the jewel case with "Sinatra" written on the front of it with the disc we'd found at Miss Magda's inside, and tucked it in my purse. I took a deep breath and threw my shoulders back, hoping that a big dose of false courage would be enough to keep me going. But no sooner had I turned to the door, when the phone rang. The machine picked up immediately.

"Miss Capshaw. You know who this is."

Yuri.

"Your little trick, it did not work so good. I am not amused. How stupid you were to think I could be so easily fooled." He clicked his tongue. "I like Sinatra, but really!"

Sinatra?

It took a second for the pieces to fall into place. When they did, my blood went cold.

With one ear still tuned to the rest of what Yuri had to say, I raced to the bedroom. Sure enough, the jewel case where I'd originally stashed Beyla's disc was gone. I hadn't told Eve I'd switched the disc for Sinatra's greatest hits. And Eve was the only one who had a duplicate key to my apartment. That meant—

I flew back in the living room just in time to hear Yuri say something about a last chance.

"You have only one hour. Then I will be forced to take serious measures."

I didn't like the sound of that.

I grabbed the phone and hit the Talk button. "Hello? Hello? I'm here. I'm listening. I couldn't answer in time."

There was no reply. I cursed myself for being so slow.

But then I heard a rustling, as if the phone was being handed from one person to another.

"Annie?"

I almost didn't recognize Eve's voice, it was so soft and frightened. My heart sank.

"Annie, it's me. I'm here with Yuri."

"Are you OK? What on earth possessed you to get the disc and take it to him? Tell him you didn't know, Eve. Tell Yuri it's not your fault. You didn't know I switched the discs."

"I didn't know you switched discs." Eve sniffled. She was crying, and I could tell she wasn't listening to a word I said. "He says he's not mad or anything and I hope you're not, either. I couldn't let you take the disc to the police, Annie. I didn't want to see you go to jail. Don't worry, Yuri says nothing's going to happen to me but . . . but . . ." She sniffed. "Annie, he says I can't leave. Not until you get here with the real disc. I don't want to stay here with him."

"Where's here? Eve, where are you? Are you—"

"You see we have a serious problem." Yuri was back on the line. I knew I had to keep the panic out of my voice—there was nothing to be gained from him knowing that I was scared to death. "You will bring the disc, yes?"

For once in my life, I didn't hesitate. "Yes. Of course."

"And you will not bring the police."

I hadn't thought of that, but now that he mentioned it, it was a damn good idea.

But again, no hesitation. "No. No police. But you have to guarantee me that Eve is going to be OK."

"OK?" I didn't see what was so funny about it, but Yuri laughed. "Of course your Miss DeCateur is going to be OK. Why would she not be? You do not think I am a . . . how do you say it? A bad guy, do you?"

I wasn't so sure, but I wasn't taking any chances. "Of course not. And I understand about how you want revenge

because of what Beyla did to Drago. But you have to understand—"

"What?"

I have never heard a single word spoken with more
venom.

I swallowed down what I was going to say—the part
about how if one little hair on Eve's head was out of place,
I was going to hunt Yuri down to the ends of the earth like
a dirty dog and hang his intestines on my Christmas tree
for garland.

"You have to understand that I need to know where to
meet you," I told him instead.

As it turned out, I didn't need to worry about the ends of
the earth. When I asked Yuri where to bring the disc, his
answer was short and sweet.

Arta.

Of course.

IT TOOK ME FOREVER TO FIND A PARKING PLACE IN
Georgetown. No big surprise there. But I was surprised when I got to the gallery and didn't find a single
light on.

I hoped I wasn't too late.

The front door was locked, so I went around to the side.
There, the door handle turned easily. I inched the door
open and toed the invisible line between the gallery and the
stone stoop outside.

"Hello! Yuri? It's me, Annie. Annie Capshaw. Are you
here?"

No answer, and no lights, either. I fished in my purse for
my flashlight and flicked it on, sending the skinny beam
skimming through the hallway that led from the side door
into the gallery. I followed it inside.

"Yuri? Eve? I'm here, and I brought the disc. The right

one this time." I took the disc out of my purse and waved it in the air. I don't know why, it wasn't like anyone could see it in the pitch dark. "You want to tell me what's going on?" I asked. "Just tell me where you want me to leave the disc and—"

My flashlight beam skimmed over a body lying on the floor, and my words evaporated in sheer terror.

Though her face was turned away from me, I'd recognize the haircut and the three-inch heels anywhere.

"Eve!" I raced over to where she was sprawled behind the sales counter. Kneeling beside her, I felt for a pulse. It was thready, but it was there, and she was breathing. I barely had time to register relief when I heard a voice behind me.

"Not dead. Drugged." It was Yuri.

I hopped to my feet and spun to face him. When the flashlight beam hit his face, he put a hand up to his eyes. "You will turn the light off, please," he said, but I wasn't in the mood to negotiate. At least not too much or too soon. I lowered the beam toward the floor.

"Drugged? Why?" I asked him. "Eve wasn't going to cause any trouble. And she's not the one who changed the discs—that was me. She didn't know anything about it."

"I thought as much." Yuri took a step toward me. When he did, the light of my flashlight glanced over something metal in his hands. A gun.

My blood rushed so loud and so fast in my ears, I could barely hear what he had to say.

"I thought perhaps that it would be quieter if Miss De-Cateur took a little nap. Then she would be less trouble and not so whiny. Poor thing. She is so lovely, but I knew she was not smart enough to change one disc for the other. But you, you are. Now, you have brought the disc with you? The proper disc?"

I put my hand—and the disc in it—behind my back.

"I brought the disc. It's outside. In the car. Here." With my other hand, I felt around in my purse for my car keys. It was the same hand I was using to hold the flashlight, and as I searched, the light was smothered. When I found the keys, I tossed them in Yuri's direction, hoping that when he went to catch them, he'd lower the gun that was pointed directly at me. Wrong. He never even tried to catch the keys. They landed on the floor with a clank.

"Come, come, Miss Capshaw. I have just complimented you. I have told you that I believe you to be a bright young woman. The least you can do is offer me the same confidence in return. I am not stupid. You have the disc with you—you said as much when you walked in. If you will hand it over, we can finish with this business."

"Not until you tell me what's going on. What did you give Eve? When will she wake up?"

Yuri chuckled. In the dark, the sound was sinister. And too close for comfort—Yuri had taken a few steps closer.

"You do not understand yet, do you?" he asked. "You think life is like the stories you watch on your American television. Happily ever after. That is what you are waiting for, yes?"

I stepped back. "You're not going to be happy, either, if you don't get this disc. How else are you ever going to prove that Beyla is guilty?"

My own words echoed back at me. And that's when it hit me.

Well, actually, *hit me* is putting it mildly. It ran into me like a freight train going full speed.

I can't say that I know what a fell swoop is, but I know for sure that's how the truth came to me. It landed right on top of me, all in one fell swoop.

"You and Beyla *are* in it together! Just like I thought when I saw you two at the restaurant. You pretended you were just there trying to find out what she knew, but you were really discussing strategy." When Yuri didn't answer, I kept right on putting two and two together. "You're the one who had dinner with Drago at Bucharest that night. Beyla couldn't have—she was at class. You're the one who slipped him the foxglove, then she picked the argument with him to throw us off track. That's why it was so important for you to get the receipt back. You knew it didn't show that I was guilty. It showed that you were with Drago the night he died."

"Brava!" Yuri could afford to give me a little bow and a smile that glinted in the glow of my flashlight. After all, he was the one holding the gun. "So, you are as smart as I thought. That's too bad, really, because it means I will have to kill you."

Talk about irony—I almost said *over my dead body*.

This was one of those times when actions spoke louder than words.

I shone the flashlight right in Yuri's eyes.

"Bitch!" He put a hand up to shield the beam, but by that time, I'd already made my move. I took off running across the gallery, switching my flashlight off at the last second so I wouldn't give away my position. A moment later, I ducked below the front windows so that Yuri couldn't see me against the bit of light that seeped in from the sidewalk that faced M Street.

"You cannot get away." From the sound of his voice, I guessed that Yuri hadn't moved far from where we'd started out, but it was hard to tell. The ceilings were open and high, and his words ricocheted against the redbrick walls and the hardwood floors. "It will be easy to find you here."

I flattened my back against a cold, stone sculpture. "I was lying when I said I had the disc with me. I left it somewhere. Somewhere safe. And without me, you'll never find it. Then you won't have Drago's inventory. That's what it is, isn't it? An inventory list of guns?"

Maybe I was imagining it, but I think the fact that I knew about the guns stunned Yuri a bit—he didn't say anything for what seemed like an eternity. When he did, his voice came from somewhere on my right. Too close for comfort. I moved from the shelter of the sculpture.

"I hope for your sake that you do not think this is the smart way to deal with our little problem," he said. "You will only make this harder on yourself. Harder on you and harder on her."

In a flash, the overhead lights came on. I was blinded for a moment, but that moment dissolved all too quickly. When it did, I saw that Yuri had one hand on the light switch. He had dragged Eve to her feet and was holding her upright with his free arm. Her eyes were still closed, and she could barely stand—she swayed back and forth as if she were drunk. Yuri put the gun to Eve's head.

"The disc," he said. "Now. Or your friend dies right here, right now, right in front of your eyes."

He might have been bluffing, but I wasn't willing to take the chance. Not with Eve's life.

I kept my place and held the disc out to him. "Here. Come and get it."

"Bring it to me."

"Move away from Eve."

Yuri laughed. "You try so hard to bargain. I am impressed, Miss Capshaw. Who would have thought that a bank teller could be so tough? But there will be no bargaining. Just as there is no escape. You know too much."

"You mean about the guns."

"The guns, yes. The guns Drago was smuggling into this country. He did not want to share the profits, you see."

"And you figured since you were partners in the gallery, you should be partners in the gun business, too. Except . . ." Another light went on, this time inside my head. "You weren't partners in the gallery. You were the one who trashed the place looking for the disc, and when you didn't find it, Beyla had to come back to look."

"Very good." Yuri's smile was anything but friendly.

"And Tyler, he said something once about how now that Drago was dead, the gallery was closed up. I should have known right then and there. He didn't just mean it was closed for the day. He meant it was closed for good, and that means that you and Drago were never partners. You were trying to take over his turf in the gun-smuggling business. You and Beyla."

"If only you had put as much thought into your silly investigation as you are now. Then, perhaps, you would not have trusted me so much. But you didn't. And now . . ." Yuri had the nerve to shrug, like we were discussing something no more important than the weather. "When the police find your bodies here, they will be baffled, yes?"

"Not so surprised. They know it is you, Yuri."

This voice came from somewhere in the shadows behind Yuri. It was distorted by the echo. Man? Woman? Neither of us had the time to analyze. His finger on the trigger, gun raised, Yuri spun around, but the person standing in the shadows had the jump on him. There was a flash, and a shot cracked the air. The noise was still bouncing off the walls when Yuri tumbled to the floor, taking Eve with him. They landed together in a heap on the hardwood floor, on top of a trickle of blood that was quickly turning into a pool.

For the third time in as many minutes, I didn't stop to think. I raced over to Eve, kneeling beside her and cradling her head on my lap. Thank goodness, except for some polka dots of blood that had spattered from the bullet that went clear through Yuri, she looked none the worse for wear. I managed to pull her aside a few feet, away from the growing circle of blood. And Yuri's corpse.

"You are all right?"

I looked up just as Beyla stepped out of the shadows, and a new instinct took over. This one was self-preservation.

All I could think about was that Beyla still had a gun in her hands. And one look at Yuri's lifeless body was all I needed to remind myself that she knew how to use it.

"You! You . . . you shot him." My voice bumped over the words in time with the heartbeat knocking around my chest.

Beyla's expression was grim. She cast a glance at Yuri's body with blank, emotionless eyes. "He would have killed me," she said. "And you and Eve as well. Like he killed Drago. Like he killed poor Magda."

Nothing was making sense. I took in a breath as I sat back on my heels. "I know he killed Drago, but don't deny that you were in on it, too. You and Yuri were trying to take over the gun-smuggling business. Is that why he wanted you dead?"

Beyla's top lip curled (in a beautiful and exotic way, of course), and she barked out a laugh. "Guns! They are nothing to me. The money is nothing. If you understood this, you would know that I could have nothing to do with Drago and his guns or Yuri and his killings."

"Then what about the disc? What about Yuri? He said—"

"Yuri is scum. Like Drago." Beyla spat on the floor. It was so uncharacteristic a gesture from a woman who was so calm and beautiful, it sent a wave of fear through me. She must have known it, because she set her gun on the sales counter. "You still do not understand," she said.

Understatement.

"But you had the foxglove."

"Yes." She nodded. "As a talisman. You know what this is? I carry foxglove for protection."

"You mean, like a spell?" We were in deep waters now, and I was having a little trouble catching my breath. Gently, I moved Eve off my lap and got to my feet, all the while keeping an eye on Beyla and on the gun on the counter. As long as the two of them (Beyla and the gun, not my eyes) weren't anywhere near each other, I could breathe a little easier.

"You mean you really are a witch, just like Eve thought?"

Beyla laughed. "There are those who would use the word to describe me. I am Gypsy. I know the secrets of the old way of life. I am not using the foxglove to protect myself, but to protect my family. Back in Romania." She pulled in a breath and let it out again, apparently ordering her thoughts.

"Drago, he hired me to take care of the books for the gallery."

I thought back to something Yuri had told me. "Then you weren't lovers? Back in Romania?"

I guess the wave of revulsion that shivered through Beyla was answer enough. "I am accountant," she said. "I do this for businesses owned by Romanians. It is easier to handle their business because we speak the same language. I was doing accounts—this is how I found out about Drago and the guns. I made a copy of the information."

I glanced down at the disc I was holding. The Sinatra jewel case sparkled with tiny drops of Yuri's blood. I dropped it like it was on fire and wiped my hands on my pant legs. "That's what's on the disc. The information you copied."

Beyla nodded. "I told Drago I would keep this secret, but he must do something for me in return. Drago is rich and powerful. I tell him he must use his influence to get my family to this country. He said he would, but he lied. This is what we argue about, that night the cooking class started. I was very angry."

Beyla drew in a breath. "Drago thought I would give up, that I would be intimidated by him. I was not."

"And Yuri killed him to take over the smuggling business."

"Yes." Beyla's brows dropped over her eyes. "And Yuri . . ." She shivered and wrapped her arms around herself. "He is even worse man than Drago. He realized I knew what was going on—Drago told him. The night they had dinner together at Bucharest. Yuri knew about the disc, too, and he wanted it. This is why he tried to frighten me at cooking school."

I remembered the exploding stove and my singed eyebrows. "*You are next!* That's what the message meant. If you didn't cooperate, Yuri would kill you, too."

"Yes. I think that was his plan. Until he came up with one that was even more sure to work. He told me that if I did not deliver the disc with the information to him, my family in Romania—my mother and my brother and his children—they would all be killed."

"And all along, Yuri acted like all he wanted was to prove that you killed Drago so he could enlist our help." I shook my head, feeling like a fool. Looking around the gallery, another thought popped into my head. "But if you copied the information onto the disc, why were you searching the gallery for it?"

"You mean, the night you were outside the window watching me?" I looked away sheepishly. Apparently, Beyla knew exactly what tripped the alarm that night. "I was not looking for disc. Not in here." She glanced around the gallery. "I was checking for . . . how do you say this? . . . for bugs. To see if Yuri had cameras hidden. When I did not find any, I knew it was safe to go to the place where I had hidden the disc."

"And Magda?"

"Magda." Beyla shook her head sadly. "Magda's death is heavy in my heart."

For a moment, I thought she was confessing to killing Magda. But then I realized there was a sheen of tears in Beyla's eyes.

"I was to give the disc to Magda," Beyla said. "And Yuri would pick it up there. Only by that time, I do not trust Yuri. The disc I gave him was not complete. I leave false disc for Yuri and hide the real disc also at Magda's so that Yuri cannot kill me and find it in my home. Yuri picked up the disc I left for him, and then he killed Magda. When he looked at the disc, he was very angry to see that all the information was not on it, but I tell him I do not care. He will not get complete information until I know my family is safe."

"But then I showed up at Magda's and took the real disc." I felt like a fool, but I knew there was no use apologizing. "Then what about the pasta sauce?" I asked. "And the time you threatened to slit my neck?"

The expression that crossed Beyla's face was nearly a smile. "The sauce . . . this, you do not understand. My sauce of tomatoes, it is very good. And your cooking . . ." She shrugged and made a face. Enough said.

"And you say I threatened to kill you?" Beyla shook her head. "No. This is not true. I tell you to watch yourself. I tell you these are dangerous people you are dealing with. It was a warning."

I guess it all made sense. Though I would have felt a little more at ease if I just hadn't seen Beyla kill a man. At the same time I wondered if I should call the cops, I wondered if Beyla would let me.

I didn't have a chance—we heard the back door of the gallery open. I was all set to duck for cover, but Beyla stopped me. "It is safe, I think," she said. "I have called a friend."

The friend in question was John, the nerdy accountant from cooking class. Who suddenly didn't look much like an accountant or very nerdy anymore. In a well-tailored navy suit, a white shirt, and a to-die-for Italian silk tie, John looked more like—

"Special Agent Derek Malchowski." He stuck out a

hand, and because I didn't know what else to do, I shook it.
He pulled a leather wallet from his back pocket and flashed
his credentials. "FBI."

My mouth fell open. "That's why you lied for Beyla
about the night Drago died."

John—er, Derek—smiled. "Sorry to make you look bad
in front of the locals. But Beyla needed an alibi, or the local cops were going to find out what was going on. We
couldn't risk it. Not that early in the operation."

"And that explains what the two of you were doing in
cooking class, too, right? It was an excuse for you to meet
with Beyla. A way for you to get together and talk without
anyone knowing."

John—er, Derek—smiled again. "We were afraid Drago
was onto Beyla, and we couldn't take that chance. She was
too valuable a source. And yes, since I know you're going
to say it, that's why we missed bread class Saturday. Important meeting at headquarters."

Suddenly, my attention snapped back to my best friend.
"Eve! we have to . . ." But Derek was way ahead of me.

"Called an ambulance," he said when I made a move to
check on her again. Eve was still on the floor, but now she
was curled up on her side and breathing peacefully.

With that worry out of the way, I had the luxury of being
mortified. "I was so stupid to believe anything Yuri said.
We almost ruined everything!"

Derek pursed his lips. "Actually, I think you conducted
one heck of an investigation. Without you . . . well, we
would have found the disc eventually, but you found it
sooner. And thanks to you, it didn't fall into Yuri's hands. If
it had, we're pretty sure he would have disappeared. We've
been expecting a new shipment of weapons, a big one. If
Yuri disappeared, we knew we'd never be able to track him
or that shipment. That's why we held off arresting Drago,
in case you're wondering."

He smiled. "You did fine there. Your only problem was assuming you knew who was guilty right from the start. Let me offer you a little professional advice, Annie: never make up your mind. Not about anyone. Not until you have all the facts." He dug a business card out of his wallet and gave it to me along with a wink. "Give me a call the next time you start on a case. I might be able to help out."

He turned and walked away just as the sound of sirens started pulsing outside the gallery. A team of paramedics rushed in and lifted Eve onto a stretcher, and I headed to the door to ride to the hospital with them.

But not before I took one last look at Yuri's body.

Once upon what seemed like a very long time before, I'd promised him that I would do whatever I could to bring Drago's killer to justice.

I wondered if he dreamed it would ever turn out this way.

I shook away the thought and stepped outside. Just as I did, a black car pulled up to the curb. No sooner had it stopped than a man stepped out of the passenger side. He waved Beyla over.

"You kept your part of the bargain." That was all he said before he opened the back door. Crowded into the backseat was a woman with iron-gray hair who looked a whole lot like an older version of Beyla, another man, and three small children. When Beyla saw them, she let out a gasp, and tears ran down her cheeks.

"Thank God!" She grabbed my hand, and honest to gosh, I think she would have kissed it if I didn't stop her. "This is my family. They are here. From Romania. They are no longer in danger."

I wasn't so sure that I had all that much to do with it, but I accepted her thanks. "I hope I can see you again," I called out as she rushed to the car door. "I've got a lot of apologizing to do."

Beyla turned and cast me a beaming smile.

"No need. And I will send you my sauce of tomatoes recipe. I think maybe it will taste better than yours." With that, she ducked into the car and from what I could see, there were tears and laughter all around.

"Just let me know when we can get together," I said, but the man who'd gotten out of the car first took my arm. He abruptly closed the car door and as soon as we backed off, the vehicle pulled away.

"Witness Security," he said. "What most folks call Witness Protection. You won't be seeing Beyla again."

Honestly, the thought made me a little sad. But in the great scheme of things, I guess it really didn't matter. After all we'd put her through, it was enough just to see Beyla happy.

Nineteen

✖

"OK, TELL ME ONE MORE TIME." EVE SETTLED HERSELF more comfortably against the pillows I'd mounded on the couch for her, but not before she leaned forward, scooped up another spoonful of peanut butter, and slopped it onto a chunk of chocolate. "You're saying that Beyla was really the good guy in all this?"

"Exactly." I emphasized my point by gesturing with the spoon I was using to do some major damage to the peanut butter myself. "Like I told you back at the hospital, we had it all wrong the entire time. I'm only glad it worked out the way it did."

"And that no one got hurt. Well . . ." Eve's complexion turned an unbecoming shade of green. "Nobody but Yuri." She shivered. "Yikes, Annie, I was that close to him when he died." She held two fingers just a tiny bit apart. It would have been easier to do if they both weren't coated with peanut butter. "I could have been the one killed."

"Not to worry." I licked the remains of chocolate off my fingers. "Beyla made sure of that. As for Drago . . ."

"He was a bad guy, too, so I guess he got what he deserved."

"And Magda."

"Poor lady." Eve lowered her spoon in tribute. "She just happened to be in the wrong place at the wrong time."

"And we just happened to have solved the case!" We clicked spoons in a toast.

"We'll have lots to talk about tomorrow at cooking class."

"Except I don't think we can." My fingers were sticky, and I wiped them against a paper napkin. "I mean, Witness Protection and gun smuggling and John the accountant not being who he pretended to be . . . Something tells me we're better off keeping our mouths shut."

"Except when it comes to Tyler." Eve's grin was wicked. "Oh, don't worry," she assured me, "I'm not going to give away any national secrets. But I think I can mention that the FBI commended us for the thoroughness of our investigation."

The way I remembered it, Derek had been commending me at the time, but since Eve had been drugged, I forgave her liberal editing.

"Tyler," I reminded her, "has peanut butter for brains."

"No way!" Eve turned her spoon upside down and licked it clean. "Peanut butter is way smarter. And tastier. I hope the man never crosses my path again."

"Here's to that." I saluted her with my mug of tea. "And here's to an end to all the danger we've been in. I don't need any more of that, thank you very much."

"Hear, hear." Eve raised her mug. "We've done our duty. No more bad guys. No more danger. No more—"

Her words dissolved in a gulp.

Because Eve had heard exactly what I'd heard: my front door creaking open.

We couldn't see out into the hallway from where we were sitting. I signaled her to remain quiet and quickly removed the peanut butter jar and the chocolate bars from the tray I'd used to carry it all into the living room, and tucked the tray under my arm. Though I wasn't sure what she planned to do with it, Eve latched onto a pillow. Side by side, we crept into the hall.

The door creaked open a little bit more. Eve and I hunkered down into our positions. When it opened all the way, we flew at the intruder from each side, our weapons (such as they were) raised and ready.

"Holy Jehosephat!" Jim slapped a hand to his heart and nearly fell back into the hallway. "What on earth are you two doing?"

"And what are you doing trying to scare us to death?" I grabbed his hand, pulled him into the apartment, and closed the door behind him. "How did you get up here? You didn't buzz."

Uncertainly, Jim eyed the tray that I had clutched in one hand. "I had the key. The one I used the other morning when I went out and bought the ingredients for the French toast. It's on an I Love Chemistry key chain."

Chemistry?

Peter, of course.

For the first time in what felt like forever, I thought about my ex without my blood pressure shooting to the ceiling and my heart feeling as if it had been ripped in two.

And it felt great.

"I thought I'd surprise you," Jim said, and he had no idea how close his words came to echoing what I was feeling. "But it looks like you've surprised me instead."

"You bet!" Eve tossed the pillow back in the living room. "And wait until you hear the rest of what happened. You'll be plenty surprised. We solved the case!"

"Did you?" When he looked at me, Jim's eyes twinkled. "I always knew you would. Tell me. Both of you, tell me everything."

"Annie will have to do that on her own." Eve disappeared into the living room and came out holding her shoes. Before I could offer a protest, she was already out the door. "I don't need to stay, so don't even say it, Annie. You heard what the doc in the ER had to say. I'm fine, and I feel fine, too. And whatever Yuri gave me, it's out of my system. I'm going to do exactly what that doctor said I should do: I'm going home to get some sleep."

"But—" I followed her to the door.

"But nothing." Out in the hallway, Eve lowered her voice. She looked over my shoulder to where Jim was waiting. "Three's a crowd," she said with a smile and headed toward the elevator.

I barely had time to catch my breath. Jim grabbed my hand, pulled me into the living room and, bless him, he didn't say a thing about the chocolate or the peanut butter. He took the tray out of my hand and set it down, then patted the spot on the couch next to him.

"I want to hear all about it," he said. "But first, I have some news of my own."

"Good news or bad news?"

"A wee bit of both, I'm afraid. You see, my Uncle Angus died."

"I'm sorry." I took his hand in mine. "Was it sudden?"

"Very. It's why I was called away from class last night, and why I canceled class today. Angus was a bit of an old codger and he didn't want a fuss made over him when he was alive or when he was dead. We've had the memorial service already, you see, and the reading of the will. I've got news, Annie." Jim tightened his hold on my hand. "Uncle Angus, he's left me his restaurant."

"His—!" A smile brightened my expression. "That's wonderful!"

Jim did his best to rein in his excitement. "It's not exactly the sort of place I've always dreamed about," he said.

"But it's a start. I can leave Très Bonne Cuisine and the cooking school. I can get started in a place of my own."

His excitement was infectious. "That's fabulous!"

"And, Annie, I want you to be my partner in the restaurant."

"That's ridiculous!" I dropped Jim's hand like a hot potato. I settled back against the couch cushions, far from him and his crazy idea. "I can't work in a restaurant. I'm a bank teller."

"You hate working at the bank."

"That's beside the point. I can't change jobs just like that, without any warning."

"They'll get along fine without you."

"But I've worked there for years."

"Then it's time for a change."

"Working for yourself . . ." My mind raced over every negative statistic I'd ever heard. "It's risky."

"Aye, but living's risky, Annie. And being your own boss, I'm thinking that's worth the risk."

"But I can't cook!" I wailed.

Jim laughed. He reached for my hand again and settled it between both his own. "I won't deny that," he said. "You are truly the worst cook I have ever come across."

"Then why—"

"Do I want you to be my partner? Because you're intelligent. And you're clever. Because you're better at numbers than anyone I've ever met, and I'm going to need that kind of talent on the business side of things."

"You mean I don't ever have to go into the kitchen?"

He held up one hand, Boy Scout style. "I swear it. You can have Angus's old office. It's in a nice wee bit of a room just off the side of the bar. You'll be snug in there, and you can organize it until your heart's content. I promise, it's far from the kitchen."

"And you'll do all the cooking."

"Cross my heart." He actually might have if he'd had a free hand. But one of them was still holding mine. And the other—and his arm along with it—had somehow managed to encircle my shoulders. "No cooking." I swear he knew what the sound of those long, delicious *ooooo*'s did to me, because he leaned in close and murmured them against my lips.

Could I argue with logic like that?

"When do we start? Not before tomorrow. Or should I say today?" I glanced at the clock over on the bookcase—it was nearly time for the sun to be up. "Tonight we have dessert class."

"Aye, dessert!" Jim moved a hairsbreadth closer, and my eyes drifted shut when his mouth came down on mine. "I was thinking we could get started on dessert right now."

RECGIPES

❊

Annie's Bacon Pinwheels

Jim's Mandarin Salad

Annie's Dilly Bread

Jim's Vegetable Mirepoix

Pasta à la Beyla

Jim's Hot Chicks

John's Steamed Mussels

Annie's Spectacular Pork Loin

Eve's Baked Apples

Annie and Eve's Indulgence

Annie's Bacon Pinwheels

Serves 4–6 as an appetizer

8 oz. cream cheese, softened

2 Tbsp chopped chives

8 slices of white bread, crusts removed

½ pound thinly sliced bacon
bamboo skewers

1. Blend cream cheese and chives in a small bowl. Spread mixture on one side of each slice of bread. Roll up each slice like a jelly roll. Cut into 1-inch-thick pieces.

2. Cut uncooked bacon into 3-inch strips. Wrap around rolled pieces of bread, so that the edges overlap slightly. Thread rolls horizontally onto bamboo skewers that have been soaked in water to prevent scorching. Grill in a 400-degree oven until bacon is crisp and bread is toasted, 10–15 minutes. Drain on paper towels before serving.

Jim's Mandarin Salad

Serves 4–6

DRESSING

¼ cup olive oil

2 Tbsp apple cider or balsamic vinegar

2 Tbsp sugar

5 shakes onion powder

1 Tbsp chopped parsley

½ tsp salt

dash of pepper

Combine ingredients in a container with a lid and shake until sugar dissolves.

GLAZED ALMONDS

1 Tbsp butter or margarine

1 Tbsp sugar

¼ cup sliced almonds

Melt butter and sugar in a small saucepan until sugar dissolves. Add the almonds and stir frequently until they turn light brown. Spread almonds on aluminum foil to cool.

SALAD

1 large head of romaine lettuce

¼ cup chopped celery (optional)

1 11-oz. can mandarin oranges, drained

1 16-oz. carton strawberries, sliced

Combine salad ingredients and half the almonds and toss with dressing. Sprinkle the remaining almonds on top. Serve immediately.

Annie's Dilly Bread

Serves 6

1 pkg. yeast
¼ cup warm water
1 cup cottage cheese, room temperature
2 Tbsp sugar
1 Tbsp butter, melted

1 Tbsp dill seed
1 tsp salt
¼ tsp baking soda
1 egg, unbeaten
2½ cups sifted flour

Dissolve yeast in ¼ cup warm water in a large bowl. Add cottage cheese. Combine other ingredients, adding flour last, slowly, using just enough to make a stiff dough. Beat well. Brush the top of the dough with melted butter; cover and set in a warm place to rise. When double in size, about an hour, beat down with a large spoon and place in a well-buttered loaf pan. Butter top of loaf again and bake in a 325-degree oven for 25 minutes. Increase heat to 350 degrees and bake until well browned, 15–20 minutes. Cool on a rack.

Jim's Vegetable Mirepoix

Serves 4–6

2 large heads broccoli
4 large zucchini
8 large carrots, peeled
3 red peppers

3 yellow or orange peppers
1 large eggplant
3 Tbsp olive oil
salt and pepper, to taste

1. Wash and prepare vegetables; cut broccoli, zucchini, and carrots vertically into 3-inch pieces. Remove seeds from peppers and eggplant; cut into 3-inch-long strips.

2. Parboil broccoli and carrots for 2 minutes in 1 inch of boiling water.

3. Heat olive oil in large pan. Add vegetables and sauté until just tender, about 5 minutes. Serve immediately.

Pasta à la Beyla

Serves 4–6

SAUCE

2 cups chopped onion	2 cups water
3 cloves garlic, chopped	1 bay leaf
3 Tbsp olive oil	½ tsp salt
3½ cups canned plum tomatoes, undrained	¼ tsp fresh ground pepper
2 cups tomato paste	½ tsp oregano

1. Sauté onion and garlic in olive oil until brown, stirring often. Add tomatoes, tomato paste, water, bay leaf, salt, and pepper. Simmer uncovered, stirring occasionally, for about 1 hour.

2. Add oregano and cook for another 15 minutes. Sauce should be very thick. Remove bay leaf and serve over pasta immediately.

PASTA

Prepare 1 pound of pasta al dente according to directions on the box.

Jim's Hot Chicks

Serves 4–6

¼ cup butter
6 Cornish game hens
5 cups water
1 tsp ground gingerroot
2 cloves garlic, coarsely chopped
2 tsp coriander seed

2 tsp fennel seed
1 small onion, quartered
½ cup chopped onion
6 cloves
¼ tsp ground cinnamon
2 Tbsp chopped or candied ginger

¾ tsp cumin
¼ tsp saffron
1½ cup long grain rice, uncooked
2 Tbsp chopped pistachios
1 cup raisins

1. In a large pot, heat 2 tablespoons of the butter. Add hens and brown on all sides.

2. Remove from heat and pour 5 cups of water over the birds. Add gingerroot, garlic, coriander, fennel, and quartered onion. Return pot to heat, and bring liquid to a boil. Cover tightly, reduce heat, and simmer until birds are tender, about 30 minutes.

3. Remove birds from pot. Place on warm platter.

4. Strain liquid from pot into a large saucepan. Wash pot and return to heat. Melt the remaining butter. Add chopped onion and cook until golden.

5. Add cloves, cinnamon, chopped ginger, cumin, saffron, and rice. Stir until ingredients are thoroughly mixed. Add 3 cups of strained liquid and bring to a boil. Cover, reduce heat to low, and cook until rice is tender, 15–20 minutes. Stir in chopped pistachios and raisins. Transfer rice mixture to a large platter.

6. Cut each hen in half and arrange on top of rice mixture. Keep hot until ready to serve.

John's Steamed Mussels

Serves 8

- 3 pounds fresh mussels, scrubbed under cold running water and debearded
- 10 Tbsp butter
- ¾ cup shallots, finely chopped
- 4 Tbsp fresh parsley, chopped
- 2 Tbsp fresh lemon juice
- 1 tsp grated lemon peel
  garlic

1. Place mussels in a large Dutch oven (or a large pot or kettle with a tight-fitting lid, so that steam cannot escape) with 1–2 cups of water. Cover and cook over high heat until mussels open, shaking the pot occasionally, 5–10 minutes. Drain mussels, preserving liquid in the pot. Transfer mussels to a bowl, discarding any that haven't opened.

2. In a small saucepan, melt butter over medium-high heat. Add shallots and garlic and sauté until tender, about 3 minutes. Add 3 tablespoons parsley, lemon juice, lemon peel, and 2 cups of the liquid from the pot. Bring to a boil and season to taste with pepper. Drizzle garlic butter over mussels. Sprinkle with remaining parsley and serve.

Annie's Spectacular Pork Loin

Serves 6, with leftovers

2 12-oz. cans frozen orange juice concentrate
5 cloves garlic, chopped
4 Tbsp honey
salt and pepper to taste
olive oil (approx. 1 cup)
2 boneless pork loins, approx. 4 pounds each

1. Combine orange juice concentrate, garlic, honey, and salt and pepper in a large bowl. Slowly add olive oil and stir until marinade thickens. Put pork loins in a large plastic zip bag and pour marinade over them. Marinate for 24 hours.

2. Grill loins on high heat until seared and juices are locked in (approx. 15 minutes), then cook over low heat for 1 hour, or until pork is cooked thoroughly.

Eve's Baked Apples

Serves 4

4 firm apples
4 Tbsp honey
butter
2 cups shelled walnuts, chopped
heavy cream

1. Preheat oven to 400 degrees. Core apples, taking care not to cut through the bottom. Pour a tablespoon of honey into each hole, and add a dab of butter. Fill up holes with walnuts.

2. Place apples in a baking pan. Add about a half cup of boiling water to the bottom of the pan, and bake for 30 minutes, or until apples are soft.

3. Cool and serve with cold heavy cream.

Annie and Eve's Indulgence

Serves . . . how much can you eat?

1 large chocolate bar
1 jar chunky peanut butter
1 large spoon

You know what to do.

A Gourmet Girl Mystery

STEAMED

Recipes Included!

Susan Conant
& Jessica Conant-Park

BERKLEY   0-425-20805-2

Penguin Group (USA) Online

What will you be reading tomorrow?

Tom Clancy, Patricia Cornwell, W.E.B. Griffin,
Nora Roberts, William Gibson, Robin Cook,
Brian Jacques, Catherine Coulter, Stephen King,
Dean Koontz, Ken Follett, Clive Cussler,
Eric Jerome Dickey, John Sandford,
Terry McMillan, Sue Monk Kidd, Amy Tan,
John Berendt…

You'll find them all at
penguin.com

*Read excerpts and newsletters,
find tour schedules and reading group guides,
and enter contests.*

Subscribe to Penguin Group (USA) newsletters
and get an exclusive inside look
at exciting new titles and the authors you love
long before everyone else does.

PENGUIN GROUP (USA)
us.penguingroup.com